BELINDA JONES

California Dreamers

HODDER

First published in Great Britain in 2011 by Hodder & Stoughton
An Hachette UK company

1

Copyright © Belinda Jones 2011

The right of Belinda Jones to be identified as the Author of the Work has been
asserted by her in accordance with the Copyright, Designs and Patents Act 1988.

A CIP catalogue record for this title is available from the British Library.

B Format Paperback ISBN 978 0 340 99445 0
A Format Paperback ISBN 978 0 340 99863 2

Typeset in Plantin Light by Hewer Text UK Ltd, Edinburgh
Printed and bound in the UK by Clays Ltd, St Ives plc

Hodder & Stoughton policy is to use papers that are natural, renewable
and recyclable products and made from wood grown in sustainable
forests. The logging and manufacturing processes are expected to
conform to the environmental regulations of the country of origin.

Hodder & Stoughton Ltd
338 Euston Road
London NW1 3BH

www.hodder.co.uk

Praise for Belinda Jones

'There is something about Belinda Jones's writing that takes you away to whatever beautiful setting she's evoking and leaves you there right until you reach the last page . . . Great fun from start to finish' *Sunday Express*

'An elegant, romantic novel that keeps you hooked right to the final bow' *Novelicious.com*

'Perfect summer reading' *News of the World*

'An entertaining beach read' *Woman's Own*

'Definitely worth cramming in your suitcase' *Cosmopolitan*

'Perfect for that girls-only summer trip' *Company*

'As essential as your SPF15' *New Woman*

'A wise and witty read' *Marie Claire*

'Fun, romantic and set in various exotic locations, it's the perfect escapist read for summer days' *Closer*

About the author

Following ten years as a magazine journalist and travel editor, Belinda Jones began writing novels inspired by her adventures. She has travelled to over twenty-five countries and hopes to write her way around the whole world by the time she's done!

She divides her time between Los Angeles, London and her husband's ever-changing naval base, and is pleased to report that since her last novel, she has acquired the dog of her dreams.

California Dreamers is her ninth novel.

Also by Belinda Jones

Living La Vida Loca
Out of the Blue
The Love Academy
Café Tropicana
The Paradise Room
The California Club
I Love Capri
Divas Las Vegas

For my husband JAG
(and all the long-distance lovers)

ACKNOWLEDGEMENTS

Sun-kissed thank yous to:

Isobel, Sara, Carolyn, Sophie, Laurence, Lucy, James, Catherine and Jaime at Hodder & Stoughton.

Cathryn, Claudia, Eugenie, Alicia and Dorian at William Morris Endeavour.

Seamus, Glenys and Usha at San Ysidro Ranch. Jim Allen and the stellar guides at Hearst Castle. Jeannie and the zebras at San Simeon. Lavender lovers Bill and Karen Evenden.

Linda Mora and Rita Marie at Joe Blasco. Jennifer and Trudy at Pryor's Planet. Cesar Millan. Alex Vlack and Damani Baker of the wondrous Bill Withers documentary – *Still Bill*.

And, finally, my lovely mother Pamela, for her eternally joyful support and insight. You're the best!

'*California became the first to discover that it was fantasy that led to reality, not the other way around.*'

William Irwin Thompson

I

Every morning, before I even open my eyes, I make the same wish: please let this be the day that something *happens*.

I no longer wish for specific things, like a lottery win or an unexpected transfer to Rio de Janeiro, and I wouldn't feel right about wishing for my best friend to move back from Spain because she relocated for *amor* and finds herself very well suited to the siesta lifestyle. There's also little point hoping that my ex-boyfriend will remember how he felt when we first met, because it's clear that we now want very different things from life. (I say that like I know what I want when really I just know that I don't want any part of what he has chosen.)

So, when I say I want something to *happen*, the truth is, I would settle for an internal shift – like when a train jolts and the passengers stumble a little before they find their footing again. Something – *anything* – to get me back on the same track as my life. Because somewhere along the way we got separated. Everyone I know seems to be heading *towards* something, but when I look ahead, all I see is blankness.

Which is ironic, considering I create images for a living.

'Morning, Stella!'

'Morning, Albert!' I hold up my ID for the security guard even though he's all too familiar with my bouffant ponytail and Coral Kiss lips. He's always my first smile of the day; the way he says my name with his cockney accent – *Stell-ahh!* – gets me every time.

Before I head into the studio, I swing by the canteen and fortify myself with two slices of kumquat marmalade on toast. (So divine! If you're ever in the Islington area, I highly recommend it.) As I swish and dunk my herbal teabag, I wonder what flawless teenage face will be greeting me today. Yesterday we were doing a shoot for *Wonderland* magazine and I had to weave around the model's iPhone wires – she was yapping away when she walked in, switched to music as she settled into the make-up chair and dialled a few more buddies as I metallicised her lids, all without looking up. Well, other than at the ceiling when I was applying pewter mascara to her lower lashes. When I tapped her hand to tell her she was done, she blinked at her reflection, said, 'That's rad!' and sneakily (and illegally, considering the magazine's embargo rules) snapped a picture of herself and uploaded it as her new Facebook profile pic. Which I suppose is the modern version of a compliment.

Of course, within the hour all my work was on a cleansing cloth in the bin.

This time I actually fished hers out and assessed it – the smudges had created an interesting pattern, like a shimmery version of the inkblot test. Who knows, maybe I'll start collecting them and framing them alongside the photographer's portrait as a new kind of art form. Wouldn't it be amusing if that was how I finally made my name in the art world? That was my original dream – to be an artist. I was going to be the Frida Kahlo of Bury St Edmunds. I only got into doing make-up as a way to pay the bills, but I have to say I was thrilled when I first made the transition from department-store beauty counters to magazine shoots – nice, flexible freelance existence and so gratifying seeing my work in print, even if it was just showcasing the new glitter liner from Urban Decay.

But now, ten years after switching canvas for skin . . . Well, after ten years even sparkle can lose its sparkle.

Last year I signed up with an agency to get into the more high-fashion side of things and then found I really missed all the 'real people' shoots. With top models it's just another day at the office, but making over harried housewives and new mums who are more likely to have puréed carrot on their cheek than blusher, is just so much more gratifying. You don't see them rushing to de-glam themselves before they head out the door. They can't wait to parade their new look – perhaps even turn a few heads in the street for the first time in years. Real people say, 'Thank you,' over and over and over. I miss that.

I take a deep breath as I prepare to enter the studio, only to recoil before I'm even through the door.

'Dear God, what's that smell?'

Photographer Adrian rolls his eyes. 'Apparently she likes her environment to smell like caramelised figs.'

'Who's she?'

'They didn't tell you?'

'Tell me what?'

He looks uneasy. 'You did bring your full retro kit, didn't you?'

'It's right here,' I say, jiggling my silver wheelie case. '1930s, right?'

'Yup, and there's this.' He hands me a disclaimer. 'We all have to sign it.'

I scan through the pages – basically I am not allowed to discuss or disclose or describe anything I see, hear or smell today. To anyone. Ever.

'What the . . . ?'

'I know!' Adrian shrugs. 'We all got them. Apparently she's highly sue-tastic, so blab at your peril.'

'Again with the "she"!' I protest. 'Who the MAC are you talking about?'

He gets a cocky look on his face, knowing he's about to get a reaction. 'Marina Ray.'

My jaw gapes. And then I laugh, a little hysterically perhaps. 'Are you serious?'

'Yes, ma'am.'

'What is she doing here?'

'Well, of course I'm putting my life on the line here speculating, seeing as they've probably got this whole room bugged . . .'

'*Adrian*!' I implore that he cuts to the chase.

'The director of the movie she wants to bag is in London to find a new leading lady to replace the one who just bailed on him at the eleventh hour. Marina Ray blew her Los Angeles audition, so now she's coming after him here, desperate for a second chance.'

'Sounds like a woman on a mission,' I note. 'So why is she spending the day with us and not him?'

'Because we are the ones who are going to provide a tailor-made head shot of her looking exactly as he wants her to look.'

'That sounds like a remarkably well-informed speculation.'

'I have my connections,' he shrugs.

'Yes,' I say, giving his groin a knowing look. And then I frown. 'You'd think she'd have her own make-up artist . . .'

'I'm sure she does, but she particularly requested you – she saw your Fred and Ginger cocktail party in *Harper's Bazaar*. I can't believe your agency didn't tell you any of this.'

I wish I could be equally incredulous. We haven't exactly been seeing eye to eye lately, ever since I tried to extricate myself from my bodice-tight contract. But let's not get into that now.

'So what's the movie?'

'Look lively – we've got company.' Adrian's assistant, Robbie, cuts in and directs our attention to a vision of neutrality entering the room.

Everything about Marina Ray's fifty-something PA is designed to cause minimal offence – plain white shirt, tailored grey trousers, varnish-free nails, squeakless loafers. I wonder if this is standard issue for a celebrity personal assistant? In order to let the star shine; you must remain flat matt at all times, 2D to her HD 3D.

As she begins assessing the food and beverage table, I scuttle into the make-up room and start unpacking my kit at double speed. Retro days are my favourites because I get to create a real back-in-time vibe. I got the idea when I went on a Golden Age make-up master class in Los Angeles and they took us to the Max Factor Museum in Hollywood.

The collection is housed in the actual art deco building where Mr Factor glamorised all the most notorious screen idols, and though it's surrounded by Hollywood tack, the second you step through the gold doors all the fake Oscar statuettes and kebab shops melt away.

The thing I loved most was the set of four colour-coded rooms. The first was painted aquamarine and labelled, *For Blondes Only* with a dressing table showcasing authentic items from Marilyn Monroe's alligator make-up case.

Next door was a dusty-pink room *For Brunettes Only* with Elizabeth Taylor memorabilia and wonderful old lipstick ads – 'The colour stays on until you take it off!'

Redheads such as Rita Hayworth had a pale apple-green room – apparently Max had a theory that if a woman could look radiant surrounded by walls of that hue, she would be able to carry off auburn hair.

Finally there was a warm peach room for the (not-exactly-common-usage term) 'brownette', as represented by Judy Garland. And me.

I suppose the fact that the word never caught on and I've never once heard a man saying, 'I've got a real thing for brownettes,' should have been a clue that it was time to revise my look, but having been through so many experimental phases over my beauty-counter years, I wanted low maintenance above all else. My job is to create beautiful looks, not necessarily have them myself. Who was really looking at me, anyway? I think in life, as in the movies, there are some people destined for starring roles and others who are better suited to looking on with mild envy.

And that's okay. The 1970s soul singer Bill Withers once said, 'It's okay to head out for wonderful, but on your way you're going to have to pass through all right. And when you get to all right, take a good look around and get used to it because that may be as far as you're going to go.'

So here I am at 'all right'. I've been here a while, so I've decided to get comfortable and make it look as pretty as I can. Since that trip to LA I've been collecting all manner of vintage perfume bottles, cosmetics and compacts. I even tracked down an original 'complexion brush' that fluffs off excess powder and looks like a doll-sized hairbrush.

When I brought my collection in to work to show Brontë the wardrobe girl, everyone – including the jaded models – was so enchanted I decided to make a regular feature of it, along with music from the appropriate era.

Which reminds me . . . I rifle through the side pouch of my case hoping to find my 1930s compilation. One day I will get round to properly labelling the CDs, or transferring them to an iPod, but the truth is, I'd be happier with a wind-up gramophone.

I pop a pot-luck disc into the slot and press play, only to feel my stomach dip and my limbs go limp. Too weak to reach out and press stop, I try instead to ride the bittersweet feeling out. It's almost like he's in the room with me. I can feel him rocking me, holding me, whispering, 'I'm so glad I belong to you.'

You know how normally when you split up with someone, people tell you there's plenty more fish in the sea? I didn't hear that after it ended with Jonathan. It was like everyone gave up hope on my behalf. Even my parents stopped asking if I'd met anyone when they made their Sunday-afternoon calls. Of course, my friends continued to cheerfully invite me to their weddings or engagement parties or babies' christenings, but there was never any question that I'd be bringing a plus one. Even now, when I bump into people I haven't seen for months, they ask me about my job but never about my love life. There's only so many times they can say, 'Never mind – I'm sure he will be along soon!' or, 'Lucky you – I miss those heady single days!' I miss those heady single days too. It's just not the same when you don't have any single friends left to go out with.

'Stella?'

I look up and find Adrian in the doorway with a look of concern on his face.

'You do remember it's 1930s today, right?'

'Yes, yes.' Finally I have the ability to press pause. 'I'm just trying to find the right CD.'

I switch to the next option – mercifully it's the right one. How can you *not* be soothed by Glenn Miller's classic instrumental 'Moonlight Serenade'? I sway dreamily from side to side and even give a little chuckle – look at me, DJ'ing for

Marina Ray! Could this be it? I wonder. Could this be the day I get jolted on to the next phase of my life? Is Stella about to get her groove back?

'No. *No, no, no.*'

'Excuse me?' I turn and find the personal assistant tutting in the doorway like a headmistress. Her look may be bland, but her tongue is barbed.

'All this junk will have to go.' She waves her arm at my most opulent treasures. 'Didn't you get the memo about her requirements?'

''Fraid not.' I grimace before defending my corner. 'I real-ise all this may seem like whimsy, but everyone I've worked with—'

'No,' she cuts me off. 'She likes the make-up room to be Zen. There's always too much going on with these eye-shadow palettes anyway.' She sneers at my pride and joy – five steps of graduating colour in every texture and hue. 'And get rid of that God-awful smell. Tuesday is figs. On Wednesdays she likes everything to be spritzed with pomegranate.'

As she turns on her heel, I take a moment to remain motionless and Not React. Just let it all wash over me. Focus on Glenn's melodic clarinet and exhale. It's no big deal. It's just one day. Marina Ray will be my first real, live movie-star face to work on, so I'll take her assistant's sniping for the novelty of the experience.

As I prepare to repack my priceless eyesores, I ponder two things – firstly, does anyone really know what pomegranate smells like, and secondly, will Marina turn up bare-faced or made-up? That's always telling. I mean, I think it must be hard for actresses when so much of their livelihood depends on their looks to walk into a room and meet people for the first time with no face on. And yet they know that they are coming here to be made up, so why add layers that will only have to be removed? That said, it's my personal worst night-mare to walk into a professional environment *sans* make-up. It's bad enough having to confront myself in the bathroom mirror in the morning, though I've done everything to take the edge off (soft amber bulbs and a pink towelling turban pulled into place the second I wake, otherwise I lose vital minutes contemplating my facial creases and the strange way my hair veers away from my crown while I'm sleeping, almost like a crop circle that appears overnight).

'Aaarrghhhh!' A blood-curdling scream from the other room yanks me back to the studio.

What now? Did they supply blueberry juice instead of acai berry?

I rush out to the studio, only to find Marina's PA tangled in – and obviously tripped up by – lighting cables. It's all I can do to hide my smirk as I see her trying to kick off the black wires as if they are live snakes. And then in walks Marina Ray.

Skinny jeans, slouchy top, huge sunglasses and a beanie hat entirely covering her crowning glory.

'Christ, Ruth, have you been drinking again?'

All eyes flash to the PA, who in turn flushes in mortification.

'Just kidding,' Marina grins. 'She's totally teetotal. I'm the one with the drink problem!' She reaches out a hand to pull up her employee. 'Anything broken?'

'I'll be all right,' Ruth mutters as she brushes herself down.

'I meant the equipment.'

An amused snort escapes Robbie before he quickly assures Marina that there's nothing more than a crumpled gel to replace.

'Phew! Now, where are the treats? I'm starving!'

We all look over to the spread of food. I can identify the seeds of sesame, sunflower and pumpkin, a delicious bowl of mung beans and half a dozen pink grapefruits.

She holds up a cellophane-thin piece of seaweed, which instantly crumbles to her touch. 'Guys, really?'

'You're supposed to be detoxing,' Ruth hisses.

Marina shakes her head emphatically. 'Nope, I'm definitely in the mood to *tox*. Whose doughnut is this?' She points to the Wardrobe girl's half-eaten sugar-sprinkled twist, left over by the kettle.

Brontë raises a tentative hand.

'Are you going to finish it?'

'Do you want it?' She looks confused.

'Thanks. You're an angel!' Marina says, stuffing the whole thing into her mouth and then pushing back her sunglasses to reveal an utterly bare face. She looks so much softer and younger in person. I think I even see a few freckles on her nose, but there's no mistaking the captivating green of her eyes.

'So listen – I'm waiting for a really important call and when it comes, whatever stage we're at, I'm going to have to take it. I just want you to know upfront so you don't think I'm disrupting things to have a chinwag with my spin instructor or anything like that.'

Once again we're thrown by her anti-diva stance.

'That's the right word, isn't it?' Her brow furrows. 'Chinwag?'

'Yes!' Adrian is first to regain his composure. 'And may I officially welcome you to the shoot today . . .'

She shakes his hand, then his assistant's and then turns to me with a look of hope in her eyes.

'Stella Conway?'

'Yes!' I breathe, amazed that she not only knows my name and my work but can pick me out in a crowd. Though the fact that I'm holding a velvet-ribboned powder puff is probably something of a giveaway.

'Ready to get started?' She moves towards the make-up room.

'Er, I just need to have a quick tidy.' I scurry after her, but she beats me to it.

Oh dear, here we go.

'Is that a lipstick case?' Her eye has been drawn to what resembles a bullet embedded in a mirrored pillbox.

'Yes, it is.' I tiptoe up beside her. 'I got it at an estate auction.'

'Amazing.' Her hands levitate over the objects as though caressing their aura. 'You know, I used to have the most beautiful vanity case in cream leather with lilac satin lining. Back then I could carry it onto the plane and even if I was wearing sloppy clothes, it made me feel like I had on a pencil skirt and seamed stockings!' She wrinkles her nose. 'Now the restrictions are so absurd – what is it, three ounces? – you'd have to scale everything down to the size of a Christmas-tree bauble!' She reaches for one of the deeper red lipsticks. 'I heard you use actual original products from past eras.'

'Well, that would be a tiny bit unhygienic' – I wince – 'but I did work hard to match the exact colour and pigmentation.'

'The packaging looks real enough.' She handles the baby-blue casing with gold squiggles. 'If a little cheap.' A tap of her fingernail confirms the plasticity.

I smile. 'Those are the real deal. Even though some of them look a little tacky, I like using them to house the new product, just to maintain some connection with the past.' I feel as if I am the one who's auditioning, though I have to say it seems to be going well . . .

But then Ruth appears in the doorway, giving me a stern look. 'Everything all right, Marina?'

'Ruth! Did you see all this stuff? It's fantastic. She's even got Evening in Paris perfume.' She claps her hands together.

'Oh, today is the day when everything starts to go right. I can just feel it!'

Suddenly I feel it too. A giddying surge of possibility.

Until, that is, Marina takes out the photograph of the woman she wants to morph into.

2

'Not exactly as much of a shoo-in as Anne Hathaway doing Judy Garland.'

'No,' I confirm as I take in the peroxide pin curls, pencil-thin brows and perfect rosebud lips.

'Do you know who this is?' Marina asks.

I shake my head. 'I mean, I'm guessing from the styling that she's a contemporary of Marlene Dietrich.'

Marina nods vigorously.

'But I don't recognise the face.'

'Which I think is in my favour – people don't have a particular image of her in mind.'

'So who is she?'

'Marion Davies. Probably the most underrated comedic actress of the 1920s and 1930s. She made over forty films, but really she's most famous as the mistress of publishing magnate William Randolph Hearst, who happened to be thirty-five years her senior.' She gives a little smirk. 'Now you can see a similarity, can't you?'

Again I'm thrown by her directness. Marina Ray's first foray into the public eye was as the arm candy of a much older and extremely powerful director – Victor Goldstein. (He cast her in the remake of *Barbarella*, knowing that the mere sight of her in Gaultier's thigh-high silver boots would make her a star.) The main difference is that Marina actually married her guy, though that ended a few years back, 'when her career took off and she didn't need him any more'. Or so the press would have it.

'William Randolph Hearst,' I repeat his rather grandiose name. 'Rings a bell . . .'

'Should do. You work for him.'

'Huh?'

'Well, of course he's dead now, but you've definitely done work for the Hearst Corporation – *Cosmopolitan*, *Marie Claire* . . .' she pauses for effect . . . '*Harper's Bazaar*.'

'Where you saw my work!'

'No small coincidence, if you ask me.'

I experience a little shiver at the connection.

'So . . .' Marina slots the image of Marion Davies into the edge of the mirror. 'Personally I think it's more key to represent the essence of the person, but of course everyone is so hung up on the visual and I know the director originally wanted Kate Hudson for the part and about ten years ago there was this movie where Kirsten Dunst played her . . . so you can see a theme there.'

'I can.' My mind is still going double time trying to work out how I'm going to pull this off. 'Is the film set in a particular year?'

'Late 1930s, I'd say. That's when they were having all the big parties up at Hearst Castle. I know they're planning to show the likes of Cary Grant and Charlie Chaplin as guests.'

'Wow!'

'I know! Better yet, they're shooting at the castle itself and it's just five hours' drive from Los Angeles, which is perfect because I have to be in California for when—' She halts herself. 'I just have to be in California for the next few months. Have to.'

'Okay,' I soothe. She's looking a little crazed now. 'I think we need to decide how we want to address the hair.'

'I'm one step ahead of you there.' She then pulls off her beanie and, instead of releasing a sheeny red river, out springs a harshly bleached bob.

I can't believe it – it looks like she tied her own hair in a ponytail and hacked below the band with kitchen scissors before diving headfirst into a bowl of peroxide.

'Who did this to you?' I gurgle.

'I did, at five o'clock this morning.' She shrugs. 'Seemed a good idea at the time.'

I bite back my thought – You've never heard of a wig? I mean, she hasn't even got the part!

'I know what you're thinking.'

'Mmm,' I try to cover my horror. 'That we need a purple rinse to tone down the yellow.'

She smiles gratefully. 'I know it's a lot to ask.'

'That's all right.' I rouse myself. 'I was only thinking this morning that I needed more of a challenge.'

'Well' – she grins wide – 'here I am!'

With the clock ticking, I'm grateful to have an extra pair of hands courtesy of Brontë, the Wardrobe girl and doughnut supplier. (She snuck out and got us a fresh batch and now all our work is accented with pink sprinkles.)

Having helped me tightly pin petite rollers in place round Marina's head, she now begins to parade the outfit options. Although I am aware of peripheral swishes of colour, my focus is on Marina's face: applying the flawless porcelain base, shaping her eyebrows into a fine pronounced arch, redesigning the shape of her mouth and then finding just the right shade of red to set off her blue lenses.

'Do you know there was actually a mouth stencil kit in the 1930s?' I say as I paint the creamy scarlet onto her lips. 'You picked one of six designs, traced the shape with a lip pencil and then filled in the rest with lipstick.' I step back to assess her face, just as an emerald silk showstopper arrives.

'I think this could be the one.' Brontë holds up the fluid yet bejewelled dress.

I eagerly agree, and Marina is so taken with it she asks if she can borrow it for the audition.

'I promise I'll get it back to you first thing in the morning.'

'No problem,' Brontë confirms. 'Trust me, I know how important a first impression can be.'

As we go through the shoe options, Marina tells us that Marion Davies would lend guests dresses from her own wardrobe if they didn't have anything fancy enough for dinner.

'And before they had heating in the castle's movie theatre, there was a heap of fur coats at the entrance and you'd just help yourself on your way to your seat. Can you imagine?'

Brontë and I shake our heads.

'Apparently everyone was very disapproving of Marion until they met her. Of course, they couldn't resist an invitation to the castle and at the end of the visit they were all won over.'

I must say I find Marina surprisingly refreshing herself. She doesn't seem at all guarded. Maybe that's why we have to sign a confidentiality agreement – because she can't be trusted to keep her big mouth shut.

I even dare to propose this as a theory.

'Oh, I can keep a secret when I have to,' she says, tapping her nose. 'Wait until the journalist gets here – you'll see.'

Often the writer does the interview while the make-up is being applied, just to make best use of the time, but Marina has requested that she doesn't arrive until the transformation is complete.

'It's part of the test.'

'Test?'

'Well, it took a bit of persuading to get the editor to go for something so highly stylised when the article is timed to publicise my wilderness movie.'

'The one about the bears?' Brontë enquires.

She nods. '*Who's Been Eating My Porridge?*'

'Nice title.'

'I've had worse. Anyway, she worried I wouldn't be recognisable, so we convinced her they'd get extra press coverage if we took the "Marina Ray as you've never seen her before!" tack. If the transformation is dramatic enough to throw the journalist off, they'll leak the photos tonight and then, with any luck, Conrad will see them as he's having his aperitif!'

'Conrad?'

'Conrad Blake, director of *Castle in the Sky*. That's the name of the movie.'

'Ohh!' I sigh, somewhat in awe of her scheming. 'You're quite the campaigner.'

'I find it takes my mind off . . . Well, you know. Keeps me busy.'

I watch as she manically checks and double-checks her phone. There definitely seems to be something nipping at her heels. But then I suspect a lot of actresses are that way – always running from something, diving headlong into the next role or co-star. This part would certainly be a departure for her – I've only seen a few of her movies, but I know she's never done a period piece before. And though she may not be the obvious choice for the era, I have to say she's pretty convincing when she regales us with one of the voiceover moments from the script.

'I took great delight in promoting romances,' she begins. 'There'd be a wedding and I would be bridesmaid again. I just did it to get a new dress. I liked a change of clothes occasionally.'

Brontë and I giggle along, eager to hear more, but Adrian's rapping at the door asking, 'How are we doing?'

'One minute!' I call back to him.

Brontë then invites the star to step into the silk dress. I give her curls a final tease and then together we turn her towards the mirror for the big reveal.

Her eyes widen, almost as large now as the real Marion's.

'What do you think?'

She gives a contented sigh as she turns first to the left, then the right. 'It's perfect!'

'Let's show the others.'

As we step out, Adrian, Robbie and Ruth all stop in their tracks, peering at Marina from every possible angle, trying to see where we've hidden the real Marina Ray. It's a rare treat to create such a stunned response, even if one reaction is notably negative.

'Your hair, Marina!' Ruth is horrified. 'Your long, glossy, red hair . . .'

'It'll grow back.'

'But not in time for the *Godiva* sequel.'

'I'll wear a wig.' She shrugs and then does a cute little flapper dance. 'Let's do this!'

She's just about to step in front of the camera when her phone rings.

'It's him!' she whoops, before skidding out of the studio and into the corridor.

The rest of us look to Ruth for a clue.

'I'm not quite sure how long she'll be. Probably best if we take a short break.'

But before we can even make for the canteen, Marina comes haring back in – her carefree face now stricken, those beautiful eyes streaming charcoal tears, her lips puffed and quivering.

She charges straight for the make-up room, and though she yanks the door behind her, we hear every gut-wrenching sob.

Awkward glances are exchanged.

I wonder if whoever drew up the confidentiality form this morning had an inkling this was coming.

'You think the audition fell through?' I suggest to Ruth.

She shakes her head. 'That wasn't the director.'

'Oh.' Now that's left me all the more curious. To hear Marina speak before, I got the impression that this role was her one all-consuming passion.

Ruth taps on the make-up-room door and then ventures in after her boss.

Adrian looks at his watch. 'This doesn't bode well. How long to redo her?'

I cock my ear – still sobbing – and then shake my head. 'A while.'

'Can we still meet the deadline?'

'What's the ice situation?' I head for the fridge, but as I pull out the trays, I slop water all over myself.

'Ruth wanted the ice cubes to be remade using mineral water.'

'Of course she did.' I sigh. 'Let me just run to the offie and get a bag of ready-mades. Robbie, can you chuck me my car keys?'

I hold up my hand ready to catch them, but as he propels them towards me, Ruth steps from the make-up room and intercepts them, rather like one of those lizards ensnaring a fly with its tongue.

'Where did you get this?' she snaps in an all-too-accusing manner.

I frown back at her. 'They came with the car.'

'Not the key, the chain.'

'Oh.' My heart sinks a little as she holds up the solid brass ring with a white-sailed ship, spread-winged eagle and outsized anchor at its centre. 'It was a present, from an ex-boyfriend. I keep meaning to replace it.'

'Your ex-boyfriend was in the United States Navy?' She is borderline incredulous now.

'Yes,' I say, wondering what the problem is. I mean, I realise it's not an obvious match, but British girls have been romanced by the American military since World War II. Or hasn't she heard?

Before I can question her reaction, she grabs me by the elbow and propels me into the make-up room, thrusting the keys at Marina.

Blinking through her blur of tears, she gasps, 'Where did you get this?'

Oh good grief! Anyone would think I had the Pink Panther diamond dangling from the chain.

'She used to date a sailor.'

It always sounds so silly to me when people say that. A soldier is so macho and tough. A marine, grittier still. A pilot, all cool and debonair. But a sailor always makes me think of little kids in white hats doing a side-jump and clicking their heels. Even if I know full well the reality couldn't be further from the truth.

'How recently were you together?' Marina wants to know.

'Couple of years ago. I've been meaning to get a new key ring.'

Marina is up on her feet now, hands on my arms guiding me over to the sofa. She asks Ruth to leave and then checks with me, 'You signed the confidentiality agreement, didn't you?'

'Yes,' I confirm.

'I need you to swear to my face that you won't repeat what I'm about to tell you.'

'Okay,' I nod. Now a little nervous.

She takes a deep breath and blurts, 'My husband is in the Navy.'

'Your husband?' My eyes rove wildly as I try to process what she has just told me. 'Victor Goldstein joined the Navy?'

'No!' she scoffs. 'Victor gets seasick in the Jacuzzi.' Then she fixes me with a hardcore gaze. 'I'm talking about my second husband. My secret one.'

My eyebrows hoick up.

'No one must know.'

'No,' I concur, and then add, 'Why is that?'

'Well, security issues aside, can you imagine the grief he'd get from the other guys? The relentless teasing, not to mention the stalking by the paparazzi, the stories claiming I was cheating on him with another guy if I so much as took a meeting on a restaurant terrace in LA?' She shakes her head. 'You know how it is in the military – the last thing you want to do is make yourself a target.'

'Right,' I say, taking a moment to imagine the classic movie-star poster taped to the inside of the metal locker, only for this guy the fantasy is real.

And then I recall Jonathan's last assignment (that I knew of) – fighting Somali pirates.

'He's okay, is he?' I ask, suddenly filled with dread. 'The phone call?'

'Yes, he's safe. It's just . . .' She throws up her hands in despair. '*Everything!* I mean, I don't get this set-up. I've always been the one going out of town for three or six months. And when I do go, I can bring people onto my set. But with him, when he's gone, he's gone! I'm lucky if I even get a two-line email. Seriously, I'd be better off if he was in the state penitentiary – even prisoners get conjugal visits! At least that way I'd know where he is – because everything is so damn restricted and confidential, he can't even tell me what part of the world he's in until he's already left that port.'

I heave a sigh. This is all too familiar.

'I don't have any say in when he goes or when he comes back and all I can do is wait and it's driving me crazy!'

'It's the lack of control, lack of a voice,' I tell her, 'the horrible realisation that your wants and needs are not remotely a factor. His priority is the Navy; he obeys the Navy. Everything to do with you has to fit in with their schedule.'

'Exactly!' she gasps.

'And you know it's not their fault, it's just their job, but some old-fashioned romantic part of you thinks that if he really loved you as much as he says he does, *he wouldn't leave you.*'

'*Yes!*'

'If he loved you, he wouldn't miss your birthday or Christmas or the time you had to rush to hospital to have your appendix out,' I sigh. 'It's the weirdest thing when you realise that the person you adore and trust the most can't be relied on, at least not in a practical sense. You can't even put them down as your emergency contact – what are they going to do, send a message to Yemen via Morse code?' I shrug. 'Whatever his good intentions, he probably won't be there when you need him the most. He won't be there to hug you after a bad day at work or help you in with the groceries or escort you to your best friend's wedding. He'll be on the other side of the world, living a completely separate life.'

She falls back on the sofa, all the more bereft.

'Sorry – I didn't mean to make it worse.'

'No, it's good to hear that I'm not being entirely selfish having these thoughts – I don't know anyone else in this position. I mean, I've looked online and thought about creating an alias so I could join one of the Navy-wife support groups on

Facebook, but then I started reading what the other women are facing and frankly it was just too depressing. I thought I was better off separating myself and pretending it's not really happening, but every now and again something happens – like the conversation I just had with him . . .'

'I take it he's away on deployment right now?'

She nods. 'It was only supposed to be three months this time, but they've asked him to stay on.' She gulps back her emotion and then grabs at my hand. 'How do you do it, Stella? How do you make peace with it all?'

I can't help but grimace. 'You did hear that Ruth said I *used* to go out with a sailor? Past tense. It ended. I'm not exactly the best person to offer any advice . . .'

'But you're here.' She grips my hand tighter. 'You survived!'

'Well, it really doesn't help when they switch schedules on you, does it?' I sigh. 'I remember flying all the way from England to be with Jonathan for a four-day weekend and we were lucky to get four consecutive hours together. I didn't even spend the last night with him – he got called back for duty on the ship. It almost seems like the Navy is deliberately trying to screw with their relationships.'

'Always moving the goalposts . . .'

I nod. 'After going out with Jonathan, my new favourite oxymoron became "military precision".'

Marina hoots with delight. 'Oh my God, you are so lucky to be British – you don't have the burden of patriotism we Americans have! I can't say a damn thing against the Navy for fear I'll get lynched.' She huddles forward. 'You know what I want to do more than anything is have a really good bitch about them.'

I smile back at her. 'Now that I can help you with!'

3

I don't know what comes to mind when you think of military guys, but I had very few thoughts on the subject before I met Jonathan.

I knew from visiting my aunt in Portsmouth that marines often got into drunken fights at the local clubs. I knew they had buzz cuts and got yelled at right in their faces by their superiors. I also, rather inappropriately considering I was eight at the time, used to know all the words to 'There is Nothing Like a Dame' because *South Pacific* was my mum's favourite musical.

As for the girlfriends and spouses of servicemen, well, in the movies their love always seems amped up, the parting only serving to accentuate the poignancy of the relationship. Do you know that at the airport gift shop in Norfolk, Virginia (home to the biggest US naval base in the world), they actually sell little statuettes portraying couples saying their teary goodbyes? Clutching and hugging so tightly, as if they are trying to lock in the sensation of the other's body, hoping they will still be able to feel them when they are gone. As if you want to be reminded of that most wretched and wrenching of moments! You really do feel as if your heart is being torn from your body, I know that now. But I never expected to be in that position myself.

I always thought of military wives as being incredibly tough – resilient, long-suffering and, well, sad. Because how happy can you really be in that situation? I mean, does anyone actually set out with that as a romantic goal? Does anyone clasp at their heart sighing, 'I want to meet a man and fall so in love with him that no one else compares and then only see him a few months of the year. I want him to spend the majority of his time hanging out with a bunch of stir-crazy guys watching porn and egging him on to get throw-up drunk as they travel to war zones around the world'?

What sane woman would choose to bring that into her life?

But of course, as everyone knows, when you're in love, all sense deserts you.

That's how it was when I met Jonathan.

I wish I could say we washed up on the shore of some desert island, but we met in a bar, just like regular civilians do.

I was in New York for a month on a MAC exchange programme and had just spent the day at their very first store in Greenwich Village, which was a trip, as it's nearly impossible to tell the women apart from the drag queens. A gang of us had gone out for drinks after and I was squeezed up at the bar trying to put in an order when one of my favourite songs came on. It has such a subtle, twinkly vibe I didn't expect the muscular guy next to me to say, 'I love this song!' at the very same moment as me.

The fact that it was called 'Just the Two of Us' proved auspicious. Our friends came and went, but we stayed in that same position long after Bill Withers finished serenading us with lyrics about crystal raindrops and castles in the sky.

Aside from his shaved head, Jonathan could not have been any less the cliché of a military man. If anything, I would've had him pegged as some cultural ambassador, he had such an innate elegance about him. And I honestly don't know the last time I described a man as 'elegant'. Despite being three French martinis down, I found myself taking care with my words, wanting to match his sophistication.

When last orders was called, I didn't think twice about inviting him back to my hotel, because he seemed such a gentleman (if not quite an officer – he was still at the training stage at this point). In fact, there was such a sense of propriety to him I wasn't even certain that he would try to kiss me.

But he did.

And what a dam-buster that was.

You know how one person can rest their hand on you and you feel nothing and yet someone else can trace the lightest fingertip and you're electrified? That's how it was with him. For once, my entire body felt invited to the party. I swear my knees actually buckled.

And then, mid-embrace, he murmured, 'How did you get to be so kind?'

Not 'You're hot!' or 'Get your coat!' but 'How did you get to be so kind?'

The fact that he even assigned value to such an outdated quality floored me. It mattered to me to *be* kind and the idea that he sensed that in me from my touch alone made me feel appreciated in a way I had never experienced before. In return he said he felt 'safe' with me, which apparently, coming from a Virgo, is the ultimate prize. I certainly felt in good hands myself. I remember when he met me the next day after work, he just took me in his arms and hugged me, right there in the street. And this wasn't a 'Hey, honey' squeeze-and-release, but a hug that held and held and conveyed so much emotion I was almost thrown. As I stood there, enveloped by him, I remember thinking, I can feel his heart. And I don't mean the physical thud or pitter-patter of it, but the nature of it, the pureness of it. It was almost as if, if I listened closely enough, I could hear our whispered pledge to each other: 'I'm going to take such good care of you.'

What he actually said was, 'I have a surprise for you,' and then he took me to this little backstreet arts centre where they were screening a documentary about Bill Withers called *Still Bill*. Both the setting and the movie couldn't have been less blockbuster multiplex and it was all the more endearing for it. Up until that night I really only knew the man's music – 'Lovely Day', 'Ain't No Sunshine' and so on – but it turns out he's such a down-to-earth, wise soul. Even casual, off-the-cuff comments hit me as so profound he became my own Dalai Lama.

'Value those who value you' was one of my favourites.

Especially after wasting far too much energy trying to ingratiate myself with men who really weren't that interested in the first place. If I ever got a tattoo, that's what it would say.

Plus there were all these weird coincidences, like Bill Withers was once in the Navy himself, and his beautiful wife described him as 'tough but sensitive', which felt like the most perfect description of the man sat next to me.

The next day Jonathan had to return to Chicago (where he was doing his training), but before he left he said, 'I'm going to fly you in for the weekend!'

He would make bold statements like that. I used to tease him that he got his good manners from Louisiana (where he was born) and his arrogance from Texas (where he grew up). He liked that. It tickled him. And I liked that he laughed so easily, that he could stand there looking dignified and authoritarian one minute and burst out laughing like a little kid the next. I loved how much he seemed to enjoy me. How much he wanted to please me. I'd never had that before.

So in among all this initial giddiness I never really stopped to think, Wait a minute – he's in the Navy. Have you really thought this through? Do you know what this would mean in the long term? I was following my heart, plain and simple. And it was leading me with superhuman force to his side.

'It was just the same with me,' Marina confirms as I bring her up to speed on my situation. 'So when did the whole Navy thing really hit home for you?'

'It was actually that first time I visited him in Chicago. Initially things were idyllic – I've never seen prettier skyscrapers and with all the fluffy white snow in the air it seemed like our own fantasyland. But then, just a few hours before I was due to leave, he said, "Listen, I have to let you know how it would be for us . . ." And then he spelled it all out – basically everything you are currently despairing of with the added kicker that, of all the military services, the Navy has the highest divorce rate.'

'Thanks for that reminder.'

I grimace. 'Sorry.'

'Go on.'

'It basically felt like the nastiest thing you could say to a girl. No sooner was he done talking, I burst into tears and ran and locked myself in the bathroom. He was obviously breaking up with me – why else would he say such off-putting, scaremongering things?' I roll my eyes. 'It took an hour for him to convince me that it was only because he had such strong feelings and because he could see a future that he needed to let me know just what the harsh reality of that would be.' I reach for one of the sofa cushions. 'I still remember his words – "You're so lovely, Stella, some part of me doesn't even want to inflict my lifestyle on you. It seems almost cruel." '

Marina sighs. 'Bless him!'

'I found the whole thing so confusing. Obviously it was the last thing I wanted to hear – I'd only just met him and was eager to spend every waking moment with him, so why was he talking about leaving me for six months at a time? Not that any of that mattered. I was already hooked.'

Marina nods. 'People always say, "Well, you knew what you were letting yourself in for . . ." but of course you really don't. I mean, you understand the *concept* of them leaving and you missing them, but at the time all you are feeling is, Whatever it takes! I'll do whatever it takes to be with this man!'

'Exactly,' I concur. 'I mean, that's what we're taught, isn't it – love conquers all.' I pick at the corner of the cushion. 'Logic and practicality go out of the window, along with any sense of protecting your heart.' I look up. 'Then again, why would you guard your heart against the very thing that is making it feel so vital and cherished?'

'I know! And, really, doesn't there seem something almost heroic about loving someone "against all odds"?' Marina ponders. 'It's so much better than saying, "Hmm, well, now you put it like that, this doesn't seem half so appealing. I'm off."'

I laugh along with her and then reach for my make-up remover so I can start removing the streaks of black from her once-pink cheeks.

'So I take it you carried on?' she asks, raising her eyes so I can wipe under her lashline.

'Well, what was the alternative – going back to the no-man's land of my love life prior to meeting him? He just seemed to be in a league of his own compared to the other men I knew.' I take a fresh cotton-wool pad and spritz it with toner. 'Even at a McDonald's drive-thru he'd say, "May I have the Big Mac and fries, please?" Who says, "May I . . . ?" any more? The idea of going back to mere mortals after I'd had a taste of his princely uniqueness was unthinkable.'

'So you didn't think it?'

I shake my head. 'I just kept moving forward, desperately trying to deflect every obstacle that arose, the main one being the end of my training stint in New York.'

'You had to return to England?'

I nod.

'So now instead of being a two-hour flight apart . . .'

'We were eight hours – basically a full day's travel door to door.'

Marina tuts in sympathy.

I don't bother telling her that the fare more than tripled, because I don't think she will be able to relate to that concern, or the fact that we had to find the money for a hotel – all on two pretty meagre salaries. But I know she is familiar with the vagaries of the long-distance relationship . . .

'Ah yes, the jealousies, suspicions and misunderstandings.' She faux whoops. 'But still you persevered?'

I sit back down beside her on the sofa. 'Every time I heard his voice I would know it was all worth it. We'd speak for hours every single night, and he was always so thoughtful and encouraging and hopeful that, even at a distance, I felt like I'd met my real-life guardian angel.'

Marina clasps her hand to her heart. 'That's so sweet!'

I take a moment to revel in just how good that felt, before I allow the smile to fade from my face.

'Then, almost exactly a year after we first met, he completed his training and he was assigned to a ship in Norfolk, Virginia. And that's when everything changed.'

Even now I still feel shaken from the jolt of going from being the centre of his universe and source of all his pleasure to a strain on his time and emotions. I'll never forget the day he turned up to meet me and he wasn't Jonathan any more. Every other time he'd come to pick me up in his regular clothes, his jeans and leather jacket, but this time he was layered in impenetrable digital-blue camouflage. Bulky steel-capped boots, cap pulled low on his forehead, collar tugged high. Only his eyes were visible, which was the worst part. They were cold and distant. He wasn't mine any more.

He belonged to the Navy now.

I don't want to inflict that chilling moment on Marina, so instead I hop back on the jolly bitching wagon. 'You know what I think is one of the most insane things about the Navy?'

'Tell me.' Marina cocks her head in curiosity.

'The fact that they have these guys enlist, put them through all that rigorous training – gas chambers and fire-fighting and dead man's float – and they never once put them on a ship! Jonathan threw up every single day it was choppy at sea, Dramamine or not. Some guys just don't have the stomach for it, and they don't even bother to check this out, which, frankly, is irresponsible, because you can't do your job and defend the realm if your head is down the toilet.'

'Sorry to interrupt the girl-talk.' Adrian pops his head round the door, clearly oblivious to our topic of conversation. 'I'm just very aware of our time constraint here.'

'We're on it!' Marina insists, hurrying back to the make-up chair, and then she turns to me. 'I'm so sorry to make you do this all over again.'

I give a shrug. 'The first was just the practice run. Now I get to do it right!'

4

The shoot goes like a dream.

I watch in awe as the digital images appear on the screen – Marina has obviously been practising poses that capture the peppy innocence of the era and she is producing winner after winner.

When the journalist – tough-cookie freelancer Karen Clark – walks in midway through the sequence, she quickly apologises and says she must have the wrong studio.

I catch her before she leaves and invite her to take a second look.

'You're kidding?'

'Nope. It's really her.'

'Wow,' she gawps. 'She must be desperate to get this role. I wonder why it's such a big deal to her.'

As Adrian calls a break to prepare for the head shots, we get the official response from Marina: 'I guess every actress feels there is some woman in history they were born to play – Madonna with Evita, Halle Berry with Dorothy Dandridge – for me, it's always been Marion Davies.'

'She's not quite so high profile as the other names,' Karen ventures.

'Well, you don't choose these people based on their star rating; it's all about who resonates with you – you see something of yourself in them and, through studying them, you understand yourself a little better.'

'For example?'

'She was a stutterer, a matchmaker and a vehement anti-vivisectionist, even if her main issue was that the poor animals didn't get a shot of vodka before they were operated on.'

'You were a stutterer?' Karen looks over her notes, as if she might have missed this detail.

'Well, it's not something I usually talk about. I've always been a bit superstitious about triggering some kind of resurgence. Not that I ever had a problem when I'm acting. Funny that, isn't it?' And then she smiles. 'There's this bit in Marion's biography where she talks about being shooed away by a fellow stutterer in the Follies – she clamied, "Stuttering is contagious, from one stutterer to another." And it's true. I've got this list of people to avoid working with – Harvey Keitel, Emily Blunt, Bruce Willis . . . There's this whole secret society of us. Even the mighty James Earl Jones!'

'The voice of Darth Vader?' Karen gasps.

'I know! Can you imagine the Dark Lord of the Sith with a speech impediment?'

'I feel a sidebar coming on!' She scribbles a note to herself. 'Anyway, back to Marion Davies – how did you first hear about her?'

'Well, I live on the same street as the AFI.'

'AFI?'

'American Film Institute. The day I went in for a snoop they were having a Marion Davies retrospective. It was fascinating watching the movies in the same sequence she made them. You can see how she was being guided down one path even though that wasn't necessarily the best choice for her. I think we can all relate to the fear of never reaching our full potential.'

I find myself nodding along, though I'm really just eavesdropping now, fixing and refixing the same curl over and over.

'So with Hearst being so much older than Marion,' Karen continues, 'are you worried that the role will invite parallels to your personal life?'

Marina sighs. 'What I'm hoping it will do is show that the public perception of a relationship can be way wide of the mark. When you see two people interacting in private, you get a whole different take on who they are and what they mean to each other – suddenly an inexplicable match can be oddly perfect.'

'For a while at least . . .' Karen shrugs.

'Marion and Hearst were together thirty-two years, until the day he died.'

'And how long was it with you and Victor?'

Marina snorts. 'I walked right into that one, didn't I?' She takes a sip of Vitamin Water. 'We were together four years. And we're still a lot closer than people might imagine.'

'So he's forgiven you for the affair with Will Ferrell?'

Marina rolls her eyes. 'There never was an affair with Will Ferrell. I mean, would you?'

'Well, no.'

'And, for the record, I haven't spent a dime of the money that I got for the movie with him. I want to do something significant to cancel out the awfulness of it.'

'Something to do with your animal charities?'

'As a matter of fact, I feel that particular film was such an affront to mankind I want to choose a humanitarian cause this time. I just haven't decided which one yet.'

'Five minutes!' Adrian calls over.

Karen cuts to the chase. 'There are rumours of a new love . . .'

'Are there?'

'Yes, but a distinct lack of paparazzi pics to back it up.' She smirks.

'Well, you see, that's all part of the cunning plan – we decided never to see each other. That way, there would be no evidence.'

Karen laughs, unsure of whether Marina is joking. 'So perhaps he doesn't exist at all?'

'So now he's my imaginary lover?' Marina looks amused and then a little sad. 'That's not so wide of the mark: I talk to him; no one ever sees him; people close to me fear for my sanity.'

I feel a pang of sympathy for Marina. It can't be easy deflecting questions when her emotions are so raw. Though I must say, she's doing a sterling job, especially when asked if there's a wedding on the cards.

'Oh, that ship has sailed,' she announces breezily.

I'm biting back a smile, but Karen looks genuinely concerned. 'You don't want to get married again?'

'I really don't. I'm done. At least, I hope I am.' She sounds a little wistful now.

'Any chance of children?'

I catch her hand trace over her belly. 'There's still a chance.'

Perhaps sensing that Marina is taking too many risks with her answers, Ruth steps in and reminds her that she needs to plug the wilderness movie. Karen duly obliges, asking her what it was like playing opposite a bear instead of her usual leading man.

'You forget I just did a movie with Alec Baldwin,' Marina deadpans.

'Now, he's hot!' Karen gushes.

'That he is,' Marina concurs, along with every woman in the room. 'That raspy voice!'

'Best older-guy hair ever!'

'Eyes as blue as a Siberian husky!'

Adrian shakes his head and tells us a) women are all mad and b) the time has come to get the cover shot.

Everyone is psyched, until the phone rings.

Oh no – *not again!*

'It's all right! It's mine!' Ruth jumps up, turning away to speak and then hurrying up to Marina. 'He's on the move.'

'Go!' Marina instructs her.

'But—'

'I'll be fine,' she assures her. 'Stella, you'll drop me at the hotel, won't you?'

'Y-yes,' I reply, wishing I'd cleaned out the car. I wasn't exactly expecting to be playing chauffeur today.

'You're absolutely certain?' Ruth checks as she fills her pockets with dried seaweed. (Well, that explains that choice.)

'We can't lose him,' Marina insists. 'You have to go.'

From that point on everything happens at double speed.

We do the shots, print out the best, then gather our belongings, scurry out of the studio and head back into the real world.

Visually, Marina is a perfect fit for the Dorchester, if only she were arriving in a Rolls-Royce Phantom as opposed to my Kia Picanto.

'I thought you liked Zen.' My brow rumples as I contemplate the *grande dame* of Mayfair through my smeary windscreen.

'Oh, that's Ruth. She likes everything so sterile she'd sleep in an operating theatre if she could. I prefer something with character. And a doorman with shiny brass buttons.' She grins as a smart fellow offers her his gloved hand. 'Can you bring the Evening in Paris perfume?' She ducks her head back into the car to me. 'I want one more spray before the meeting.'

'I'm coming in with you?'

'Of course!'

Ah, the presumption of the privileged. I couldn't possibly have anything more important planned! And indeed I haven't.

As we enter the lobby, we garner a few looks, but I'm pleased to say they're a mixture of curiosity and admiration as opposed to recognition. So far so good.

'I'm just going to get an update from Ruth.' Marina hurries into a corner while I take in the luxuriously carpeted 'Promenade' of the hotel.

Apparently this society salon is the same length as Nelson's Column. But with fewer pigeons.

I always wanted to have afternoon tea here. I wonder what I was waiting for? Why do we always say, 'Someday I'll . . .' as opposed to picking an actual date, however far in advance? Even now I have a portable calendar, the only thing I ever write in are dentist appointments and 'rent due'. I really need to be more proactive. Why not pepper the year with fanciful treats?

'Ruth reckons he'll be here in under ten!' Marina flusters back in my direction.

'And breathe!' I lay what I hope is a calming hand upon her arm.

'I have to get this.' She grips on to me, looking earnestly into my eyes.

I nod, understanding how urgently she needs to forget her lonely Navy-wife persona and become Marion Davies, if only for a matter of weeks.

'I don't know much about the casting process, but I can say you totally look the part.'

'All thanks to you,' she pips. 'I'm so grateful for all you've done today.'

'My pleasure.' I smile. 'I really hope it does the trick.'

'If it does, you know you're coming with me to California, right?'

I expel a snuffle. 'If only that were even possible. My agency own me right now.'

Marina swats away my concern. 'Listen, I may not be able to spring a certain person from an institution that shall remain nameless, but I can get you out of some flimsy agency contract. Trust me on that.'

'Well . . .'

'I can't tell you what it would mean to me to have someone who understands my situation by my side.'

Does she really mean this? She looks sincere.

'And you know I intend to find you a man?'

I give a merry hoot of disbelief.

'I'm serious,' Marina insists. 'There is no reason why you should be alone. I won't have it.'

Suddenly it's my turn to twang with emotion – the idea that someone I barely know is stomping their foot over my solo status is surprisingly touching.

Of course, my friends have all at one time said they can't understand why I haven't met someone, but it's in that subdued, tutting-yet-resigned way. No one has ever logged an official protest. Until now. If only she meant it. What a champion to have! What an endorsement: 'As recommended by Marina Ray'.

Uh-oh. She's started chewing on her thumb. I gently extract it before she smudges her perfect lip-line. She barely even notices, her eyes are trained so intently on the door.

'So when he arrives, do I just wait here while you two—'

'Oh no. I need you with me to stop anyone else getting in the elevator.'

I frown, trying to make sense of what she just said. 'What exactly are you planning to do in there?'

'My audition.'

I blink back at her. 'Your audition is taking place in an elevator?'

'Well, hopefully we'll progress to his suite, but that's the best I've got for now.'

'Wow,' I marvel. 'You know a director is busy when he actually schedules appointments for the ride to his hotel room!' No response. 'How many floors do we have?'

'I'm not sure. Ruth is still trying to find that out.' She checks her phone, but there are no new messages. 'We'll just push the top floor to cover all bases.'

I get an uneasy feeling. 'This isn't a hijack operation, is it?'

Marina cocks her head. 'Well, it hadn't occurred to me to press the emergency-stop button until now—'

'Marina,' I cut in, 'does he even know he's seeing you tonight?'

'No!' she cheers. 'And that's the beauty of it. He doesn't even know I'm in the country, so I will have a real chance to appear to him as someone else, no preconceived notions.'

I stumble backwards so I can support myself on the nearest marble column – she flew all the way to London for an audition that doesn't even exist!

'Wouldn't it be simpler to just announce yourself?' I say. 'I mean, you're Marina Ray!'

She shakes her head in an emphatic no. 'We already tried that. He said he wouldn't want to waste my time seeing me again.'

'What exactly went wrong at the first audition?'

She looks instantly deflated. 'It was so unfair – I only found out about it while I was doing promo shots for *Porridge*, so there I am with a head full of cave-woman hair extensions, looking like I've just got done mud-wrestling, trying to learn the lines in the car—' She stops herself. 'Basically I blew it. That's why it has to be this way.'

I nod understanding. 'All the same, it seems a little precarious.'

'It's all I've got. They are so close to the start of filming now. I have to get in before some hot new Carey Mulligan type steals the part from me. Oh my God!' She startles as her phone buzzes. 'He just left the restaurant. He'll be here any minute!'

I don't know whose heart is beating louder now as we head back to the lobby for our high-heeled stakeout.

It's then I realise that I don't have a clue what Conrad Blake looks like.

'You can't miss him,' Marina assures me. 'He's super tall with this whisked-up white hair and never goes anywhere without his pocket watch.'

I get a sudden image of the White Rabbit from *Alice in Wonderland* and then I find my eyes drawn to the spiky gold hands on the grandfather clock. Strange to think that both our fates will be determined in just a matter of minutes. I hope I'm not being excessively gullible, but I'm beginning to believe Marina would try and take me with her – as she said, I'm a two-for-one service: make-up artist and Navy empathiser. Dare I even imagine how incredible that experience could be? To step out of my whitewashed cube and become part of a living, breathing moving picture? I'm as invested in this now as she is. I just wish it wasn't such a long shot.

'Oh, where is he?' Marina is getting increasingly agitated.

'Don't lose your Marion-ness,' I remind her. 'Carefree with a side of wanton. Come on, let's get a little closer to the revolving door.'

Marina surprises me with a smile. 'You know, when I was a child, my mom worked in an office building with a revolving door and she used to make a game for me, getting me to enter as one person and come out as another.'

'Like a superhero?'

'Oh, we did everything! I'd go in as a waif, come out as a princess; in a toddler, out an old lady . . . I'd even do relatives – in as Cousin Mandy and out as Uncle Clive!'

I chuckle at her repertoire. 'So you were a good mimic?'

'I guess. I remember the security guard telling my mom, "That girl's got talent, Mrs Ray." ' She turns to me. 'What about you? If you could go in one way and come out another, what would you choose?'

'Interesting concept,' I muse.

My first thought is that I would like to shake off my disillusioned self and emerge as one of those sunny people who wakes up in the morning and smiles before they've even opened their eyes.

'You don't think of yourself as a happy person?' Marina seems surprised.

'Well, I used to be. So maybe I should be more specific – I suppose I would like to forget Jonathan.'

'Really?'

'Well, at least that way the rest of the world wouldn't keep falling short. If I forgot what it felt like to be loved by him, then everything else wouldn't feel so pointless or less than. If I couldn't recall his face, then I might be able to look at another. If it was no longer possible for me to conjure his touch, then maybe the wanting would go away . . .'

'Wow.' Marina shakes her head. 'You're making me feel like I've got it made!'

'Well, everything is relative.' I shrug. 'The better it is when you are together, the worse it is when you are apart.'

'It's just been so long.'

'I know, but you don't want to get into that frame of mind now.' I give her shoulders a light jostle. 'You'd better take a twirl and come back out as Marion!'

Just as she steps into the glass section I see Conrad Blake enter the opposing panel. I gesture wildly to Marina, who promptly stops and tries to reverse, only to jam the revolution of the door.

Oh no! He's already out and striding towards the lift.

'Go after him!' I see Marina mouthing frantically.

His gait is so elongated I have to break into an unladylike trot.

'Hold the door!' I call ahead. It's closing, closing . . . but then a paw extends and blocks the gap.

'Th-thank you!' I gasp, scooting inside. I turn back to find the button to hold the doors open for Marina, but we're already in motion.

'What floor?' he asks me.

'Er, er, twenty,' I blurt, before noticing that it only goes up to nine. 'What am I saying? That was yesterday in Paris!' I tinkle. And then I spot that he has already illuminated seven. 'Oh, what a coincidence – we're on the same floor.'

'Everything all right?' He seems to sense my distress.

I turn to him and look into those eyes that have observed some of the world's greatest actors in motion. How can I possibly compete? Honesty has to be the best policy at this point. Well, semi-honesty . . .

'Mr Blake, my friend would very much like to audition for you. She was just—'

'Have her call my office.' He turns his face towards the doors.

I puff with frustration. 'She was literally the other side of the revolving door when you came in. If we just nipped back down, you could meet her.'

'Not tonight. I've had a very long day.'

Ping! Seventh floor.

'After you.' He motions for me to step out first.

Darn it! Which way to go? I step out and stall, pretending to be rummaging for the room key in my bag. Like he doesn't know my game. I'm just craning my neck, watching his progress down the long corridor, trying to see which door he is about to enter, when a voice cries, 'Wait!'

We turn and see Marina bursting from the stairwell. So much for making a nonchalant entrance – she's red in the face, panting and barefoot.

'What the . . . ?'

'Please, Mr Blake' – I turn back to him – 'all we need is five minutes of your time.'

'It's going to take her longer than that to catch her breath.'

Suddenly she's bolt upright, reciting her first line.

He holds up his hand. 'Stop, please.' He looks her up and down. 'If you're willing to gallop up seven flights of stairs after me, then the least I can do is offer you a glass of water.'

And with that he turns and opens the door to his suite.

5

Twenty-one hours later we are on a plane to Los Angeles, California.

Yup, that's right – *we!!!*

Marina was as good as her word, both in her promise to take me with her and to extract me from my agency contract. (Apparently celebrity trumps legality.)

It seems unfathomable that my life has broken into a sprint from such a plodding state. After the audition, I literally had to tear home, layer anything vaguely summery into a case, reorganise my kit, empty the fridge of any perishables and then try to grab a couple of hours' sleep – aka lie in bed in a state of disbelief. I must have nodded off just before the alarm because I remember waking up with the usual plea – Please let this be the day that something happens – and then thinking, Wait! It already has! Everything has changed!

And then I couldn't get out of bed quickly enough.

On the way to the airport, I made a few calls – 'Hi, Mum. Just letting you know I'll be out of the country for the next couple of weeks . . . Not exactly a holiday – I've got a job on a movie set in California! . . . Yes, I've got travel insurance . . . It's with Marina Ray . . . No, she actually seems very nice.'

I got more of the reaction I was hoping for from Brontë. 'This is it, Stella,' she told me. 'This is your ticket to a better tomorrow!'

I actually got to see Brontë in person for a few minutes, dropping the borrowed dress back to her riverside shoot in Chiswick, an easy stop en route to Heathrow.

'So I take it the audition went well?'

'Honestly, it couldn't have got off to a worse start,' I confided, reviewing the moment up until Conrad welcomed us into his suite.

Once inside, Marina began with her spiel about how similar she and Marion are, but it was only when she copped to the fact that she too had had a relationship with a considerably older, highly influential man that Conrad finally realised who he was dealing with.

'Marina Ray, you have a lot of nerve,' he said, 'and I mean that as a compliment.'

But before she could even do her scene for him, he said he had to be upfront about the money – apparently he'd blown the budget on a hot male star to boost female ticket sales, thinking he was going to cast a newcomer as Marion.

Marina insisted she didn't care about her fee. 'I just want to do the work. This work. *Your* work.'

And so, finally, he let her read. He took the role of Hearst and suited it rather well. All gravitas and lofty values. Marina was the perfect contrast to his imposing ways, like a frothy frill of cream to his chunky apple pie.

I didn't know she was capable of comedic performance, but she was really spot on, and far giddier than she is in real life.

Still Conrad seemed to be holding out on her. That's when she suggested he added a new scene.

'I wondered if you might make a little feature of her dachshund, Gandhi?' she began. 'Everyone thinks of Marion Davies as so flip and flighty, and I know that's a lot of fun, but we also want to see that she has a heart. So at first you'd see her joking with the little dog, calling him Mahatma Coatma Collar Gandhi, and then we would cut to the day he got sick when she was told he would have to be put down.

' "Over my dead body!" ' she read from Marion's memoir. ' "But it all happened too fast. I saw Gandhi looking up with those two appealing eyes. The nurse gave him a shot and he went. Well, I tore the place apart. I broke everything I could lay my hands on. I almost killed everybody, I was so furious. If they'd left him to me, I could've taken care of him." '

She looked up at Conrad. 'I know I couldn't think of anything worse than someone taking my baby from me before I was ready. Don't you think the audience will be able to relate to her on this?'

Marina later told me that she knew Conrad had recently lost his spaniel, so if that didn't get to him, then nothing would.

'It's the softest part of the person – the relationship they have with their pet,' she told me. 'The least cynical, the most loving.'

And she was right. I could see him mellowing before my eyes.

She then finished him off with a quote from Hearst about the death of his dachshund, Helen: ' "An old bozo is a nuisance to almost everybody, except his dog. To his dog, he is just as good as he ever was, maybe better." '

'Okay,' Conrad conceded, briskly wiping his eyes. 'You got me.'

Though I stepped outside to let him reveal just how small the fee was, apparently it was enough for her to negotiate me into the deal – she said she couldn't conceive of playing Marion Davies without me.

'And he believed you?' I was incredulous.

'Listen, Al Pacino was just at the Emmys thanking his make-up artist above all else in his acceptance speech. It's de rigueur to cop to the collaboration. Besides, it's true.'

Then she told me there was one other thing she needed from me besides my make-up skills – my candour.

'I know you're English and have an inbred nimbleness when it comes to avoiding hurting people's feelings, but I need you to let that go when you are with me. I want you to be blunt to the point of rudeness.'

'Well . . .'

'I'm serious. I have enough "yes people" in my life. I don't want any more. I'll only be offended if I think you're telling me what I want to hear. Just come right out with whatever is on your mind, okay?'

'Okay,' I told her.

Though I am a little worried about putting this to the test, it does explain why Ruth gets away with being so curt.

'Upper class was full, so you're going to have to fly coach,' is how she greets me at the airport.

'That's more than fine, honestly,' I insist, embarrassed that they may even think this is an issue.

'Tell you what, Ruthie, why don't you trade with her?' Marina proposes. 'You sleep the whole journey anyhow; this way, I'd get some company.'

'Oh no!' I'm aghast. 'I couldn't possibly.'

Despite my extremely 'blunt' protestations, Marina won't be swayed.

'Can I have a word with you, Marina, in private?' Ruth takes her over to the automatic door. I can't hear what they're saying because the door keeps opening, letting in more travellers and outdoor noise. Eventually Ruth is on the other side of the glass door and Marina is coming back to me.

'Well, that solves that – she's not coming with us.'

'What?' I am stricken. 'Marina, I absolutely do not need to be travelling upper class—'

She shushes me. 'She just said that she's always wanted to see the Lake District and seeing as you were travelling back with me, this was the perfect time for her to take a couple of days to do that.'

'But we leave for Hearst Castle the day after tomorrow.'

'Well, I'm sure you don't mind running the odd errand for me, do you?'

'How odd?' I want to ask. Mind you, so far Ruth seems to be the more high maintenance of the two.

'No, of course not,' I tell her. 'I'd be happy to help with whatever.'

'Anyway, don't worry. I made Ruth agree that we can call her anytime, day or night – you know, because of the time difference.'

I don't quite see Ruth propelling her mobile into the nearest bin, but as she leaps into a taxi, her body language seems to be screaming, 'Free at last! Free at last!'

'Come on.' Marina links arms with me. 'Let's go buy every Hearst Corporation magazine for the flight!'

No sooner have we taken off than Marina suggests a cocktail at the petite sci-fi bar.

'This is just so cool having no one recognise me,' she giggles. 'I feel like I'm playing hooky or something.'

'What can I get you, ladies?' the server enquires.

'What would Marion drink?' I turn to Marina.

'Hmm. Champagne, of course. Gin fizz. Maybe a sidecar?'

'How about one of each?' the server teases.

'As a matter of fact, I think that's very her!'

If keeping Marina company means matching her drink for drink, I'm in trouble. Fortunately her bladder is less robust than her liver and while she's in the loo, I tell the server to make the rest of mine virgins.

'I'm teetotal too.' The guy next to me leans in a little too close.

Fearing he's one of those Americans who confess their alcoholism at the drop of a swizzle stick, I merely say, 'Good for you!' and then flip open the first of our stack of magazines.

I don't even have to feign interest when I see Milo Vallis staring back at me – how many men could make a threadbare denim shirt look so good? I always think of him as freshly sunkissed, as if he spends his days lying in a field staring up at the sky with a sleepy smile on his face. When he's not acting in blockbusters, of course. I love his movies. He always brings an effortless charm to them – one of those guys who saunters through life one hand in his pocket, the other skimming a pebble across a lake or stealing some fabulous jewel, as he was in his last outing. He looked so good in that black polo neck . . .

'Thieving bastard.' Marina seems less enthralled when she rejoins me. 'That's the son of a gun who's taken most of my salary.'

'What?'

'He's playing some kind of movie-star amalgam so they can get away with his character behaving outrageously without being sued.'

If I knew where the cargo area of the plane was, I'd crawl in and whoop my head off. Is this even possible?

'Are you saying that he'll actually be with us, at Hearst Castle?'

Marina frowns at me as if I'm a little slow. 'Yes, of course.'

I reach for a slug of gin fizz only to be greeted with soda water and lemon juice. Backfire!

'Have you met him before?' I ask, battling to keep my voice at a level pitch.

'Yeah, we did a movie together a couple of years back. Never got a major release.'

'And did you . . .' I pause '. . . get on?'

'You mean *get it on*?' Marina smirks, beckoning the dish of peanuts. 'As a matter of fact, the bastard turned me down.'

'Really?' I brighten, unconcerned that she's dropped two 'bastard's in as many minutes.

There is nothing more appealing to me than a man who will turn down a stunning woman. I mean, is that not indicative of depth and discernment – a desire for a connection beyond the physical? I feel a kind of elation and have to reach for a mouthful of peanuts myself now, just to hide my smile. Oh wait. There could be a less thrilling reason for this.

'He's not gay, is he?'

'Oh no. He chose one of the prop master's assistants over me. Can you believe it? Crew over talent? No offence.'

'Absolutely none taken,' I assure her with undisguised glee.

'Which reminds me, I must get them to send me an advance copy of the tech list – there's this sound guy I worked with on the last movie and if I wasn't married, I would definitely have gone for him. I'd love to see you guys get together.'

'Mm-hmm,' I feign interest.

'Or maybe even one of the set decorators – you paint faces, he paints facades. How d'you like that?'

I play along, but little does she know any matchmaking is redundant now. Nothing could compare to an in-person crush on Milo Vallis. Just the chance to be around him, be in his presence, listen to him talking and maybe even catch a stray smile or two. Who knows, maybe he'll feel like slumming it with a 'crew' member again!

I feel a new surge of energy and all I want now is for Marina to stop talking so I can go back to reading the article about him. Eventually, mercifully, she decides it's movie time.

The way our 'seat suites' are positioned, she can't see what I'm up to, not that it's a crime to read a magazine, but it certainly feels like an illicit activity to be researching Milo. The more I read, the more I like him – so natural, so playful – until I read about his taste in women. Of course, it's just a magazine article, not a binding contract, but here it is in print – just how much of a sucker he is for the black hair-blue eyes combo.

'Add a pair of metallic stilettos – you know where it looks like she could snap the heel off and use it as a weapon? – I see that and I'm done. Seriously!'

I look down at my bendy ballet pumps. Oh dear.

Of course, I reason to myself, people rarely end up with their 'type'. I mean, just think of Marina and her Navy guy. Me and my Navy guy for that matter. Not that mine was a happy ending.

I carefully extract myself from my pod so as not to disturb Marina (who appears to have nodded off) and then shut myself in the plane toilet and assess my reflection.

My crumpled dress-for-comfort form couldn't look anything less like an assassin. I peer closer. It's been a long time since I had an actual hairstyle. Yes, my bouffant ponytail has become my signature, but only because it hides a multitude of sins. Every now and again I get the urge to try something radically different, but I had this secret notion that if I returned to looking as close to my real self as possible, that this man – my true soul mate – would have an easier job finding me. If I was disguised as a wispy blonde or a glossy chestnut filly, he might glance my way, but ultimately he would pass me by, thinking, That can't be her – the description specifically said, 'Tawny.'

52   *Belinda Jones*

Or is it that I want to look exactly the same as I did the last time I saw Jonathan? Am I afraid to try any other style because what if we were in the same room and all he saw was the back of my head and it was burgundy and shaved to the nape? How would he know then to come up behind me and put his arms around me and tell me he was home for good?

I heave a sigh. I don't want to be this person I see in the mirror any more. This girl does not look ready to take on Hollywood. She's too bland, too forgettable. When I think of the lengths, or rather the shorts, Marina went to for the part she wanted – hacking off that beautiful red hair and bleaching it to brittledom, putting on a vintage gown and striding right up to the man who could make her dream come true and demanding he make it happen. And it worked!

How far would I be prepared to go to separate myself from the lonesome person I can't seem to shake any other way?

I know change is supposed to come from within and in a way it is – a strong inner desire to be reinvented is what is making me consider a physical transformation of my own. A need to look in the mirror and not see the woman Jonathan left but someone I barely recognise, someone bold enough to embrace a new life.

I don't know yet quite what form my new look will take, but I do make a pledge to myself that, from the moment the wheels touch down in Los Angeles, I am going to be a new woman.

6

What actually happens is that I am greeted by a new Los Angeles.

Last time I exited this airport I was part of the shuffling, stiff-legged masses waiting to board the blue and yellow shuttle bus. This time I am ushered directly into a low, svelte limo.

Last time I was gawping up at the giant billboards advertising the latest blockbuster. Now I am sat beside the magnified star (though, as is so often the case these days, she actually looks better without the air-brushing).

The last hotel I stayed in was one of those trendified motels that still has echoes of a stale-shirted drunk watching TV over the top of his belly. This time I've got the ultimate upgrade – a movie-star mansion!

'Nearly there,' Marina tells me, after half an hour of bombing along the multi-lane freeway gawping up at the vast splendour of the pink and gold sunset through the open sunroof. We're now turning onto the broad boulevard of towering pines, fanning palms and pointy cypresses that borders Griffith Park and its iconic white-domed observatory.

'Hard to believe that somewhere this close to Hollywood could be this green, isn't it?'

'It's gorgeous,' I concur, feeling a definite sense of vitality.

'This is actually the very street I lived on when I first moved to LA – Los Feliz Boulevard. I was in one of the cute apartments further down – they've got it all here: Italian courtyards, faux-French turrets . . . There's even a Southern plantation one with a real, live cannon!'

'You're kidding!'

'Well, not live as in it fires, but you know what I mean. Ernesto, can you slow here?' she instructs the driver.

'This was my one . . .' She points to a striking art deco building featuring the trademark stepped angles and bands of milky-jade tiles. 'I felt like a starlet every time I went through that front door.'

Maybe that's where I've been going wrong, I decide to myself. My place in London looks like a crack den from the outside.

As we weave around the side streets, I am charmed by even the boxiest blocks on account of the authentic 1950s lettering and starbursts set on the front panels.

'You know where you would love?' Marina gets excited. 'The Dresden – it's so kitschy-retro with this old piano duo singing "Fly Me to the Moon" and Ric, the barman, mixing crazy-strong drinks. Whatever hellish mood you arrive in, he makes it right just by saying, "What'll it be, baby girl?" '

'Sounds like heaven,' I sigh. 'Last time I was here, all us make-up girls got dollied up for a big night out at the Standard and they wouldn't even let us in.'

Marina rolls her eyes. 'No velvet ropes in this hood. I rarely even see a stiletto, unless it's on some pierced rock chick.' She looks wistful. 'I missed that laissez-faire vibe when I was with Victor in Beverly Hills. I was so used to heading out not thinking twice about what I was wearing, but within a week I felt obliged to buy a whole new designer wardrobe.'

'Like Julia Roberts in *Pretty Woman*?'

'Just what exactly are you implying?'

For a minute I think I've crossed a line. 'I-I didn't mean to suggest that you were in any way pimping yourself out to Mr Goldstein.'

'Oh stop.' She nudges me. 'I'm just messing with you!'

'Oh right.' I swallow back my palpitations. 'So after the divorce you moved back here?'

She nods. 'Most of my best friends still live in the area, so it seemed natural to come back to the nest. Plus I think having so many memories of when I was a poor wannabe helps keep me grounded.'

She almost had me convinced, until she tells me why she is now instructing the driver to step on it.

'I just remembered I asked Inez to go to Mexico City and get us my favourite burritos – with any luck they'll still be warm.'

I blink in disbelief. Now that's a job I would like – flying to different countries on the culinary whim of a superstar. I picture the scene.

'Hmm, I'm in the mood for pizza today.'

'Well, for the best I'm really going to have to go to Naples, so, if you like, I could swing by Paris on the way back and get a lovely tarte tatin for dessert.'

'Sounds good. Hurry back!'

The truth is, I probably *would* want to hurry back to this place.

The minute the gate slides closed behind us, I feel as if we've been spirited away to an exclusive chateau – a vast vine-clad building with black-shuttered windows, multi-level balconies and terraces trimmed with citrus trees and rose bushes.

'White roses are my mom's favourite – they make me feel as if she's still with me.' She smiles, before adding, 'The lemons and limes are great for cocktails.'

While Ernesto deals with our luggage, Marina leads me through the giant white-glossed front door to a lobby seemingly revolving round a fabulous purple glass chandelier.

As I gaze up at it, I start to sniff the air.

'What are you doing?' I catch Marina giving me a concerned sideways glance.

'Just trying to figure out the fragrance of the day – I know Tuesday is figs and Wednesday is pomegranates, but I have no idea what flavour Thursday is.' And then I gasp. 'Is it my job to spritz?'

Marina rolls her eyes. 'I told Ruth to take that nonsense off the rider. She is naughty. She only does it to torment people.'

'Don't you mind?' I ask, surprised by her blasé attitude.

'I should, shouldn't I? It's just she keeps threatening to retire and I'm so attached to her schoolmarm-ish ways.'

'But it's your reputation at stake!'

'They'll only make up some other diva story anyway. At least that stuff is fairly harmless.'

'Oh.'

'I don't mean to be defeatist. Besides, I'm really hoping this movie will change the way people look at me. I've just got a feeling.'

'But it won't be out for another year,' I protest. 'Couldn't you do one of those sit-down interviews with Diane Sawyer or whoever and set everyone straight on all the false rumours about you?'

'My management would love that, but I signed a pre-nup with Victor and I can't discuss anything to do with our marriage ever, even after his death.'

'That's a shame.' I grimace. 'I mean, with the possible exception of Jesse James, the viewer always ends up liking these supposed sinners.'

She smiles. 'Now, Miss Sandy Bullock is the ultimate role model for a dignified public persona, and you know what she would say if she were here right now?'

'What?'

'Let's eat!'

Marina hustles me through to the kitchen, where I am immediately confronted by the most gargantuan fridge – basically the size of most people's wardrobes but with a built-in vodka-chilling unit, complete with frosted shot glasses.

'Looks like a fun crowd.' I peer at the photo collage magnetised to the side.

'Oooh!' She veers away from the microwave, where she's zapping the burritos. 'Let's pick out a man for you. Sit, sit . . .'

She ushers me onto one of the breakfast-bar stools and then begins a process of 'What about this one?' running back and forth, brandishing pic after pic, rather in the way a dog eagerly drops a chew toy at your feet.

Frankly the men are in about as good condition.

'Marina, these guys look like they've been gnawed on and spat out!' I complain, getting ever more bold with my bluntness. 'Don't you know any clean men?'

'Still hankering for a bit of military polish?' she teases me as she hands me my plate.

I give her a dark look. 'I don't need a crew cut and shiny boots, but if they could've at least bathed in the past month . . .'

'These are hipsters,' she huffs. 'It's just their look. It's not dirt in their hair; it's product. You of all people should be able to distinguish the two.'

'I can. Trust me. There is a distinct absence of Fudge Hair Varnish on these follicles.'

'What about this guy? He's really smart and witty—'

'Too skinny,' I wince, mouth now full of chicken.

'This one?'

'Is he posing outside a rehab facility?'

'Yes, but he only went for fun because one of his best mates was going. He doesn't really have a problem.'

I raise an eyebrow.

Marina scoots together the pictures with a sigh. 'I can see I'm going to have to cast the net a little wider.'

If I was being truly blunt, I'd be obliged to note that Marina has very different taste in friends to her idol. I was perusing Marion Davies's infamous biography on the flight and the woman literally dined with everyone from Winston Churchill to George Bernard Shaw, but, as far as I'm aware, she didn't spend too much time in the company of indie bands and graffiti artists. All I can think is that Marina must've led quite the double life when she was married to Victor – I can't see him getting loaded in some dive bar. Same goes for the Navy officer, for that matter.

'So where's your guy in all this?' I ask as my burrito starts shedding rice and crinkles of lettuce.

'I don't keep pictures of him out any more,' Marina replies, handing me a napkin. 'I found that every time I'd catch a glimpse of his face, I'd get this horrible pang and end up missing him all the more.'

'But you carry a picture of him with you?'

She nods, but she doesn't offer to show it to me. Maybe she thinks I'll be able to identify him by face alone. Truth is, I couldn't even pick out Jonathan's shipmates in a crowd. We never socialised with them. Which makes me wonder . . .

'Have any of your friends actually met him?'

'Oh yes,' she confirms. 'A select few.'

'And how did he manage fitting in with them?'

'I must confess there was some initial resistance.'

'Go on.'

'Well, before they met, my friend Dylan swore blind all Navy men were gay – "Why would you sign your life away unless being confined on a ship with two hundred other sex-starved men appealed?" Once I'd clarified that Jeff was most definitely heterosexual, he just moved on to the next round of clichés – "Surely he must be some undereducated redneck with an NRA membership." '

'NRA?'

'National Rifle Association.'

'Oh. So what happened?'

'He just played with them – saluted everyone as he walked in the room, showing off this big anchor tattoo he'd drawn on his forearm, just like Popeye!'

I chuckle along.

'He'd brought over this fifty-seven-year-old rum and basically got them all trashed. By ten p.m. their disdain had given way to fascination: he's talking about manually hauling fuel ships alongside his own and chemical-warfare drills and I'm looking at Dylan, with his smudgy eyeliner and girlie hair band, thinking, Who's gay now?'

I can't help but laugh. Then I inform her, 'You know the tradition of sailors and rum actually came from the British Navy – when they captured Jamaica?'

'Is that so?'

'They found that grape-based spirits like brandy went off in the heat, but the rum actually improved.'

'Oh, you have to see this!' Marina hops off her stool and opens up a mirrored cupboard filled with an array of high-end booze. But there beside the Grey Goose and the Ketel One is a giant plastic economy-sized bottle labelled, 'Military Vodka'. She hoicks it down and dumps it beside me, pointing out the painted images of an army tank, fighter jet and black combat boots on the label.

' "Do not drink and operate heavy artillery"!' I read with a hoot.

'You want a little hit?'

I hesitate. 'Maybe just enough to dip my tongue in.'

But she goes the other way, inadvertently glugging out far too much, drenching the table. 'Oh God, it'll probably take the surface off!' she panics, quickly reaching for a cloth.

I'm actually rather impressed that she knows where to locate the cleaning products.

'I would've imagined you have staff . . .'

'Oh, I do. Inez runs the show. But we were getting in late – I didn't see any point in them coming in until tomorrow.'

'Plus she must be tired after her trip to Mexico.'

Marina looks confused. 'She's from Pasadena.'

'I thought you said she'd been to Mexico City to get the burritos?'

Marina doubles up with mirth. 'Honestly, Stella, what do you take me for?'

Her phone goes.

'Come on.' She jumps to her feet and bids me follow her, back out into the night. 'Now I have two things to show you . . .'

The first is a restaurant. Stone flagging on the exterior, predominantly red on the interior, name of Mexico City.

'This is where the burritos came from.'

'Ohhhhh!' I cover my face, feeling rather foolish.

'Though I like your version better. Oops, mind out!' Marina pulls me out of the way of a guy skittering by on his skateboard, oblivious to us, as he is texting.

'What about him?'

'He can't be more than seventeen!' I protest.

'Not the skateboarder, that guy.' She nods across the road to another restaurant, rather more upscale with linen table-cloths even on the pavement seating.

The guy in question is well dressed and apparently well heeled – the valet parker has just swung his BMW up to the kerb.

'Well?'

'Please tell me you're not picking strangers off the street now.'

'I'm just trying to get an idea of your taste,' she defends herself. 'I still don't have a clear picture.'

I want to refer her to the magazine photo of Milo Vallis, but instead I tell her that I've given up on types. 'Honestly, I just want someone whose face lights up when they see me, someone who gives me huge, heartfelt hugs, someone I can trust but who also makes me laugh.'

'A doting but playful life companion?' she summarises as she sets me in motion, back up the hill. 'Maybe also someone you feel will protect you and stand by you and never leave you?'

'Yes,' I confirm, thinking she is looking into my very soul.

'You want a dog.'

I roll my eyes.

'No, seriously. You should probably get a dog first. That will take care of some of your basic needs and then you won't ask so much of your man.'

I go to argue back, but actually I think she makes a fairly good point. Instead I tell her that I'm surprised she doesn't have a Cesar Millan-style pack of dogs – wouldn't they be excellent company while Jeff is at sea?

'Funny you should say that . . .' she replies, stalling beside an archway and then pointing up to the sign above our heads: 'El Perro Feliz Dog Sanctuary.'

'El Perro?' I frown.

'It's Spanish for "dog". "*Feliz*" means "happy".'

'The Happy Dog.' I smile, but only for a second – the minute Marina opens the gate we are greeted by a chorus of frantic barking.

'It's okay – they're not running wild,' she assures me.

'How come you have a key?'

'I own the place.'

'What?'

Marina gives a nonchalant shrug. 'I came in looking for a dog and basically opened my big mouth telling them they needed a larger play area, somewhere potential adopters could hang out with the dogs, maybe even with a second-hand sofa to see how the two of you fit together in repose, and the owner just laughed at me. Where were they going to get the funds for the expansion? They couldn't even afford the second-hand sofa! Within a week I owned the whole place.'

'They sold just like that?'

'Well, the owner was nearing retirement and I promised to keep the staff intact and make some major improvements that she would oversee, so actually, she was pretty happy about the whole arrangement.'

'And when did all this happen?' I know I haven't read about this in the gossip magazines.

'Just coming up to three years. But it's a secret.'

'*Another one?*'

'I don't want looky-loos traipsing in and out all day – you know, people coming here hoping for a sighting, pretending to be looking at the rescue dogs, getting their hopes up, getting *my* hopes up . . .'

'People might think a little more favourably of you if they knew . . .' I venture.

'Oh, I've long since stopped worrying about what people think of me. Besides, they'd only accuse me of exploiting the dogs to try and improve my image or some such nonsense. Things are going well as it is – Kendal's doing a fantastic job running the place. She lives out the back here . . .' Marina guides me through. 'She's been looking after my boy while I've been gone.'

My jaw drops.

'And before you go thinking I've got a secret son, I mean my dog, Bodie.'

Right on cue a dog that looks like a cross between a teddy bear and a pot-bellied pig barrels up to Marina, in such a tizzy of excitement he doesn't know whether to jump or lick or come or go – he ends up bending his body into a croissant shape in a desperate bid to get both ends of his body close to her.

'Officially I am supposed to wait until he calms down before I give him affection, but I usually succumb ahead of time – right about now!'

She bends down and wraps her arms around him, though he can barely keep still enough to accept the hug, as his tail is going like a manic windscreen wiper.

'He's so compact,' I marvel. 'What exactly is he?'

'Pretty much anything you want him to be – a lot of people say Akita or dingo, but the vet says he's most likely a mix of chow chow and pit bull, neither of which has the best reputation, but put them together and all you get is goofy love.'

Right on cue he slides onto the floor and offers up the blond fluff of his belly.

'That's the spot – ooh, right there!' Marina laughs as his back leg starts twitching agitatedly. 'Feel free to join in – he's a more-the-merrier kinda guy.'

'Thing is . . .' I hesitate '. . . I'm really more of a cat person.'

'Oh, he'll turn you around,' she insists. 'See, you can do anything with him.' She smooshes his face into velvety folds. 'He'll never bite.'

Gingerly I move in. 'He's so soft!' I gasp as I run my hand along his back. I thought his short hair would be coarse, but in fact it's Pantene-silky. 'And so smiley!' I laugh as he grins up at me with his big upturned mouth and warm brown eyes. 'What are those spots on his tongue?'

'That's the chow in him. They have these purplish-black tongues. His is spotted on top and striped black underneath. Here, give him this treat.'

Marina hands me a dog biscuit in the shape of a fire hydrant.

'Can you sit for Stella?'

He slams his furry bottom directly onto the ground and looks up at me with rapturous expectation.

'Should I just . . . ?'

'You can put it right in his mouth.'

He takes a gentle chomp and then leans heavily back onto my shins to enjoy it. I feel my heart twang – sold!

'I'm so glad you guys get along.' Marina beams. 'He's coming with us on our little jaunt up the coast!'

'They allow dogs on the set?'

'When you're getting paid as little as I am, they're more flexible with the perks. Heyyyy! There you are!'

Marina throws out her arms to embrace a tall, curly-haired woman, who, in turn, introduces herself to me as Kendal.

'That's quite a do you've given Marina . . .' she says as she leads us through to her comfy living room.

'Oh!' I startle, not necessarily wanting her to think this is representative of my best work. 'We're still working on the colour . . .'

'I like the cut. Ever groomed a dog?'

'Kendal!' Marina tuts. 'She just stepped off an eleven-hour flight.'

'I'm just saying . . .' She pulls a face. 'Andy is on holiday and we've got three desperate for a trim – already shampooed, ready to go.'

'Um . . .'

'Oh my God!' Kendal suddenly diverts herself. 'I wanted to tell you in person – I think I've found the perfect Gandhi!'

Marina turns to me. 'Remember Marion's little dachshund?'

'Of course,' I say. Slightly ashamed that, at the time, I thought Marina was being rather mercenary using Conrad's recent loss as leverage.

'Dachshunds are Kendal's weakness. She's rescued how many?'

'Forty-nine.' She blushes.

'So tell me . . .'

'Okay' – she sits forward in her armchair – 'so his name's Frankie. He's old, probably only got three more years tops, so nobody wants him, but I figured if we could get him a cameo in the movie, all of a sudden he's a celebrity . . .'

'We could get a still from the set and put it up on the website. Maybe even get Milo holding him – who could resist that?'

Not me, I think to myself.

'So can I meet him?'

'He's with a foster family and I don't want to remove him until you get the go-ahead, but I'll drive him on up to the castle as soon as you're ready.'

'Fantastic! And did he get along with Bodie?'

'Perfectly. You know how rambunctious your boy can be, but he was totally respectful. There was even a little facial licking.'

'Awww.'

As the pair of them chat, with Bodie now sleeping half in Marina's lap, half lolling off the sofa, I wish I could beam this scene to the world and they could see she's not the opportunistic gold-digger so often portrayed. Forthright?

Yes. Ambitious? Yes. Mouthy? Absolutely. But my, what a big heart she has. Look at her now – absolutely ecstatic to hear that some Rhodesian ridgeback named Jack got paired with an adoring family who live walking distance from the shelter.

'You don't know how long we've been waiting.' She turns to me with shiny eyes.

'It's not just people you like to matchmake, is it?' I tease.

'Well, I owe this place some major payback.' She smiles. 'This is where I met Jeff.'

7

It was a cool, crunchy-leafed October evening, Marina tells me. The sanctuary had closed for the night, but Kendal had a special case coming in – she'd been working with dog expert Tamar Geller on *Operation Hounds & Heroes*, which basically matches wounded military members with shelter dogs that also need rehabilitation. Jeff had come along to support his buddy Lance, who had post-traumatic stress disorder and was being paired with a very jittery vizsla. As the dog was especially timid, they felt it was important for Lance to really take his time bonding, so Jeff asked if he could visit with the other dogs.

'Of course, at this point we didn't know him from Adam, so Kendal had me monitor him on our security system.' Marina smiles. 'He was just a natural – such a calm authority about him, which I suppose reflects what he does for a living. You could almost hear the dogs exhaling and saying to each other, "It's okay. Our pack leader has arrived. No harm will come to us now." '

'How long did you watch him for?'

'A while,' she admits. 'I suppose it was a kind of role reversal: me falling in love with a man on the screen! Though the big difference was, he was playing himself.' She chuckles to herself. 'It was like dominoes out there – even the dogs that had been up on their hind legs barking at face level were down on their backs in seconds, all soppy and relaxed. I didn't want to spoil the moment, but I really wanted to meet him, so I put on a set of Kendal's scrubs, tied my hair up under one of the surgical caps, which had a Halloween bat print, so you can imagine how ridiculous I looked . . . Anyway, the fact is, he had no clue who I was – he'd been stationed out in Bahrain for the past four years and preferred reading to movies, so I could've gone out dressed in my Barbarella outfit and he still wouldn't have recognised me.

'Turns out he'd grown up with dogs and said the worst thing about being in the Navy was not being able to have one of his own. We decided there should be some kind of dog-share programme on the bases whereby the guys in the barracks get to live with a number of dogs and then switch over with a new set of guys when they have to go to sea. I was telling him I'd seen an episode of the *Dog Whisperer* where a Los Angeles fire department had taken in a Dalmatian and they took turns looking after him according to their shifts and he thought that was brilliant.

'Especially for the guys who don't have any family or loved ones to come home to – can you imagine the comfort of knowing something warm and furry was going to bound up to you and want to hang out with you and sleep alongside you? So many guys just go into an Xbox coma – how much better would it be for them to be out in the air giving the dog what it needs the most – exercise!

' "That's our biggest problem here," I told him. "Getting these dogs their daily walks. We're always looking for more volunteers." And he said, "Can I volunteer right now?" and so we started taking them out in pairs, just strolling them around the neighbourhood. It was dark by then, but of course the dogs were just as sniff-happy as ever. I was happy too – turns out we're both from the Midwest and he was just so easy to talk to, I felt like I'd known him for ever. In fact, as we traded each set of dogs for the next, it was almost like we'd had all these different lifetimes together – our poodle life, our terrier life, our German-shepherd life. And then came our Bodie life . . .

'He had far and away the most energy. I told Jeff I couldn't understand why he hadn't been adopted – he was like the entertainments director at the shelter, always raising the spirits of the other dogs, springing around, engaging them in play. Jeff thought he was just hilarious the way he'd pogo on his hind legs with this manic look on his face at the sight of a squirrel.

'I told him sometimes people would come around the corner and think I was taking him for a vertical walk!

'And then I said I thought what he really needed was a runner, someone who could take him out for a couple of miles every morning and he'd jog alongside and then come home with his tongue lolling out to the side and sleep for the rest of the day. Jeff said he was a runner, had been doing it since he ran track at school. Well, when it came to saying goodbye to Bodie, he looked like his heart might break.

' "One day I'm going to have a ranch and rescue a dozen dogs who've been cooped up in tiny concrete cells and give them never-ending fields to run in, cool streams to drink from and warm blankets to rest upon."

'And all I could think is that I wanted to be there with him – setting out their food bowls and grooming them and cuddling up before an open fire with a dozen sleeping mutts at our feet.'

I sigh. I have to say it sounds pretty appealing, even to a city girl like me.

'So what happened next?'

Marina sits forward. 'I made him an offer he couldn't refuse: what if we co-adopt Bodie? What if he had custody when he was in town, and when he was gone, I would have him?'

'Good thinking!'

Marina looks chuffed. 'So that was our first date – me bringing Bodie over to his home on the base. I told him there was a great dog beach just an hour away, in Santa Barbara, and he said, "Let's go!" Honestly, Stella, I think it was one of the best days of my life. We stayed at that beach till sunset. Then the three of us got burgers from the Boathouse and we just sprawled there in a contented, sandy heap. I remember thinking, This is it – it doesn't get any better than this.'

'Marina?' Kendal calls through to where we're sat on the floor beside the very cage that used to house Bodie. 'I need to go through some business stuff with you before you leave.'

Marina jumps to her feet. 'Do you want me to drop you back home? This could take a while.'

Of course, nothing could be more appealing to me right now than collapsing on what I'm sure will be the most spectacular mattress, but instead I ask for the names of the dogs that need a trim.

Marina looks thrilled. 'Really?'

'I'll need to borrow Andy's kit.'

'No problem!' she pips, skipping through to tell Kendal the good news.

'Okay, so let's see . . . Mitch, Sonny and Lucy.'

I begin by checking out their charts to see who sounds the easiest to work with. Mitch is apparently cat-friendly and kid-friendly, though I can't help but wonder how they assess this. Do they bring in a cat with nerves of steel? Some reinforced child with arms coated in rubber tubing?

The Airedale terrier cross has unsightly stains in his beard, like he's been slurping Scotch broth directly from the bowl.

He's easily freshened up, though I am tempted to squirt a little leave-in conditioner on his wiry coat.

'Next!'

I look at the array of bows set aside for Sonny the shih-tzu.

'You're a boy, right?'

'I knowwwww!' he seems to say.

'Tell you what, why don't you wear this red one like a bow tie and we'll give you a trendy little crop on top?'

He rewards me with a lick.

'Why, thank you. Now, Lucy. Gosh, you've been here the longest of all of them,' I say as I read her chart, feeling bad that I too left her until the end.

I'd heard about black-dog syndrome – typically last to get adopted, possibly because they don't tend to photograph as well as their lighter counterparts or people think they have less sunny dispositions.

'Let's see if we can't turn your luck around with a new look.'

As I sweep up Mitch and Sonny's clippings so Lucy has a pristine salon experience, it occurs to me that we can both relate to the feeling 'No one chose me.' Or if they did, it was only temporary. Twice Lucy thought she had a new home, had a taste of another life, of love, and then something happened and she was returned to the shelter.

'Been there, sister,' I tell her. 'I know what it's like to be road-tested and then told, "This isn't going to work." '

I suppose the more surprising thing is all the people who pick a dog out in a few minutes and then cherish them non-stop for the rest of their life. It would seem love at first sight really does exist when it comes to animals. Not to mention a greater sense of commitment.

'That's what you're all wishing for, isn't it?' I look around me at their motley collection of faces, some more hopeful than others, the majority now asleep.

I suppose the main difference between us is that I can actually go out and try to meet someone; they have to wait for someone to come to them.

That's actually a policy I was trying to adopt of late – letting the man come to me. I've chased down one too many in my time, made it far too easy for them. Jonathan was the first guy who came to me. God, that felt good – to know that he was actually attracted to me rather than a case of seeing-as-you're-offering.

Now, if I could just get Lucy to come to me . . . I try to lure her with the diced apple her chart says she adores, but still she resists.

'Is it the scissors?' I ask her. 'They do look rather menacing, I have to admit, but honestly, they won't hurt at all.'

She looks at me with profound scepticism, or at least that is what her body language conveys: I can't see her eyes at all.

'Come on, you saw the boys were fine.'

The wariness remains.

'What if I just started with some light feathering . . . ?'

She writhes away from me.

'God, you're worse than the girls on *America's Next Top Model* on makeover day,' I complain. 'Look . . .' I pull out a side strand of my hair and chop it off.

This she can't believe.

'It actually feels good,' I say as I take out another chunk.

I can see now how Marina got so daring during her 5 a.m. hack-a-thon – it feels so illicit and daring! I snip again; Lucy's wagging tail eggs me on. And on. Before I know it, I've given myself a raggedy fringe and lost several inches from the back. I'm just trying to neaten it into something a little less lopsided when I sense a paw upon my arm.

'Now you want a go?' I grin back at her, amazed at how still she sits during the snipping. She even raises her chin, as if making sure the cut will flatter her jawline. 'Talk about hiding your light under a bushel,' I gasp as my clipping reveals the most soulful pair of eyes. 'These are what are going to win over your new owner,' I assure her. 'One look and they'll be smitten.'

Her mouth parts in a smile and my heart swells – suddenly I wish it could be me.

'Come on, let's go and show the others.'

'Oh my God!' Kendal startles as we round the corner. 'Who's been styling who?'

'I thought if I showed her what I had in mind . . .'

Marina bursts out laughing. 'Stella, you're crazy!'

'Suits you, though,' Kendal muses. 'Got a kind of asymmetrical Rihanna vibe going.'

Marina reaches over and pulls some of Lucy's longer strands over towards my face. 'Maybe you should go black too.'

My heart skips a beat. 'Really?'

'Do it!' she cheers. 'We can be like yin and yang!'

Now it's my turn to burst out laughing. This makeover is taking on a life of its own!

On the way back home, Marina tells me that she'll be doing 'table reads' with the actor playing Hearst for most of tomorrow, so I'll have plenty of time to get my hair professionally finished.

'And if you are going to go darker, you might want to look over your wardrobe. All my redhead outfits look bizarre with this blonde. It's a good thing I'll be in costume most of next week.'

'Hmm, I wouldn't mind getting a sundress or two – it's even hotter here than I imagined.'

'I'll give you the name of my favourite vintage shop. You'll be spoiled for choice. And there's a great mani-pedi place next door. And a cupcake shop across the street.'

Sounds like the perfect day. Maybe there will even be time to pop back and visit Lucy. Not that I should be getting attached to an American furball when I live in England. But isn't that so like love? There's no rational reasoning behind it. I bet several people told Marina that the world is full of dog-loving men, so why did she have to fix on Jeff? As for me, I always thought that if I ever had a dog, it would be a classic golden retriever, but tonight I would've chosen Lucy over any breed.

Suddenly my attachment to Jonathan doesn't seem quite so unfathomable after all.

'Okay, so this is your room.' Marina ushers me inside an aqua-accented haven. I sink ankle-deep in white carpet as I step towards a bed that, frankly, has more square footage than my entire flat back in London. 'Sleep well,' she says, somewhat redundantly.

'And you,' I reply. 'You too, Bodie.' I bend down and give his head a final rumple. He yawns directly in my face, his pink tongue rolling out of his mouth, extending like a moist strip of Hubba Bubba.

'It's way past his bedtime!' she laughs, nudging him on his way.

'Marina?' I call after her.

'Yes?'

'I just want you to know how grateful I am, for everything.'

'Oh, you're going to earn it.' She gives me a knowing wink. 'Trust me, before the week is out you'll be cursing that we ever met!'

8

I wake up the next morning to see a pair of dancing brown eyes and perky gold ears greeting me.

Bodie's front paws are up on the edge of the bed, his back paws disappearing into the carpet. I wonder how long he's been standing like this, waiting for me to wake up. For a second my eyes flicker back closed, but immediately there's a high-pitched nasal whining.

'What is it, Lassie?'

The whining gets more urgent. I reach out my hand and stroke his rucked brow and it instantly ceases.

'Is that all you wanted? Some lovin'?'

He drops down, takes a few paces back and then propels himself onto the bed.

'Oh my goodness!' I gasp as he rolls onto his back, demanding his tummy be rubbed within an inch of its life. It's quite the role reversal for me to be on the receiving end of the 'love me, love me, love me' behaviour. I rather like it, especially since with this morning's love-fest I don't have any concerns about how I look. Then again . . . I wince a little as I remember what I did to my hair last night.

Bodie scurries into the bathroom after me as I inspect the damage. Can you imagine if I was required to show up at any of Marina's meetings? 'Oh yes, this is my new make-up artist. Yes, she's terribly avant-garde. With the emphasis on "terribly".' I'm not sure about asking Marina for a hairdresser recommendation since I've most likely taken her job. Oh well, I'm not going to be short of options – this is LA, after all, the most image-conscious city in the world.

After one of the most luxurious multi-angle showers – further enhanced by foaming lemongrass soap – I rummage through my case in search of something to cover my hair. My sequinned beret only draws more attention, so I settle instead for tying what's left of the length in a ponytail and then binding a blue silk scarf round the rest. I keep my outfit simple – a cream peasant top, cropped jeans and my usual ballet pumps, albeit in gold. Well, I am heading to Hollywood.

Now comes the awkward bit – leaving the room. This is my least favourite aspect of staying at someone else's house. Especially someone I've never stayed with before. The dreaded morning after, when you're not sure if it's acceptable to waddle out in your PJs or you are expected to emerge all fragrant and ready to face the day. Should you be peppy or respectfully low-key? Is it okay to put the kettle on without asking permission first? What about raiding the cereal cupboard? I have no idea what Marina will be like first thing in the morning. So many people wake up grumpy. I don't want to do anything to get on her bad side.

'Morning!' I chirp as confidently as I can when I head into the kitchen. 'Oh!' I jump when a woman, clearly not Marina, turns to face me.

'Inez?'

'Beatrice,' she corrects. 'I cook your breakfast. What do you want?'

'Um . . . is Miss Ray joining us?'

'She work out. After she eat.'

'Oh. Should I wait?'

She frowns at me.

'Pancakes!' I say, which isn't the norm at all for me, but it's the most American thing I could think to order.

'What flavour?'

'Um. Gosh. Banana?'

'Sit.' She motions to a beautifully laid table in a sunny alcove.

'Oh, this is lovely!' I gasp.

'Tea or coffee?'

'Tea, thank you.'

'You choose.' She pushes a wooden box towards me.

'Blueberry cheesecake!' I marvel. 'Blueberry-cheesecake-flavour tea?'

Beatrice pulls a face.

'Oh. You think the ginger peach is better?'

'I don't have to drink it.' She shrugs.

'No,' I agree. 'Well, I think I'll give it a try.'

I take a deep breath. This really is surreal. Here I am in Marina Ray's mansion in Los Angeles having breakfast in the sunshine. My heart feels all skippity. I'm going to breeze through the day with a new kind of elite serenity.

'There you are!' Marina bursts into the kitchen. 'Get your kit. You've got ten minutes to fix my face.'

'Wh-what?'

'They've pulled the first meeting forward. I've barely got time to shower.'

'Oh God!' I leap up, clanging my shin on the table leg.

'What about the pancakes?' Beatrice looks devastated.

For a second I hesitate – they look so beautiful and golden, oozing maple syrup.

'Stellaaaa!'

'I'll be back!'

But the fact is, I'm still working on her face as we step into the limo, and all the way to her first meeting. It's a good thing the windows are blacked out. God only knows what people would think if they could see the way I'm straddling her and gripping the back of her head, all in a bid to steady her face and give her a perfect lip-line.

'There! You're good to go.' I finally release her.

Marina checks her reflection and exhales. 'Nice job.' She reaches for my hand. 'Get Ernesto to drop you wherever you want. I'll see you back home tonight.'

I nod, not sure if I should tell her to 'break a leg' or whether that is purely for theatre use, so I just give her an idiotic thumbs-up.

'Where to?' Ernesto addresses me via the rear-view mirror.

Before my beautification begins there is one place I just have to return to . . .

'To 1660 North Highland Avenue, please.'

'Certainly, ma'am.'

He called me 'ma'am'! I giggle as we roll by the pedestrian crush of Hollywood Boulevard.

Even with the revampings since my last visit, it's still got a slightly grubby-tacky feel. So not representative of Los Angeles as a whole, yet such a draw on account of those iconic pink and black stars – I see you can now even get a picture of yourself kneeling beside one with your own name spelled out in gold. I'm oddly tempted, but the lights are green and Ernesto is already making the turn.

'Here we are,' he says as he opens the door for me.

I step out, mortified as a group of tourists peer excitedly only to tsk when they realise I am a mere mortal.

'Here's my card. Call me when you want to relocate.'

'Thank you.' I smile gratefully. 'Next stop will be a hairdresser!'

He nods politely.

I take a breath and look up at the deco grooves of the Max Factor Building, now the Hollywood Museum.

It's a good few years since I was last here, but I am as excited as I was the first time I entered the marble foyer, with its glass display cases and the step-back-in-time music. I pay the entrance fee and then smile at the familiarity of the colour-coded rooms. Today I head directly to the pink room designated *For Brunettes Only*.

With no one else in the room, I dare to sit in the canvas chair in front of the mirror and mentally try on the looks surrounding me.

Although I'm willing to risk Ava Gardner's colour, I can't see any of these roller-set retro styles looking good on me. But the yesteryear eyebrows I love. They really knew how to shape and fill them back then. I study image after image, admiring the precision of the tapering, and then I take out my own eyebrow pencil and experiment with one of the vixen-esque arches.

What I'd really like to do is reach beneath the protective glass and give myself a little squirt of Hypnotique – 'For the woman born to enchant men.' Well, I don't know if I fit the bill there, but I very much like the idea that it has the power to make him 'concentrate, concentrate, concentrate on you alone'! Hmm, I wonder if these cabinets are alarmed.

When a tour group spoils the illusion that this is my own private boudoir, I move on, drawn into a darkened screening room where a documentary on Max Factor has me instantly spellbound – can you believe that Max was just eight years old when his parents sent him to work as an apprentice in a pharmacy? I'm guessing the child labour laws were rather different in the Eastern Europe of 1885. Mind you, this did lead to a gig at the Russian royal palace, which sounds like a fairy tale until you learn this was an anti-Semitic regime and

Polish-Jewish Maximilian Faktorowicz had guards escorting him at all times. The czar even forbade him to marry. Not that he took any notice of that – he snuck a rabbi in for a wedding with his hometown sweetheart and had three children with her on the quiet!

By the age of thirty he was understandably desperate to break free and rather ingeniously used make-up to engineer his escape, painting his face to give himself such a sallow, sickly complexion they were convinced he was dying and sent him to a spa in Germany! From there he gathered his family and kept on going – all the way to the US!

How has there not been a movie made about this man?

At the time, the only women who wore make-up were stage actresses and prostitutes. The most 'nice girls' wore was moisturising cream and a little powder. I shudder at the thought of being that restricted. I mean, I love make-up's transformative powers, but I also appreciate it as an equaliser – how those of us with less than perfect complexions, stunted lashes or uneven lips are now just as free to join the pretty party. The mere thought of how you look first thing in the morning being as good as it gets chills me.

As I continue to watch, I realise I never actually connected the cosmetic revolution to the movies, but it all started with Max and his problem-solving at the advent of Technicolor – traditional shiny greasepaint absorbed surrounding colour, so if an actress was filmed beside a blue wall, she would appear blue. Max came up with a matt 'pancake' and it was such a success actresses started stealing it from the make-up department because they wanted to look as gorgeously flawless off screen as on.

He went on to invent lipstick in a hard stick form (previously a soft pomade) and the mascara wand, not to mention all the signature, star-making looks from Joan Crawford's broad, straight-across lip-line to Jean Harlow's platinum-blonde waves. In return they were more than happy to appear in ads that promoted his products (and their latest movie) and for this he paid them $1. Compare that to the $50 million Julia Roberts reportedly earned to be the new 'ambassadress' of Lancôme and you see just how savvy and forward-thinking he was. By 1938 Max Factor was one of the richest men in Hollywood.

I'm eager to learn more, but Marina is buzzing on my phone, so I stumble from the darkness to a corridor lined with retro ads.

'How funny is this?' I chuckle as I greet her. 'I'm standing right beside this illustration of a naval officer looking up girlfriends in his little black book and it says, "Whether she's a blonde, brunette, brownette or redhead, there's a Colour Harmony make-up for her!"'

The hearty laugh I was expecting doesn't come.

'Of course, that's terribly outdated to suggest that sailors have a woman in every port.'

'Stella?'

'Yes?' This doesn't sound good.

'I just want to let you know that I may have slightly exaggerated your experience in the movies.'

'I have no experience in the movies.'

'My point exactly. So this is what I want you to do – my friend Elena has agreed to give you an immersion session this afternoon. She's all up to date because she's just taken a camera and lighting class, which really offers an edge in terms of understanding the lenses and the kind of shot they are going for.'

'Sounds complex,' I grimace. 'How long was her class?'

'Six months.'

I feel sick. Sicker still when I realise I have yet to sort my hair.

'Oh, she can do that for you too.'

'H-how much should I pay her?' I ask, my head still in a spin.

'I got it. Don't worry about it.'

'Are you sure?'

'Yes, yes, just be a sponge. Not a make-up sponge, because they're just little wedges, but a big natural sponge freshly harvested from the Aegean Sea. Soak it all up!'

'Okay,' I quaver, fumbling for Ernesto's card. 'I'll head there right now.'

'Good girl. Hopefully you'll still have time for a bit of shopping after. See you later.'

Ernesto says he'll be with me in ten, so I use these last minutes to stand amid the hundreds of black and white shots of movie stars – Lana Turner, Hedy Lamarr, Ginger Rogers – they're all here. Some pictured at their surprisingly modest Beverly Hills homes, some at the Brown Derby restaurant, others straightforward studio head shots. Just as I stare at them, so their eyes seem to be meeting my own and I try to imagine them infusing me with all their knowledge and experience.

Of course, it's really Max himself that I want to channel. I move along to study the pictures of this little man at work in his barbershop coat and round spectacles, and take a moment to process where I am – this is where movie make-up began, not just Los Angeles, right here in this building! Who knows whose footsteps I am walking in right now.

It's only then, on the way out, that a particular movie still catches my eye. It's in the Joan Crawford display case and not separately labelled, but if I'm not very much mistaken . . .

'Excuse me,' I summon the well-groomed man on the ticket desk. 'Could you tell me who this is?'

'Marion Davies,' he replies without missing a beat.

I look back at the shot. In a place where every other woman looks picture- and pose-perfect, she's captured in character looking scrappy of hair and decidedly unpolished. It feels good to see a fellow misfit.

I take a breath and tell myself, I can do this! as I step back into the limo.

The limo indeed. Well, even if I am heading for a fall, I'm doing it in style!

9

Elena is great. A petite yet curvaceous Latina, she tells me she's cut back on movies since the hours are so long and she needs to be home to raise her teenage daughter, but she still does TV (her back catalogue includes *Dancing With the Stars* and *Ugly Betty*) because they are only seventeen-hour days.

'What?!'

I can't resist asking her if Vanessa Williams is as fabulous as she appears ('Even more so'), but then we get straight down to business.

We decide to use indigo to dye my hair to give it a real jet gleam and then opt for a cut that can be worn choppy and edgy but could still be Marcel-waved if I'm feeling too irreverent amid the vintage stylings at Hearst Castle. Throughout the process I am snacking on crispy artichoke pizza and Elena is describing what I can expect on the set. The more she tells me, the more I realise just how much there is to know, but she gives me some good pointers, like palling up with the lighting guy (who has the power to make your star's baggy eyes and double chins disappear) and understanding that not every actor wants to chat while you are making them up, as they will most likely be going through their lines in their head or trying to get into character.

'You're probably going to bear witness to a greater range of emotions than at a photo shoot and, remember, the face you create has got to look good from every angle, not just one split-second snap.'

'Good point.' I've certainly done a fair few eye-make-up designs that really only looked appealing with the model's head tilted back looking askance at the camera.

'Hygiene is major for me,' Elena continues. 'Nothing gets me more riled than seeing make-up artists with dabs of colour up their arm. Use a palette. Clean brushes. No double-dipping.'

'Got it,' I say.

She's just giving my hair a finishing spray when she casually asks, 'You do have your make-up itemised, don't you?'

I look back at her. 'How do you mean exactly?'

'Well, on a movie set they pay you a daily rental fee for the usage of your kit, so the payroll department needs an inventory sheet to justify the cost.'

I take a deep breath. 'I'm not sure I even want to know how much I've spent on my kit. How much is yours worth?'

'My basic one? About seven thousand dollars.'

'Gosh. Good thing my phone has a calculator function.'

I can imagine it's going to take me hours to list everything so, after I've given Elena a grateful hug, I ask Ernesto to take me back to Marina's, doing something of a double-take as we draw level in traffic with Gwen Stefani. She looks pin-up perfect, possibly just having come from some photo shoot. Now I realise why so many celebs set up home in LA – it isn't just a case of the movie or video-music industry being based here; it's the light. The illuminating, glamorising sunlight. You could never look that gorgeous on a drizzly day – grey does nothing for one's complexion or hair tone. And of course everyone looks cooler in sunglasses.

I slip on mine and, as the gate pulls back, imagine that Marina's mansion is in fact my own.

What must it be like to live with this level of grandeur every day? The first few months of stardom must be dizzying, not least for the ability to spend freely . . . I think of the rush I get on a spree at the mall and imagine that times a thousand. When would you ever stop? *Why* would you stop? I just read that Barbra Streisand built a little cobbled shopping village in the basement of her dream home so she could display all the fabulous antiques she had bought on her travels. Then again, how many stars have wardrobes resembling boutiques?

The biggest fly in the ointment of all this deluxe living seems to be human relationships, in as much as no amount of money, fame or beauty can protect you from heartache. When it comes to love, we're all equally vulnerable.

As the front door opens, I nod hello to some raven-haired hipster in the hallway, before realising that I just greeted my own reflection. Is this really me?

'Wow. I mean WOW!' Marina rotates me when she returns home, inspecting me from each angle.

Then she walks us over to a large baroque mirror. 'I think they might put out a missing persons on Marina Ray and Stella Conway – they are nowhere to be seen!'

I give her a wobbly smile. 'Do you think it's too extreme? I'm not entirely sure I can carry it off.'

'You have to drop any uncertainty right now,' she barks. 'Claim this new you! Own it!'

I'm a little taken aback by her intensity.

'You can't be a wimp about these things. Do you know how many actresses I'm competing with for every single role? I have to believe more than anyone that I am right for the part and then do whatever it takes to get it.' And then she softens. 'You know, that's actually one of the things Jeff likes about me – my proactive nature. He says he wouldn't put it past me to turn up on an enemy frigate just so I can give him a passing wave!'

I give a little chuckle.

'Anyway, I need your help – the only thing they weren't sold on was the blue of my eyes. They're reading too dark and flecked on camera, whereas hers were very pale and clear. Can you go through the options with me?'

'Of course,' I say, following her up to the hair and make-up section of her dressing room and then gawping at the rows of wigs, hair accessories and colour-coded lipsticks. 'How many terracottas do you have?'

'No idea, but I always use this one.' She pulls open the drawer and shows me a further twenty in the same colour. 'Just in case they discontinue it. Pisses me off that they never give you any warning when they do that.'

'Me too!' I groan. 'I'm still lamenting the demise of Estée Lauder's Pink Glaze.'

'So here's the selection.' Marina brings out a tray of coloured lenses.

'Now that's impressive.'

'Well, I like to mix things up according to the audition – anything to get me looking less like me and more like the character. I also use this.' She switches on a lamp and a camera linked to the wall-mounted TV. 'This should help us decide.'

As she begins going through the blues, I marvel at the ease with which she applies them.

'You've never tried? Oh, it's fun! Give these Halloween ones a go.'

After some initial faffing, blinking and frustration, I succeed in getting them in place.

'Oh my God,' I squeal, frightening myself with the yellow and black cat's eyes. 'That is so freaky.'

As I hurry to remove them, Marina ponders, 'You know what would look divine with your new hair colour?'

Say blue, say blue!

'Violet. Like Elizabeth Taylor. What could be more alluring?'

I hoick up my lids and blink the lenses into place, then look up, quite taken aback at the transformation.

'I hardly recognise myself!'

'That's one of the best things about being an actress – getting a break from being you.'

'Now that sounds appealing,' I sigh.

'So why not go for it?'

I look back at myself. Or whoever this new Stella is.

'It might be fun,' Marina suggests. 'Just to see the different reactions you get.'

I know it's ridiculous to be thinking of Milo right now, but all he said in the interview was black hair and blue eyes. (And violet is close enough.) He didn't say skinny or stunning. And then I smile as I recall my teenage self squeezing to the front of multiple Take That gigs, convinced that, should Mark Owen throw a lyric my way, he would fall instantly in love with me. I never thought I'd get to experience the grown-up equivalent of that fantasy. Though I have to confess a huge part of the appeal is how far-fetched it is – I can honestly say I'd rather ogle Milo from afar than have Marina set me up on a date with a real man with real prospects.

And I wonder why I'm still single.

'Are you sure it's okay for me to borrow them?' I remove the Liz lenses and pop them back in their case.

Marina nods her head, unable to speak as she is now midway through an enormous, jaw-cracking yawn.

'One more pair,' I persuade her.

Thankfully they are the ones.

'Praise be!' she cheers. 'I can barely keep my eyes open. Stay and play if you want. I'm going to bed. Oh, and see that box over in the corner?'

I nod, fully expecting her to ask me to sort through the jumble and find the appropriate position in her wardrobe, but instead she says this: 'That's all stuff I've been sent but will never wear. It's all going to charity, so if you want to pull anything out, help yourself.'

Now it's time for my jaw to extend. Movie-star freebies? I really am in LA.

As it happens, everything is too small for me. Everything except the shoes . . .

I hold up one pair of killer black stilettos. They look pretty fancy. I'm guessing she rejected them for their lack of red sole. I take a breath. Dare I?

'Oh hellfire!' Marina calls out from her room.

When I hurry to her side, I find her looking testily at her phone.

'What is it?'

'They've sent over more line changes – just when I thought I had it down.'

'Oh no!' I sigh. She really does look exhausted. 'Maybe it's better to read them when you're fresh in the morning?'

'Maybe. Or perhaps I'll go to sleep with the new pages under my pillow – you know Marion actually tried that once. Can you imagine?'

I tsk along, but it doesn't stop me from going back to my room and tearing out the magazine picture of Milo and placing it under my sheeny aqua pillow.

Every time I shift in the night and hear the paper crackle I smile because, regardless of how fanciful my crush may be, at the end of our 230-mile drive tomorrow, I will be meeting Milo Vallis. In person. Face to face.

Make that 80 miles.

I've set my alarm to get me up a good hour ahead of time – there's no way I'm missing my pancakes two days in a row – and head down to the kitchen dressed for car comfort in a polka-dot sundress. I'm just swirling on my syrup when Marina oh so casually announces that we will be picking up Milo from his family's ranch en route.

'W-what?'

'You might want to stop at the third pancake 'cos he's invited us for lunch and it's only about an hour and a half away.' She throws down her napkin and jumps to her feet. 'I'm going to give Bodie one last pee – see you at the car!'

When I finally regain the power of speech, I call after her, 'I'll just be a minute! Forgot one thing . . .' And then slam my suitcase on its back and go rummaging for my heels, kicking off my ballet pumps and squishing them in the front panel before I make my uneven stagger out to her gold Mercedes – a present from MGM.

'Are you going to be all right driving in those?' Marina looks concerned.

'Oh, I always drive barefoot,' I tell her, already relieved to be removing the stiff leather after twenty paces.

'Okay, here we go!' Marina cheers as I set the car in motion.

I'm desperate to ask more about Milo but decide to begin by asking how she got on with her lines last night.

She rolls her eyes. 'Shame I can't drive or you could've run the scene with me. I really should go over it a few more times. Mind if I disappear?' she says, holding up her headphones.

'Of course not. Go ahead.'

'Okay, just stay on the 101 until I say otherwise.'

I happily bomb along the freeway, passing signs for Hidden Hills, Thousand Oaks and the 'Premium Outlet Stores' of Camarillo.

I find everything fascinating for its sheer American-ness – we may be heading off to one of the most cultural landmarks on the West Coast, but I find myself experiencing an opposing desire to shop at Wal-Mart and eat a bowl of radioactive macaroni cheese, or 'mac'n'cheese', as they say here.

As we draw level with the rather unlovely named town of Oxnard, Marina perks up and tells me that we're just minutes from her beloved's naval base at Port Hueneme.

'It's pronounced "Why-knee-me",' she educates me.

But the fact is, I already knew that. Sometimes Jonathan and I would have flights of fancy where we would pretend that we actually had some say in what happened next for us – and him being based in California was the best-case scenario for us both – his sister, Delana, is based in Los Angeles, and if ever there was a town that embraced make-up . . . I shake my head at how absurdly optimistic our ideals seem now.

Marina presses on her chest. 'It gives me such a pang just seeing the name.'

'Me too,' I mumble.

But then I get a surge of resistance.

It's a strange thing to wish for – for love to leave your body – but, even though I fear my heart would shrink to the size of a pea if I release the feelings I still have for Jonathan, I do wish them gone. I just don't know how to make that happen. What would it take to get me over him once and for all?

'Milo Vallis.'

For a minute I think I might have answered my question out loud.

'Ah, here he is!'

I cast a glance to my side and see that Marina is locating his address on her phone.

'In a few miles you want to exit onto 33 North.'

'To Ojai?' I read the sign overhead.

'It's pronounced "Oh-hi",' she corrects me.

'Is that Spanish?'

'It's actually Native American Indian. I think it means "moon" or something. "*Hueneme*" is one of their words too . . .'

As she chatters on, I try to raise myself up in my seat so I can discreetly check my reflection in the rear-view mirror. I could do with a chin blot and a sheen update on my lips.

'Turn off here!' Marina keeps me on track, guiding me off the zippy freeway to a quieter country road.

'I would've pictured him as more of an ocean-view kind of guy . . .'

'He is,' Marina confirms, 'but his mom lives here. He always checks in with her before a shoot – the calm before the storm, he says.'

I can't help but smile to myself – Milo Vallis just became human in my eyes: he has a mum!

'It's this one – take the next left.'

We've barely ground onto the rubbly road when Marina makes me jump with her sudden exclamation of 'It's him! It's him!'

My eyes dart every which way, fearing I'm about to run over our leading man, but then Marina slaps her phone to her ear. 'Baby?'

Baby?

'Jeff!' she mouths at me.

The inevitable cooing ensues, but it is short-lived: 'Hello? Hello?' She looks frantically at her phone and then screeches, 'Stop the car!'

I slam on the brakes and obey her cry of 'Back up! Back up!'

'What's the matter?'

'I've lost the signal. Keep reversing. More. More. There! Phew! The bars are back. Thank goodness for that.' She goes to open her car door.

'What are you doing?' I make a grab for her.

'I'll wait here. You go on ahead.'

'B-but—'

'I'll be fine. Bodie will be with me,' she says, stepping out and releasing him from the back seat.

'But what about lunch?'

'Just bring me a doggy bag. Pardon the pun!'

And then her phone rings again and she's gone, deep in Jeff world.

I'm reluctant to move on. How can she be so casual about this? Sending me off to rendezvous with Milo Vallis as if he's a mere mortal or something.

Maybe I could suggest we pack everything up and take it to eat picnic-style back with Marina. I'm sure he won't mind some perfect stranger telling him what to do with his freshly baked victuals. Oh God!

Gingerly I roll the car forward. The road begins to weave and become bumpier and dustier. I see a ranch house up ahead and proceed with the driving version of tiptoeing. Am I really allowed here unattended? Is it okay if I park directly outside? I suppose it makes sense if he's going to be loading his luggage. I faff around aligning the boot with the front door, hoping no one is watching me from the window, and then turn off the engine and stall for another moment. My hands are actually shaking a little as I reach for my shoes.

This is not a date! I remind myself.

No one but me knows the fantasies that have been playing in my mind, and no one need know. If I can just keep from blushing and stammering and maintain some air of professionalism . . .

'Hello?' I call after ringing the doorbell and knocking oh so politely garners no response. I try to peek in through the window, but the rooms look empty. I suppose this is the right house. Could there be more than one? I'm walking round to the side, trying to see if I've missed something, when my nostrils flare.

What's that lovely smell?

A few more paces and my question is answered by a haze of purple as far as the eye can see: *lavender*.

Suddenly I'm transported to a field in Provence, half tempted to take out my make-up kit and do an impromptu painting using eye shadows in lieu of pastels. What a sight. I take a step closer – having always imagined lavender grew straight upwards, I am surprised to see bushes fanning out like those fibre-optic lamps from the 1970s. I reach down and rub the bristly little buds between my fingertips.

'Mmm,' I sigh as I inhale the sun-warmed perfume, and then an even longer 'Mmmmmm' on the exhale as I spy a figure standing knee-deep in purple.

It's the man himself.

Milo turns round before I can compose myself, his loose shirt revealing a golden chest, his blue linen trousers slung low on the ridge of his hips. His head is tilting, looking at me with curiosity and beckoning me to join him.

This is more than I could've ever hoped for, but the dreaminess of the scene is slightly compromised as I take my first step and feel my spindly heels sink into the dusty earth, dropping me 3 inches. Oh no. I dislodge them and try to move forward, this time attempting to put all my weight on the balls of my feet. Not exactly the most seductive of walks. But then I realise the lack of grace is the least of my problems – every bush is buzzing with bees.

'It's fine,' he assures me. 'They won't bother you if you don't bother them.'

I step boldly into the fray, only to catch my dress on a cluster of stems. Darn it! I backtrack to free my hem, but within seconds I sense a bee tickling my thighs.

'Oh my God! Oh my God!' I flap, swishing the fabric in a desperate bid to whisk the insect out from where it really has no business being. I can only imagine what this must look like to Milo. I may as well just break into the Can-Can and have done with it.

I'm just trying to recall what underwear I opted for this morning when I remember he doesn't actually know who I am.

And breathe . . .

I push my hair back from what I'm sure is a very pink face and try to sound charmingly nonchalant as I pant, 'I'm Stella.' Shortly followed by, 'Oh my God, there's another one!'

They're all making a beeline for me now – that'll teach me to spritz perfume at the back of my knees.

Before my tizzy escalates any further, Milo swoops in, whisks me off my feet and starts to carry me back to safety. Just like that. I am in his arms, my dress securely pinned to my legs by his palm, my hands very aware of the strength in his shoulder, my face just a few inches from that legendary jaw.

As he sets me down on the solid ground of the patio, I stumble a little. He holds my forearms until I am steady. 'Okay?'

I nod a yes. This is all too surreal. 'Marina sent me on ahead,' I attempt to speak again. 'I'm her make-up artist.'

'Stella,' he repeats my name.

I nod.

'I'm Milo,' he says, and then he leans in and kisses my cheek. 'Pleased to meet you.'

Is that normal, to kiss someone you are meeting for the first time?

I feel my face prickle with heat, though I doubt it's noticeable since my initial flush has yet to subside.

'It's so hot today!' I attempt to fan myself.

'Isn't it just?' he says, eyeing me up and down. 'You look so much like . . .'

'Yes?'

He shrugs and then husks, 'Someone I wish I knew.' And then guides me into the shade and invites me to take a seat. 'I won't be a moment.'

Someone I wish I knew. I mull over his words as I catch sight of my alter-ego reflection in the windowpane – this could well be my greatest makeover to date!

A chinking of ice cubes announces his return – with a large pitcher of lavender lemonade. He pours me a glass and watches as I sip and rapturise.

'You like that?'

'I really do!'

'Good thing you like lavender – everything here is flavoured with it. Lavender tomato jam, lavender grilled salmon . . . We even have lavender chicken dog biscuits for Bodie.'

'Hold on!' I can't help but interrupt. 'Did you say lavender tomato jam?!'

'It's not as bad as it sounds.'

'Are you sure about that?'

'Okay, now you're going to have to try it.'

'I don't know if I can!' I squirm as he reaches for the jar of soft red sludge.

'It's not like I'm trying to get you to eat sea urchin or horsemeat sashimi.'

I frown back at him.

'I just did a movie in Japan.'

'Oh!' My nose wrinkles. 'What does sea urchin taste like?'

'Sort of fishy peanut butter.'

'Gross!' I sputter. 'Do I even want to know about the horse?'

'Oh no, I didn't try that, but I suspect that tastes like cruelty.' He then gives a playful jiggle of his eyebrows. 'This is looking pretty palatable by comparison, isn't it?'

I take a breath and accept a bite.

'You like it?'

'It's actually not bad,' I'm forced to admit.

'Told you,' he says, going to put the lid back on.

'Wait! Let me try a bit more.'

'You do like it!' He smiles.

It's not going to knock kumquat marmalade off the top spot, but it might come a close second.

'So your mum actually makes this?'

He nods and then tuts himself. 'I missed a trick there, didn't I? Should've passed this off as my own recipe. Then you'd have been terribly impressed.'

'I'm still impressed,' I tell him. His chest puffs up until I add, 'Just with your mum.'

He hesitates for a second and then bursts out laughing. 'You're English, right?'

'Yup,' I confirm.

'I know your people all too well . . .'

He then proceeds to startle me with a series of 'innit', 'know what I mean?', 'geezer' phrases.

'Oh stop!' I beg. Although he's actually doing a pretty good job of the accent, it's totally ruining the fantasy for me.

'Come on, let's hear your American accent!' he cheers.

'Oh no, I couldn't!'

'Go on!'

I shake my head and purse my lips.

'It's funny, you guys always either do some kind of *Sopranos* Noo Yawk-Italian accent or a Southern drawl.'

'Actually mine is pure trailer trash,' I counter.

He raises an eyebrow.

'I picked it up from this TV show about a Nevada brothel. There's one catchphrase in particular that stuck with me. It's not too polite . . .' I look around for ears to offend.

'My mom is in town for the Lavender Festival,' he assures me. 'Let me have it.'

It's only three words long, but I just can't seem to spit it out.

'Would this help?' he says, extracting a bottle of wine from a nearby ice bucket.

'Has this got any rogue flavours I should know about?'

Milo smiles. 'If I said lemon curd and pine, you might baulk, but wait until you taste it . . .'

The sun streams through the pale gold fluid as he pours. The glass he hands me is as fine as spun sugar, the taste so crisp and refined. And that's when it blurts from me: 'You snaggle-toothed whore!'

Milo's wine comes shooting out of his mouth in a spray, dripping down his chest and his shirt.

'Oh no!' I gasp, offering my napkin for mopping duty, but he's one step ahead of me – whipping off his shirt and using the whisper-thin linen to blot his body and his chin.

'Damn!' He laughs as he sits back down in the chair, brazenly shirtless. 'I hate to waste good wine!'

I quickly jump up to replenish his glass, desperately trying to control the excited shaking in my hand. 'Here! Pretend it never happened.'

He shakes his head. 'And you seemed like such a nice girl.'

'I am!' I protest.

'Let me see your teeth,' he demands.

'What?'

'I want to see if there are any snaggles there!'

'No,' I giggle, squirming and covering my face.

'What are you hiding?' He looms over me, prising my hands away from my cheeks.

I put my hands out to bat him away, but they instead find their way to his chest. His skin is so soft yet toned it wipes the smile off my face. I haven't felt naked human warmth like this since Jonathan.

It feels sublime.

At such a moment you don't expect yours to be the sensuality-sabotaging voice, but that's exactly what mine is.

'Why don't you tell me more about the lavender you grow here?'

He looks at me as if to say, 'Really?'

'It looks like you have different types.' I gesture wildly at the surrounding bushes.

'As a matter of fact, we do,' he confirms. 'English, French and Spanish . . .'

His talking gives me a chance to get a grip, especially when he's telling me of lavender's antiseptic properties and how it was used in World War I to disinfect hospital walls and floors.

However, every time he looks away I find myself gazing back at that chest, wondering what it would be like to lie upon. And kiss. I'm almost relieved when he nips inside and puts on a fresh shirt. Now we can get back to normal conversation, and dip the fresh batch of sweet-potato crisps in lavender aioli. Mmm-mm.

'You know I still get batches of Walkers crisps sent over!' He chuckles. 'Nothing compares to their prawn cocktail.'

As we talk more about his last trip to England, I keep wanting to pinch myself. I'm listening to him speak and making all the right sounds, but inside I'm squealing, still trying to reconcile the fact that this is the face I've seen magnified so many times on the big screen. Just looking at him gives me a kind of electrical charge. But, every now and again, I forget to be in awe and simply enjoy his company. I think it's the setting – so rustic and relaxing with just enough breeze to soothe my fevered brow. He seems to be having a good time too. Which is crazy! But thrilling. And I never want to leave. I want this to be my life now. I want to sit with him on this patio and eat lavender tomato jam and pixie tangerines (his family's secondary line of produce) for as long as we both shall live.

'Is that your phone?'

I really have got to change the ringtone from 'Together We Are Beautiful'. Adrian chose it for me, saying it was appropriate seeing as I'm in the beautification business, but, for moments like this, it's mortifying. Though Milo seems to be rather amused . . .

'It's Marina,' I tell him as I answer. 'Yes, yes, of course. Be right there.' I look back at Milo, trying to hide my dismay as I tell him that she's ready to hit the road.

He nods but doesn't move right away.

This is our first moment of silence.

I wonder if he is sharing my regret that we can't sit here sipping wine until the sun sets. I envision him noticing my goose bumps before me and then inviting me inside, wrapping a soft, fleecy blanket around my shoulders, then pulling me close to him to imbue me with some body heat.

'And so to work,' he sighs, finally.

'Back to reality?' I say. Though of course his reality – a glamorous movie set – is hardly the norm.

I'm about to kick myself for making such an inane comment when he comes back with this: 'Love is the only reality.'

I blink in amazement – that's exactly what I think. I've just never phrased it quite that way!

' "Love is the only reality" . . .' I find myself repeating his words for the second time today. 'That's wonderful.'

'Just something I heard on *The Bachelorette.*' He shrugs as he gets to his feet.

I'm not sure if he's joking, trying to play down a poignant moment, but I don't get the chance to ask, because he's already heading into the house. 'Do you want to pack Marina a little picnic while I grab my things?'

'Sure!' I say. Teamwork. I like that.

I slice and spread and stack the goodies and then pause and take a moment to imprint the view on my memory.

'Where did you guys meet?' I imagine people asking.

'In a lavender field,' we'll sigh as we give each other a suitably dreamy look. Glossing over the whole incident with the bees, obviously.

'All set?' Milo asks as he throws a large sports bag into the boot of the car.

'You travel pretty light,' I marvel.

'Well, I spend all day in clothes supplied by Wardrobe, so all I really need is some sloppy hang-out gear. Besides' – he smiles as he heaves a crate of wine in alongside it – 'all the more room for the vino.'

I raise an eyebrow at him.

'It's from a local vineyard,' he says. As if that makes it on a par with soda pop. 'Let's go and get Marina before the vultures start gnawing on her carcass.'

11

As soon as the former co-stars reunite, I take a back seat. Quite literally – me and Bodie in the back like the kids while the adults talk shop upfront. Their conversation is nothing I can join in with – all names and places and situations I've only ever read about in passing. Bodie places a paw on my knee as if to say, 'I know! I get this all the time.'

We're settling in for the duration – which by the way is not too hellish, with coarse green hills to our right and the ocean glinting like a sheet of dimpled metal to our left – when Marina tells Milo that she needs him to make a quick diversion, there's something she needs to show me.

As we exit the freeway, I straighten up, eagerly looking for clues as to what could possibly warrant delaying our arrival at Hearst Castle.

Even Bodie seems more alert – his wet black nose undulating as he takes in the change in the breeze.

Until this moment I never knew trees could look upper class, but the ones crowding this roadside are decidedly plush – rich, dense greens accented with pink and white frills of silk.

We pass signs for Mimosa Lane, Bolero Drive and Laguna Blanca School, which sounds so beautiful it almost makes me want to shrink back to my eight-year-old self and skip through the gates with a leather satchel and clean *blanca* socks.

'Right here,' Marina instructs.

Milo is blithely following her directions while discussing the latest script change, when suddenly he slams on the brakes. Jeez! I'd have worn a neck brace if I'd known there was going to be more of this.

'I can't go any further.'

'What do you mean?' Marina adjusts the seatbelt currently slicing her at the diagonal.

'I'm going to have to drop you girls here.'

I look out of the window at the hand-carved wooden sign announcing the San Ysidro Ranch. What I now recognise to be Spanish lavender bushes nestle at its base and extend the length of the driveway – is this perhaps some kind of herb rival?

Marina appears to be equally mystified until Milo reminds her that he has been banned from the property.

'What did you do?' She squints at him. 'Ohhhh! I remember – Gwyneth Paltrow's wedding—'

'No need to relive the details,' he says, casting a discreet look in my direction.

'But that was years ago.'

'They were quite emphatic.'

'Okay, well, if you don't mind waiting ... We won't be long.'

It seems most odd to leave Milo skulking down in his seat, but Marina is a woman on a mission and there is no way Bodie is getting left behind. He's been doing his high-frequency nasal whining since we stopped, desperate to get out of the car.

'I take it he's been here before?'

'Oh yes!' Marina grins. 'This is his happy place.'

'A better class of tree to pee on?' I suggest as we pass a row of dainty olive trees.

'You have no idea,' Marina concurs as she waves ahead to the gatekeeper, who in turn throws up his arms in glee.

Just when I think he's going to swoop in and hug her, he throws himself down to Bodie's level. 'I didn't know you were coming, buddy boy!'

'We're actually just passing through – I wanted to show my friend here Eucalyptus Cottage, if it's not occupied?'

'Let me check,' he says, raising his walkie-talkie and exchanging some coded words. 'Teresa will be there with the key – do you want me to send a buggy for you?'

'No, no, we're fine walking.'

I must have emitted a whimper of anguish because Marina turns and looks at my feet and then asks if he can arrange to have a pair of slippers waiting for us.

'No problem,' he acquiesces. 'May I get your name, ma'am?'

'Er, Stella Conway,' I reply, wondering if he's planning on having them embroidered with my initials.

Marina goes to walk on, but the gatekeeper calls after her, 'Um, Mrs Arnett?'

'This is the only place where I'm known by my married name,' she explains before turning back. 'Yes?'

'Would you mind if I got a quick picture with Bodie?'

'No, of course not. Stella can take it. She's the one with the artistic eye. Though I can't promise he'll do his move!'

'Oh, that's all right,' the gatekeeper laughs. 'Just his smiling face is enough.'

'They seem to be a little confused over who is the celebrity,' I comment as we proceed up the drive.

'Oh, Bodie totally trumps me here. On the last visit, we got him a pet massage and snapped him doing this incredible yoga pose – sort of upward dog – so now they have the picture of him and Glenys the masseuse on the pet welcome letter!'

'Are you serious?'

'Absolutely! Hamming for the camera runs in the family.' Then she stops. 'What do you think of this?'

I look up and see the ultimate cross between an English country garden and California sunshine, and ahead of us, a picture-perfect white bungalow erupting with vivacious pink bougainvillea.

'What is this place?'

'Well, in essence it's a hotel, but most of the rooms happen to be individual cottages. This one over here is where John and Jackie Kennedy honeymooned.'

'Really?' I coo, following her over.

'We stayed next door in Rose the first time – it's just darling.'

The flower names keep on coming as we wend our way up the hill – Geranium, Jasmine, Honeysuckle – putting me in mind of the enchanting *Flower Fairy* books of my youth.

'Isn't this adorable?' Marina points to the daintily arranged organic vegetable garden with little hand-painted signs for beets and chives and Cherokee purple tomatoes, which sound like something Milo's mum might grow.

We continue on past a grassy level I imagine being used for a wedding marquee or game of croquet and then she stops.

'I wanted to take you up to this point just so you can see all the layers of the view.' As she turns my body, my gaze tumbles down the hill and then climbs in stages back up to the sea – the palest wash against the hazy sky.

'Are those ships?' I point to four smudges on the horizon.

'Oil rigs,' she corrects. 'They look so intriguing out there, don't they?'

I nod.

'You okay?'

I can't help but wrinkle my brow. 'I used to love staring out to sea – just like everyone else, I used to find it so serene.'

'But now?'

'I can't help but wonder where he is.'

Marina sighs. 'Even after all this time?'

I shrug. 'I suppose I'll always wonder a little.'

'When was the last time you went on a beach holiday?'

I give her a bemused look. 'I don't know. Probably not since a family holiday to Corfu. You think I should work on getting some new associations with the sea?'

'It's a thought.'

'Bodie!' Another fan hurries up for a cuddle.

'He certainly knows how to work the public,' I note, as he flips onto his back and writhes enticingly.

'Such a flirt,' Marina tuts. 'Come on, we can cut through this car park.'

Mercedes, Mercedes, Mercedes . . . all brand spanking new. And then more cottages, including one named Wisteria, which obviously puts me in mind of *Desperate Housewives*.

'You know Milo has a cameo coming up on that show?'

Before I can reply, Marina is fanfaring our arrival at Eucalyptus.

I'm actually more excited about the towelling flip-flops presented to me by a diminutive woman whom Marina introduces as 'the lovely Teresa'.

'Put them on, put them on!' she urges.

My feet have just died and gone to heaven.

'Thank you,' I say, a little teary-eyed with relief.

'Where's Mr Arnett?'

'Far away,' Marina grimaces.

'Oh, that's no good,' she tuts. 'Why don't you come stay with us? We just had big wedding cancellation for the weekend. You can have any cottage you like.'

'If I didn't have to shoot a movie, I'd be unpacking right now,' Marina assures her. 'Sadly we only have time for a quick glimpse.' She steps aside and bids me open the gate. 'You go first.'

At the top of the steps, before I can even set a toe on the decking, I do a double-take – there beside the door is a wooden sign reading, 'MARINA STELLA BODIE'.

'What?' I hoot. 'How did this happen?'

'They do it for all the guests, so that it feels like your very own cottage.'

'B-but they only found out my name at the gate!'

'They're individual letters,' she explains. 'They just slot them in.' She then reaches up and traces her fingertips along the indentations. 'This is the moment Jeff said he knew he was going to propose – when he saw our names side by side like this and it just looked so right to him.'

'So it's your happy place too?'

She nods, a little teary herself. 'This is our home from home. I couldn't stay on the base; he couldn't come to mine . . .'

'Paparazzi?'

She nods. 'This was just heaven – like our own little cottage in the country.'

As soon as I step inside, I see how this place would be the perfect choice for a couple of displaced lovers – it really does have the look of someone's home. Just after the cleaner has been.

Even though we are surrounded by wood – the timber of the ceiling, the dark hardwood floors, the antique warp of the desk and tables – the dominant feature is the vast, chunky stone fireplace. The sofa and chairs set to admire it are outsized and inviting. I run my hand along the claret fabric as I take in the adroitly positioned ornaments – sufficiently quirky to give the impression that they come from a personal collection: braying camel in bronze, Dalmatian bookends for the dog-lover and, my particular favourite, a patterned china pig sleeping with his head resting on a soft cushion.

'You've seen the décor in my house – I love all the Hollywood Regency glitz and my big purple chandelier, but even though I would never pick out floral curtains or put a blue cockerel on my mantelpiece, I feel more at home here than I do in my own place.'

'It almost feels like your parents' house,' I observe.

'Not my parents'!' Marina scoffs.

'Well, some lovely old relative then, one who has lots of spare pairs of Wellington boots and an amazing cheese board.'

Marina bursts out laughing. 'What on earth are you talking about?'

'You know those people who have found a life they are comfortable with and are really living it instead of thinking about what they're missing out on or trying to keep up with the Joneses?'

Marina nods. 'I do.'

'I mean, there's nothing modern here, nothing that yanks you back to the outside world. No wonder you felt so content – it takes you back to simpler times.'

'Well, that and the heated floor in the bathroom.'

'What?'

'Take off your slippers and walk on that.' Marina ushers me onto the tiles.

'Ooooh!'

'Yes?'

'Oh yes!' I enthuse. 'It's like a hot-stone treatment.'

'Wait till you try lying out on it.'

'What?' I laugh.

'I caught Jeff doing this once and now I'm totally hooked. Come lie down!'

Even Bodie joins us, the three of us revelling in soothing warmth. They both have their eyes closed, but I'm taking in the claw-foot tub and multi-jet shower. Jonathan would love that. The man was never happier than when he was in the shower. I remember on Valentine's Day weekend he booked us a room at the Blackstone Hotel in Chicago and scattered dark red rose petals from the bed to the bathroom, then lit little candles and arranged a plate of chocolate truffles. That was my first experience of a man being romantic in the classic sense. I have to say chocolate-flavour kisses as water cascades over you is one of life's great pleasures.

'I'm so glad you're here, Stella.' Marina brings me back to the present.

'Well, it's always nice to have someone to lie on the floor with.'

'No, I mean on this trip. Just having someone around who actually gets the Navy thing . . .'

I sigh. 'I know what you mean about that – I used to think, It's all right for him – he's with a bunch of guys all in the same boat!'

'Literally!' Marina laughs, and then she turns to face me. 'I'm sorry you didn't have anyone around when you were going through it. Maybe there would've been a different outcome if you had.'

Now I feel uncomfortable. I haven't exactly told her the whole story of why we split up.

'Gosh, have you seen the time?' I sit upright. 'We should probably get back on the road.'

'One more thing to show you.' Marina jumps to her feet, crosses the sitting room and then opens the patio doors.

As I follow, the first thing I see is a giant hot tub.

'This is where we got married.'

'In a Jacuzzi?' I splutter.

'No!' she scolds. 'I mean this patio area, though technically there is enough room in there for a priest and a couple of witnesses . . .'

As she ponders the perils of a wet white wedding, an outdoor 'raincloud' shower catches my eye – that and the little shelf of Bulgari toiletries.

'We kept the ceremony very simple,' she recalls. 'I mean, you hardly need to decorate when Mother Nature has already done such a magnificent job. We didn't even need confetti – see these flowers?' She plucks a luminous purple-blue petal and hands it to me. 'Last time we were here, I took a few samples and had a sash made for my dress. On the day, I wore one flower in my hair and Jeff had one in his buttonhole.'

They say the brain can't distinguish between real and imagined thoughts and looking at the dreaminess on Marina's face now, you would think Jeff was standing beside her.

'Other than our first-dance song we didn't even have any music because we just love the sound of the creek rushing by below,' she continues.

I peer over the fencing at the boulder-strewn stream.

'And instead of white doves . . .'

'Hummingbirds!' I smile delightedly as I watch one perform his shimmering green vibrations.

Bodie, meanwhile, is more interested in trying to snap passing flies in his jaws.

'It's when he starts going for the wasps that we get in trouble. Oops, phone.' She looks at the display. 'It's Ruth. I'm going to take it in the bedroom. Make yourself comfortable.'

I settle into one of the padded recliners, taking in the giant eucalyptus trees, with their flaking layers of papery grey bark, and then chuckling as Bodie disappears into the hedgerow, rustling his way along the bushes to appear on the other side with a couple of leaves woven between his whiskers. Suddenly I understand those people who commute into London from the countryside. Waking up on a Saturday morning to peace and greenery must make it all worthwhile. I know Jonathan and I felt closest when we ventured out of the city – one time we stayed in this lovely B&B in Wisconsin called Lazy Cloud . . . They offered in-room picnics complete with red and white checked tablecloths and the best caramel apple pie in the world. I even remember the make – the Elegant Farmer – because the name was so charming. That was Jonathan's first time in a hammock and our first starlit deer-sighting. And then I catch myself. Oh my God! I may not be physically revisiting the places Jonathan and I have stayed, but in my mind I am always popping back and hanging out there. No wonder I can't move on! My brain believes I am still with Jonathan!

Suddenly I'm more eager than ever to get to Hearst Castle – I've never known how to stop my mind from wandering back to those memories, but now I see a way forward: if I can just fill up my head with enough new experiences, I won't have to keep reviewing the old playlist. Like right now, I'm going to switch from the Lazy Cloud picnic to my recent lavender lunch. In fact, how about I go and pick a little sprig of the stuff and then every time I feel myself backsliding I can sniff it and transport myself—

'Oh!' I collide with Marina, returning from her call. 'How's Ruth?'

She gives me a smug look. 'See how she makes out that she can't stand me, but when it comes down to it, she can't keep away? She's heading off to Windermere tomorrow. Loving it but finding it a little strange not having a million things to do each day. She wanted to know if there was anything I needed arranging, but I think we're good, right?'

'So far, yes.'

Marina takes a breath and then returns to her state of reminiscence. 'This is where we had our first dance as man and wife.'

Oh, here we go, she's off again.

'Why don't you tell me more as we head back to the car?' I suggest, taking her arm and guiding her over to the front door.

' "Beyond the Sea", that was our song,' she sighs, placing her hand on my forearm, making me feel a little like the father of the bride. 'I chose the Harry Connick Junior version because Jeff's hair used to be just like his when he was younger. Of course, now it's cropped and all grey, but he's still as handsome as ever.'

I meet a little resistance as I try to move Marina past the gate, but after a long look back we progress down the hill, Bodie bringing up the rear like a sheepherder.

'What about you and Jonathan?' She turns to me. 'Did you guys have a song?'

I nod, hoping her enquiry won't start the track playing in my head. ' "Just the Two of Us", Bill Withers.'

With barely a moment's pause Marina starts singing, amazing me with her voice and perfect recall of the lyrics.

'Oh my God – castles in the sky!' She stops suddenly. 'How apt is that!'

'Mmm,' I mumble. 'I'm surprised you're so familiar with the song . . .'

'One of my earlier movies had "Lovely Day" in the soundtrack – I'd spend my breaks listening to the rest of his catalogue on YouTube.'

'Do you know that he was a stutterer?' I ask.

'Is that so?'

I nod. 'In the documentary I saw on him, he visited this theatre group in New York and all these kids were coming up to him, trying to introduce themselves, and you could see the strain of them trying to get their names out and the huge compassion in his eyes. I remember him saying that they had to learn to be that little bit more civil and forgiving than the people who teased them.'

'So true.' Marina looks misty-eyed.

'Do you know something else crazy? He was in the Navy!'

'Get outta town!'

'For nine years.' And then I find myself chuckling. 'There was this other bit where he got together with his old Navy pals and they're talking about when they were deployed to the Pacific – someone told them, "In Guam, there's a woman behind every tree." And then they add, "But there's only two trees!" '

'Oh, that's hilarious!' Marina claps her hands together. 'I have to tell Jeff!'

As she stops in her tracks and starts typing him an email, my hand goes to my own phone. It's such a long time since it would buzz all day long with playful texts that would put a soppy smile on my face – wait! I'm doing it again! I look around me and then tug a handful of lavender from the nearest bush.

When I turn back, I find Bodie leading Marina in the wrong direction, away from the car.

'Marina!'

'Quickest stop at the gift shop!' She bids me follow. 'Gotta get Bodie a Bow Wow Beanie.'

I frown back at her.

'You know, like Beanie Babies but for dogs. He's had Stinky the Skunk and Nuts the Squirrel—'

Before she can complete the list, Teresa hurries over and presents one of the very items Marina was describing, only this one is in the shape of a dog.

'Is that a dachshund?' Marina exclaims. 'Stella, did you see this?'

'Yes, ma'm, this is Weenie,' Teresa confirms.

'You have no idea what a good-luck charm this is!' Marina hugs Teresa tight. 'Thank you, thank you!'

Bodie is even more enthusiastic, snatching it from her hands and squeaking it so frantically it sounds like the horn on a clown car.

That's going to be fun in an enclosed space for the next three hours.

12

As it happens, Weenie has to be put in the glove compartment as Milo has conked out in the back of the car.

'Seems a shame to wake him,' Marina decides, settling into the passenger seat with Bodie, as I return to the wheel.

Even though Milo looks deeply (and beguilingly) in REM, I want to make sure Marina doesn't discuss anything personal in front of him – no talk of recent makeovers or proposed matchmaking – so I ask her to tell me a little bit more about William Randolph Hearst.

'I think the interesting thing is how widely the descriptions of his character vary according to who you ask' she begins. 'Most people mistake him for the ruthless megalomaniac in *Citizen Kane*; his staff say he was most benevolent, paying them over the odds, throwing fun parties for their kids, et cetera. His newspaper colleagues would refer to him as "the Chief", but Marion would call him "W.R.". She thought of him as a great mind and a huge heart.' Marina readjusts her seatbelt to turn to face me. 'You know what I think was one of the sweetest things he ever said to her?'

'What's that?'

'Well, this may sound weird, and maybe it's because my mother is gone . . .'

I give her a glance of encouragement.

'Well, when Marion's mother died and Hearst was comforting her, he said, "May I be a mother to you?" I just think that's so touching, this big burly man of six feet four offering to take such a nurturing role. Which is why I find it hard to get my head around the rumours that he was implicated in a murder.'

'What?' I gasp.

I look over at Marina, thinking she's overdoing the dramatic pause, only to find she's fallen asleep, all but mid-sentence. Even Bodie has succumbed, letting his head fall between the seat and the armrest, rucking his facial fur into soft pleats.

I don't mind too much – the changing scenery has me riveted, in particular a glorious view of Lake Cachuma, and – I swear – John Corbett (aka Aidan from *Sex and the City*) weaving through Los Olivos on a bicycle. He must have wondered why I was looking so gaga at him when I already had a hot actor in the back of the car.

I glance at Milo in the rear-view mirror – I can't believe I am currently the sum of his and Marina's entourage, though I suppose there will be people to meet every need on the movie set. I wonder if they ever get first-day nerves at the start of a new film? I suppose it helps that they've worked together before. I must check the script to see if they have any romantic scenes together. That would be strange, knowing their history. That said, there does seem to be more of a blasé palliness between them as opposed to any sexual tension.

'Mmmhh.' Milo shifts, turning his body to face the back of the seat, and in doing so bares his bronzed lower back.

Eyes on the road, eyes on the road! I tell myself as I swerve into the oncoming lane.

I'm on the 101 freeway now, passing Los Alamos, Pismo Beach and a sign offering ten avocados for $1 – what a bargain! I could get twenty for the price of the last one I bought at Waitrose!

I'm just transitioning onto the infamous Pacific Coast Highway – aka PCH – when the fuel light starts flashing. Everybody is still out for the count, so I take the initiative and stop to fill up the tank in Morro Bay. Still nobody stirs. Would they even notice if I nipped into the brilliantly named Touch & Go massage parlour to ease my munched-up shoulders? I can feel myself getting ever more tense with every misrouting on the town's small but absurdly hazardous roundabout.

Back on the designated road (praise be!), I'm getting used to the repetition of the sloping sun-bleached grasslands when I round a corner and the scene opens out before me like a pop-up storybook – greeny-blue sea with a ruffle of white foam, seagulls evenly perched along the wooden fencing, then, on the other side of the highway, sprucey-looking trees giving way to distant purplish mountains.

A while back I saw a sign for Montana de Oro, and the hills leading to the mountains really do appear to be carpeted in gold, albeit worn bare in patches. The jet-black cattle are in stark contrast – sleek oblongs with heads grazing so low they appear to be attached to the bottom corner of their body. I'm just thinking how honey-hued Bodie could run undetected for miles around these parts when suddenly it's my turn to cause the whiplash, or in Milo's case, the slamming into the seatwell.

'Ooomf!'

'Sorry, sorry!' I squeak.

'What is it?'

'I thought I saw. It can't be, *but it is . . .*'

We all look up from the layby I've skidded into. There, just a few feet away, is a zebra. No mistaking its tapered stripes. *And another and another.* Even a baby one, keeping pace beside its mother.

Bodie starts barking, but Marina quickly shushes him.

'He's the same way with horses,' she explains.

Judging by the way these striking beasts are grazing along-side the cattle, I'd say that's exactly what they think they are, only more mellow.

'It's like they have absolutely no idea how fabulously exotic they are!' I gasp as another car pulls over to join our gawping. 'How is this even possible?'

Milo explains that, back in the day, Hearst had his very own safari with camels, kangaroos, emus et al roaming free on his hillside, and zebras are one of the few animals that have endured.

'So we're close?' I surmise.

'Did we pass Cambria?'

'Yes,' I nod, 'and several signs for Moonstone Beach.'

'Doesn't that sound romantic?' Milo yawns, extending his arms in a stretch.

I am momentarily distracted, but then Marina confirms we are only a few miles from our destination and the butter-flies in my tummy become a swirling tornado.

Back in the car, everyone is upright and alert – even Bodie has his ears pricked, paws up on the dashboard, mouth open in an expectant pant.

Personally I find it hard to believe that a place of such legend is positioned off a simple two-lane road, especially when the surrounding terrain seems so deserted.

'I just keep going straight?'

'See the pier up ahead?' Milo points over my shoulder. 'The driveway is just opposite there. Anyone want a Mento?'

We both say yes. He pops one into Marina's palm, and even though I have my own hand extended, he places not one but two in my mouth. I want to burst out laughing, all girlish and giddy, but I don't want to let on my 'condition' to Marina, so I act unfazed and offer a simple 'Ta!'

'Remind me again of the difference between "ta" and "ta-ta".'

Before I can reply Marina has started rapping on her window, cheering, 'La Cuesta Encantada!'

I strain for a glimpse but see nothing except green-tufted hills.

'Turn right here,' Milo instructs.

We pass through a modest gateway and then are obliged to slow first to 25 miles per hour, then 15, dragging out the anticipation.

'Apparently there will be someone to drive us up from the Visitors' Centre. Here we are . . .'

At first I am reluctant to give up my celebrity chauffeuring duties – we've come so far, what's five more miles? – but they seem fairly insistent that we should make use of the assigned driver.

Within minutes I can see why. My ears actually pop as we make our grindingly steep ascent, veering round extreme bends with absolutely no safety barriers. At one particularly treacherous bend I get a vision of us plunging to our deaths, my body smooshed against Milo's as the car compresses around us. Noticing me flinching, he reaches out to grip my hand in reassurance.

'Their hands were entwined,' the newspaper report noted.

Now I am trembling all the more. I don't think I've had the chance to have any eye contact with Milo since lunch. He's either been driving or sleeping or out of range. Now I daren't look because I don't want him to see my nerves, not about the journey – as majestically knuckle-gnawing as it is – but about the prospect of losing him to the masses on the film set. Marina showed me page after page of the crew list this morning. Never mind the rest of the cast and all the extras ... The numbers hadn't really registered until now, when I see a whole convoy of vehicles heading up the hill and suddenly I wish I could rewind our three-hour journey. I should've slammed on the brakes a lot sooner or, at the very least, pulled into a drive-thru Starbucks and caffeinated everyone to a state of chattiness. Only now does it seem like a terrible waste of quality time.

'Look down there,' Milo urges.

'I don't know if I can,' I bleat wimpishly.

Gently he guides my chin towards the window. My stomach swoops down the expansive Santa Lucia Mountains, all the way to the sea. It's such a vast, splaying, untarnished view I can't help but be filled with wonder.

'Neat little front yard, huh?' he smirks.

'I can't believe no one has built around here – not for as far as the eye can see.'

'That's because they own all the land.'

'What?'

'Hearst's father bought a quarter of a million acres back in the day – for seventy cents an acre!'

'Seventy cents?' Marina hoots. 'For prime California coastline?'

'Remember, this was back when the PCH was just a dirt road.'

'So this really *is* their front yard?'

He nods. 'It's ranch land, plain and simple. Hearst was fifty-six when he inherited it and if you look up, you can see what he and his architect, Julia Morgan, spent twenty-seven years building . . .'

This time I obey without question and there it is – the infamous castle, a cross between a fairy-tale palace and a Mediterranean villa, accented with the tallest, skinniest feather-duster palm trees.

'You like it?' Milo asks, with the same personal concern as when I tasted the lavender tomato jam.

'It's stunning,' I breathe.

And then I smile to myself. Maybe it's going to be okay. Maybe our bond, however brand new, is secure.

'Hey, Milo,' Marina calls from the front seat, 'here's a girl for you!'

I look out of the window and there to greet us is a large pair of breasts. Yes, they are attached to a young woman, blonde, naturally. Well, not naturally blonde but basically ticking every cliché box going. Her make-up is a fright – impenetrable orange foundation, baby-pink Tippex lips and more kohl than Cleopatra. Where she did apply the 'less is more' concept is her clothing – a stretchy halter-neck top and the miniest of miniskirts.

As we step out of the car, Marina whispers to me, 'Someone should explain to her the difference between Hearst and Hugh Hefner. I think she's come as a Playmate.'

I have to believe that Marina is purely teasing in terms of matchmaking Milo, but the girl in question – name of Orla – seems to think it is a terrific idea.

'I'll be showing you to your rooms,' she says, addressing only Milo, with an annoyingly self-conscious flick of her hair. 'Let's start with the ladies, shall we?'

I love the way she a) calls us 'ladies', as if to emphasise the fact that she is considerably younger, and b) has already strategised that if she dumps us first, she will end up alone with Milo in his quarters.

It's been a long time since I felt possessive and/or competitive. And I don't do competition. I always back down. It just seems so undignified, scrabbling for a man. Besides, I don't think I'd fare well in a catfight – I always have to keep my nails short for make-up application, so my weapons are no match for her reinforced talons.

It's therefore a wonderful bonus to see that Marina seems to want to obstruct her at every turn.

'Why don't we see Milo's room first? It'll save me nosing later!'

'Well, his is in the Casa Grande—'

'The big house. How fitting!' he swaggers. 'So these two are in one of the guesthouses?'

Orla goes to speak.

'Wait – don't tell me. Casa del Sol?'

'Yes!' Orla looks a little surprised by his intuition.

'Well, it makes sense – Ms Ray in the House of the Sun!'

Orla laughs excessively and then informs Marina that they have met her request for adjoining rooms.

'You know, I still can't believe they're letting us stay here, this place is practically a museum.'

'Of course, it's just the principal actors and the director with that privilege.'

'And me!' I pip.

Orla's face sours all the more. 'The rest of us are at the Cavalier down the road.'

'Oh, what a shame,' Marina crows before she can add her room number. 'You'll miss all the corridor-creeping going on here!'

I see Orla's jaw clench and then she decides to retaliate by flouncing five or six steps ahead, thus giving us a clear view up her skirt.

I have to admit she does have a near-perfect rear – I can't even imagine what it must be like to have a shiny bottom. And she's obviously been wearing her toning trainers because her calves are so shapely—

'Check this out!' Marina taps me.

It's only now that I realise I alone have been transfixed by

Orla's physique. Both Milo and Marina have turned to gaze upon what they tell me is the Neptune Pool but immediately puts me in mind of Caesar's Palace in Las Vegas with all the dramatic pillars, statues and colonnades.

The water is a perfect turquoise rippling over the bold black and white geometric tiling. I am in awe, seriously doubting there could be a more appealing pool with a grander panorama in the world.

'Look how white these sculptures are.' I step closer. 'There's not an imperfection or a grey vein to be seen. Is it even marble?'

'Finest Italian Carrara,' Orla chips in.

'Bodie, don't drink that!' Marina yanks his lapping pink tongue back from the pool.

'It's all right, it's pure artisan spring water.'

Marina smirks back at her. 'Someone's been doing their research.'

'I came in a few days ahead of time to take all the tours,' she explains. 'The most amazing thing to me is that these pillars here are nearly two thousand years old, but everyone just wanted to know how deep the pool is.'

'And how deep is it?' I ask.

'Three feet in the shallow end, ten in the deep.'

'You've got a good memory,' I find myself complimenting her, and then realise she's probably a wannabe actress trying to prove that she can memorise lines. Until, that is, she says she was a history major, adding, 'So this is my thing.'

Neither of the others hears our last few exchanges, so I have no one to widen my eyes at, no one to ask why, when you can actually talk knowledgeably about Graeco-Roman architecture, would you be the girl wearing the titchiest toga at the party?

'So,' Milo returns to my side, 'what do you think?'

I take a deep inhalation. 'That the gods themselves must bathe here.'

'You know, my mom came to a fund-raising gala a few weeks back and they auctioned off a swim here for five thousand dollars!'

My mouth falls open.

'I should add that it was for a party of ten and included cocktails and the use of the deco dressing rooms.'

'You know, if I was rich, I'd probably pay that,' I decide. 'I mean, that would be a once-in-a-lifetime experience.'

'Well then, we'll have to see what we can arrange . . .' He gives me a mischievous look.

'Count me in!' Orla flips back to bimbo mode. 'I've got my bikini all ready to go.'

'Aren't you already wearing it?' Marina deadpans.

'Onward!' Milo decides to lead the way this time.

Now all three of us have our eyes trained on his behind, no doubt each pondering the apparent absence of underwear beneath those crumpled linen trousers. Not that I'm surprised. Milo strikes me as the type who sheds his clothes the second he gets home. Jonathan was the same way. He'd even iron naked, which is a very bold choice.

'Whoa!' I exclaim as my ankle snaps to the side. Oh great. The heel tip of my shoe has decided to come loose, leaving me afraid to place the protruding nail down upon the stone steps – this is not the place to be etching my initials. I wonder if I can just jam it back on? If I twist it back into place and then just stamp – 'Oh noooo!' I gasp as I feel my body unbalancing . . . I make a grab for the stone handrail but miss it – all I can do now is wait for the crack to my skull, then the splash into the pool, corrupting the crystalline water with a dark seepage of murky red.

What actually happens is that I fall into Milo, who has leaped to my aid and is scooping me up into his arms for the second time today.

'This is getting to be a habit,' he husks. 'Maybe I should just carry you everywhere we go.'

'Yes, please!' is the first response that springs to mind, but instead I settle for a rather breathless 'I think you just saved my life.'

'You make me feel like a superhero!' he chuckles.

'Well, that was a pretty swift save.'

'Now, if I could only fly you the rest of the way,' he says, contemplating the remaining twenty or so steps.

'You can put her down now,' Orla snips as we round the corner and discover a glorious courtyard brimming with pink flowers. 'Casa del Sol is right here.'

But instead of releasing me, Milo insists on delivering me all the way – carrying me across the threshold that leads directly into the first bedroom. My bedroom.

The only reason I know I'm not dreaming is that he sets me down on the Persian rug, as opposed to propelling me onto the hand-carved bed.

Which, though imposingly dark and solid, is tiny.

'You know this is actually king-size?' Marina and I go to dispute the fact until he adds, 'Back when kings were this size.'

I hate to look as ingratiating as Orla, but now it's my turn to laugh out loud. He's a funny guy, this Milo.

'The freakiest thing is that all this stuff is the real deal.' Marina peers at the religious artwork and china ornaments.

I give them a cursory glance, but what has me leaning on the desk for support is the ceiling – an intricate, almost geometric lattice inset with panels of sky blue and burnt orange featuring ever-more ornate designs in gold. Real gold.

'I'd say the ceilings are the signature item at the castle,' Orla announces. 'Each room is different and you'll see everything from cherubs to shields to seahorses.'

'I heard that Hearst would buy entire fifteenth-century ceilings from Spain and then chop them down to fit the room,' Milo adds.

'It's true,' Orla confirms. 'You can understand why people joke that he was travelling around Europe with a crowbar in one hand and a cheque book in the other, but in fact most of these pieces are from auction houses in New York.'

'You know what tickles me?' Marina chimes in. 'That Hearst calls this a "guesthouse" – for most Americans, that means some garage conversion at the bottom of the garden, but this place has how many rooms?'

'Eighteen,' Orla confirms. 'And it's not even the biggest.'

'You have guesthouses in England, right?' Marina turns to me.

'Well, we really use the term for B&B-type accommodation.'

'Ahhh yes,' Milo enthuses, 'the B&B! That's where all you Brits go for your smutty weekends.'

'Dirty,' I correct him.

Now it's Milo's turn to burst out laughing. 'It sounds so prim the way you say it, "Duh-tea"!' he mimics. 'You need to say it in your trailer-trash accent to really get the full effect, "Dur-dee"!'

'So this is your bathroom,' Orla tries to break up the banter with the glare of white tiles. 'It leads straight through to Marina's bathroom and then her bedroom.'

'Oooh, I got a pool view!' she cheers as she runs ahead.

Marina's room is considerably larger, with a striking cobalt-blue and gold fireplace, two floral velvet armchairs and a low window-side sofa where one might recline in a silk robe and pearls, and admire the vista. Her bedhead is a tapestry, her side table a Moorish hexagon, and dangling from the ceiling is something the Pope himself might waft incense with.

Both our rooms seem insanely, intensely elaborate and yet at the same time extremely *cosy*. As with the San Ysidro Ranch, you can tell this place was decorated with absolute confidence, if not a little audacity.

'Take this real Ch'ing dynasty vase,' Orla continues. 'Hearst casually drilled a hole to accommodate electrical wires so he could turn it into a lamp!'

Marina is making blah-blah-blah motions, but the truth is, if Orla were an audio tour rather than an assault on the eyes, I think I'd actually enjoy her depth of knowledge. My only disappointment is that, considering this place was built throughout the 1920s and the 1930s, there are not more deco items.

'Well, of course that would've been considered modern at the time and he favoured antiques,' she explains. 'There are a few items dotted around – one of my favourites is a lamp depicting Cupid trapped behind prison bars.'

So that's why he's been lagging behind in his work. Must try and spring him at the earliest opportunity.

'Mr Vallis, are you ready to see your room now?'

Milo is over by the window, framed and lit so beautifully I feel I ought to page the cinematographer and get him to capture this moment on film.

'You know, my dad first brought me here when I was ten years old.' Milo looks uncharacteristically wistful. 'William Randolph Hearst was the same age when he did the Grand Tour of Europe with his mom. The two of them were gone a year and a half, visiting London and Venice and the mist-shrouded castles in the Black Forest, whereas our tour lasted just an hour and a half. But, to me, the experience was just as impactful.' He smiles. 'I remember my dad seemed so impressed that Cary Grant had stayed here. It struck me that Hearst liked inviting movie stars to visit more than anyone else, so that's when it became my dream to be an actor, so I would get invited to magic hilltop castles that had flags in the dining hall and blue billiard tables, and one day my dad would be as impressed by me as he was by Cary Grant.'

There's a brief silence when we all contemplate the sensuality of his mouth and the mysterious depth to his eyes . . . but then Orla's walkie-talkie crackles and ruins the moment.

'Excuse me.' She flushes, hurrying outside.

No sooner is she through the door than Marina reaches for the ice-packed champagne. 'I think we need a toast!'

Three glasses are filled, three raised and three chinked as our voices unite: 'Here's to all our dreams coming true!'

13

For a brief, delirious moment I feel like a guest of Mr Hearst himself – sipping champagne and gossiping with the Hollywood elite.

'You realise, of course, this would've been a highly illegal move back in Hearst's day,' Milo notes as he tops up our glasses. 'Drinking in one's private room.'

'Not that W.R. disapproved of alcohol per se,' Marina clarifies. 'Cold beer on tap in the kitchen all day long, martinis in the Assembly Room prior to dinner with wine—'

'Which David Niven said flowed like glue!' Milo interjects.

'He just wouldn't tolerate drunkenness.'

'I heard Errol Flynn lasted four hours.' Milo smirks. 'Of course, Niven was an altogether more debonair drunk – managed to sneak in his own liquor and get away with it.'

'I didn't realise he was a boozer.'

'You're kidding, aren't you? He named his beach house Cirrhosis-by-the-Sea.'

'Oh!' I chuckle.

'Of course, the irony being that Marion Davies was the thirstiest of all, in fact—'

We're interrupted by a knock at the door.

It's Orla, letting me know that I'm wanted in the make-up trailer for a meeting with my new boss. Great. Always good to turn up to your first day drunk.

Experiencing a flurry of nerves, I turn to Marina. 'Wish me luck!'

'You'll be fine,' she assures me. 'Any problems just refer them to me.'

'Thank you,' I say to her, and then turn and repeat myself to Milo. 'Thank you. Really. I'd be in intensive care right now if you hadn't intercepted my fall.'

He shrugs. 'It feels good looking out for someone.'

My heart skips a beat.

'Ready?' Orla hustles me.

I actually feel like I'm floating as I follow her across the main courtyard and down a fragrant, citrus-lined path.

'Are these limes?' I enquire, feeling I should make some attempt at conversation.

'Tangerines. Hearst couldn't see the point of green fruit on a green tree. He was a big fan of colour.'

'I don't think I've ever seen so many butterflies,' I say, brushing the trailing purple lantana with my fingertips.

But all sensory pleasure ceases when I come to replace my shoes. My feet are in an even worse state than I imagined – rubbed-raw skin and harsh indentations from the stiff leather. I'd wear the San Ysidro Ranch slippers if I hadn't left them in the car. Oh well. Here goes nothing – what choice do I have?

'Wait!' Orla halts me. 'Don't do that.'

I look up at her wincing face.

'I'll lend you a pair of my flip-flops. Let me just run to my locker.'

Though she is just gone a matter of seconds, in my eyes she has transformed from a dollybird Playmate to a radiant angel. Even if the flip-flops are pink wedgies jangling with candy-coloured charms.

'I'm so grateful,' I breathe. 'You have no idea.'

'So how long have you known Milo?' she asks, eyes glinting with intent.

'Not long,' I chirrup, not even caring that she obviously has an ulterior motive for being nice to me – the squishy foam feels sooo good.

'You seem quite familiar . . .'

Oooh! She's noticed the chemistry between us. Maybe I'm not imagining it!

'Well, he's easy to get along with.'

'Is there anything going on with him and Marina?'

Oh. Now I see where her concern lies.

'No.' I shake my head. 'They're just friends – they already know each other from another movie.'

Why did I say that? I should've kept her guessing.

'So, as far as you know, he's single?'

This feels very uncomfortable, as if she is preparing to stake her claim. Obviously I can't say, 'Forget it – I saw him first!' but equally I don't want to encourage her.

'Stella?'

Fortunately our conversation is cut short by a woman who is the antithesis of Orla – short but substantial, with an air of authority and an array of communication devices strapped to her ear/wrist/hip. She introduces herself as Carrie, the production manager, and then goes to open the door of the trailer, letting me know that Mr Lloyd Anderson, head of the make-up department, is waiting for me.

My nerves have just magnified tenfold. I pray he's not going to put me to the test – at the moment a lip-line would come off like the manic jiggle of a polygraph test.

Of course, I am the last to arrive. And not just today. I know from my chat with Elena that Lloyd will have been meeting with Conrad and the more established members of the cast for the past several months to discuss the precise 'look' for each character. They will have done screen tests and detailed visual presentations and here am I, swanning in the day before shooting begins and claiming the leading lady. On the upside, Lloyd looks a convivial enough fellow, broad of girth and unruly of hair, cream shirt-sleeves rolled up and Paisley cravat tied loosely at his neck.

'Okay, so as you know, Ms Ray has brought in her own personal make-up artist – everyone, this is Stella.'

Mixed mumblings as I find myself a seat.

'As we have an ever-expanding number of extras, we are going to need you to contribute to the bigger picture, as it were.'

'Absolutely. Happy to.'

'Some of the lookalikes will invariably appear less convincing than their promo shots . . .'

As he hands me copies, I instantly recognise Gary Cooper and Bette Davis.

'. . . so you might want to gen up on who they are supposed to be looking like. If you want to print out images, they'll be happy to oblige in the office next door.'

'Can I do Clark Gable?' a camp twenty-something asks.

'I'll make my assignments when I've had a look at them all tomorrow, but that should be fine, so long as you behave yourself.'

'Me?' He looks mock-scandalised.

'Moving on.' Lloyd looks back at his notes. 'Obviously I'll be taking Charles Dance.'

'Gosh, was he a guest here? I wouldn't have thought he was old enough.'

There's a titter at my ignorance.

'He's playing Mr Hearst.'

'Oh, of course!' I tut myself.

'Francesca, you'll have Milo Vallis.'

My heart sinks as I see the girl in question give a covert low five to her neighbour. Naturally she would be the prettiest girl in the room. Dark, petite and cool-looking with a rose and thorns tattoo wending up her arm. And to think I was worried about Orla! Aside from the fact that she's not even his type, why would he bother with someone so trashy when, really, every woman is equally available to him?

I'm just thinking it's going to be torture working alongside them when Lloyd lets me know that Marina has her own private make-up trailer. Of course, I understand she wants to be able to talk freely about Jeff, but—

'Stella?'

'Oh, thank you.' I accept a printout of the schedule.

'This is going to be an intense week. The State of California has permitted us just seven days to shoot here and then we do the rest on sound stages back in LA. So this is how the schedule is looking so far . . .'

I can barely take in what Lloyd is saying but busily scribble notes, hoping that at some point this will all make sense.

'Saturday, we have the day off because they insist on opening for the public on their busiest day. I suggest you all get some rest because Sunday is going to be a doozy – it's the big masquerade-party scene. All hands on deck.

'Any questions?'

I would like to know when my head will stop spinning but decide to keep that query to myself.

'The rest of you can go, but, Stella, I think you should go through Marina's wardrobe so you can coordinate the make-up colours.'

'Right!' I say, wishing I knew where Wardrobe was.

Fortunately Carrie is on hand to give me a map. 'As far as the property goes, I think it helps to think of it as a

Mediterranean village, so you have the main plaza and the big church-like building, which is the Casa Grande, and then the three guest cottages, which are named according to their view. Remind me which one you're in?'

'Casa del Sol.'

'So that's obviously the sun. Then we have Casa del Mar, view of the sea, and Casa del Monte, view of the mountains. That's the one Conrad is staying in, so you want to be particularly quiet in that area.'

'Gotcha.'

'As far as everything to do with the film goes – the trailers, the office, catering, et cetera – that's all down here by the fire station.'

'There's a fire station?'

'Well, you've seen how much wood is in the guest rooms. The whole place is heaving with it.' She flips the sheet over. 'Here are the floor plans of the Casa Grande. That's where most of the filming is taking place. We're putting up signs as well, but if you get lost, just call this number and Orla will come find you.'

If she's not mooning over Milo.

'So Wardrobe would be . . .'

'Right behind you!'

Marion Davies's outfits surprise me. Considering she was essentially a showgirl-made-good with an unlimited budget, she seems rather conservative in her personal taste – lots of Peter Pan collars, puff sleeves and Argyle cardies . . .

'She was not a provocative dresser,' Nora, the Wardrobe head, confirms. 'Not like Jean Harlow.' She holds an ultra-sheer number out to me. 'You know Conrad had a ball casting the actress for this!'

'Who is it?' I'm intrigued.

'Just an unknown with killer boobs, but the amazing thing is, she actually has Harlow's cleft chin!'

I chuckle. 'This is going to be so much fun – who doesn't wish they worked on a Hollywood movie in its heyday?'

'These are all the evening options we have for Marina . . .'

'Has she seen these?' I say, admiring the slink of one ruby-red satin number.

'Well, I asked her if she wanted to come down tonight, but she said she was already in bed.'

'Oh,' I say, a little dismayed to hear that the champagne party is over. 'Well, just so as you know, it's jet lag rather than lack of enthusiasm. She's over the moon to have this part.'

'I bet,' Nora smirks. 'She is certainly at home around rich, older men.'

'You mean Victor?'

'I'm sure he wasn't her first sugar daddy.'

I'm not quite sure how to respond to that – should I defend her? But then I decide it's better for her to find out for herself how sweet Marina can be. She wouldn't believe me anyway.

'Okay. Well, thank you for showing me everything. Hope you manage to get some sleep tonight.'

I'm just exiting Wardrobe when I collide with Lloyd.

'Oh good, you're still here.'

'Everything all right?' I feel a little nervous.

'Yes, yes. I just wanted to let you know that you'll actually be doing Milo tomorrow.'

I blink back at him.

'You must've made quite an impression – he has requested you himself.'

It takes all my strength to keep my facial muscles from springing up into an exuberant grin. He chose me! He wants me!

'So get Marina done first thing and then get straight on Milo.'

'I will,' I assure him.

I wait for him to return to the make-up trailer and then throw my arms up in celebration. *Yes!* It's as good as a date! Tomorrow I will get to caress that beautiful face and run my fingers through his hair – oh, I can't stand it! This is all too glorious! I don't so much run back to my room as gallop, complete with audible whinnying. Once inside, I throw myself onto the bed, only to roll and grab the covers around me until I am bound like a burrito. Panting a little, I look up at the intricate artistry of the ceiling, both dazed and amazed. How often in life do you get to say, 'Well, things were going great and suddenly they got better'?

Tomorrow morning I'm going to get up an hour early just to revel in the delicious anticipation of seeing, and touching, Milo. I squeal again, reaching a new level of shrill.

'Stella, are you all right?'

I look up and see a concerned robe-clad Marina staring down at what little of my face is peeking out from my fabric wrap.

'Are you in pain?'

I try and sit up and release myself, but my binding is too secure and now I feel as if I'm sitting here in a giant hot-dog costume.

'I'm fine,' I puff. 'I just can't believe I'm going to be working on a real Hollywood movie!'

She nods. 'I remember when I felt the same way.' She looks wistful for a second, as if it's been mildly downhill ever since. 'Well, I'm going back to bed.'

I hesitate. I don't want anything to ruin my mood, but she is definitely looking a bit sad.

'Everything okay?'

She shrugs. 'I'm just a little irritated with myself – you know, this is a complete dream come true for me and yet here

I am, pining for my husband.' She fiddles with the bedpost and then adds, 'I think seeing Milo again has reminded me of where I was at before I met Jeff.'

'Not good?' I ask as she gives a little shudder.

'It was something of a low point for me.' She tries to sound breezy. 'Newly divorced from Victor, everyone saying I'd got the career leg-up I needed and then left him, which wasn't the case at all.'

'What did happen?' I ask. 'I mean, I know you can't discuss this in public, but it's just you and me here.' I pat the bed.

She slides herself onto the corner, looking a little unsure.

'Well, in a nutshell, I was away promoting the movie, going to premieres all over the world, and when I got home, I found out he'd been having an affair with one of those interchange-able LA bimbos. I'd say she looked like Orla, but they all look alike – that's the point, isn't it?'

'Oh no!' I sympathise.

'I should have seen it coming. I was the first non-blonde he'd ever dated. I thought we had something real – he said I'd woken him up from a forty-year stupor. But it's hard to trump those gold-diggers, because they're not looking for an equal relationship. They'll say and do anything to win over the guy, be anything he wants them to be, espe-cially in the bedroom, as long as their shopping habit is paid for.'

'And so when you met Milo . . .'

She gives a little smile. 'He seemed like the perfect anti-dote to my misery – all party all the time. There's something so bacchanalian about that man. Even seeing him today just made me want to drink and make merry!'

I raise an eyebrow.

'Not that kind of merry. I drank far too much the first time around with him. Made a fool of myself. Got rejected.' She shakes her head. 'I was so lost then. Just wanting to escape what my life had become. I don't want to feel like that again. I just want to be Mrs Arnett.'

I reach over to give her hand a squeeze.

'It makes perfect sense that you don't want to go back to that, but maybe you should think of going even further back,' I suggest. 'Like another seventy-five years or so.'

She gives me a quizzical look.

'For this one week we get to live in the 1930s. Why don't we forget all our modern-day concerns and just immerse ourselves in this experience? I need a break from thinking about Jonathan; you need a break from missing Jeff. Now, I'm not suggesting you have an affair with W.R., but just enjoy being Marion for the week.'

As she considers this, her faces catches the light and I notice she's still wearing her make-up.

'I've got cleansing wipes by the bed,' she dismisses my concern.

'Come on, why don't we do it the old-fashioned way?' I suggest, leading her back to her bedroom.

I cover her hair in a towelling turban and then gently massage cold cream into her skin.

'Mmm, I love that smell.'

'Well, the best thing is, it will linger, so what I want you to do is lie back and let that scent take you to a time before you and Jeff were even born. Close your eyes and dream a Marion dream – how about before she even met Hearst? Didn't you say she used to be in the Ziegfeld Follies?'

Marina's face brightens. 'Yes.'

'Well, put yourself in her dancing shoes!'

She settles back into the pillow looking content.

I mouth, 'Sleep well,' and then tiptoe towards the door

– just reaching for the handle when she calls after me, 'What about you? What are you going to dream about?'

I think for a moment, so many fantasies to choose from.

'A midnight swim in the Neptune Pool,' I decide. And then, on the other side of the door, I add, 'With Milo.'

14

'Stella!'

I wake up to the sound of Marina calling my name.

I squint at the clock – 5.34 a.m. This can't be good.

Scrambling out of bed, I hurtle through to her side, grabbing a handful of tissues from the bathroom en route. But when I reach her bedside, her eyes are dry, if a little bleary.

'Could you be a doll and take Bodie for a walk? He refuses to go back to sleep. And take the Chuckit with you – he loves the thrill of the chase!'

I pull a face at the plastic arm designed to propel tennis balls with extra force. 'I'm not sure that is an entirely wise idea,' I say, having visions of toppling statues and shattering glass.

'Oh no, I wouldn't use it round here. One of the runners is going to take you down to the beach. If you go right to the far end, you can let him off the leash and there's nothing to hit there except for the odd tree.'

The beach. Just one day after confessing how melancholy a sea view makes me. *Really?*

There's a rap at the door. 'Miss Conway?'

'There he is now. Better jump into some clothes.'

And with that she snugs back down into her nice warm bed.

Well, I suppose as assistant duties go, it could be worse. Plus the saltwater might be good for my wounds, I decide as I reach for my rubber flip-flops.

Jeans, T-shirt and fleece. Nothing I can do with my hair or face in the time given.

'Right, Bodie' – I grab him and head out through the door – 'let's go!'

'So you're the make-up artist?' The runner looks unconvinced.

'One of them,' I reply. 'Please bear in mind I was asleep five minutes ago.'

'I'm going to drop you at the beach and then come back in half an hour.'

'Half an hour!'

'Is that okay?'

'I guess it will have to be.'

We ride down the hill mostly in silence. There's a haziness to the sky today – like viewing everything through gauze. I'm glad of the familiar sight of the pier or I might fear that Bodie and I would be enveloped in sea mist, never to be seen again.

'I'll pick you up right by this sign,' he announces, halting the car.

' "William Randolph Hearst Beach", ' I read. 'So he owns this too?'

'Well, the State does now. Part of the package with the castle,' he replies. 'Just follow the path down. I'll be back at six thirty a.m.'

'Well, he was a laugh a minute,' I mutter to Bodie. But before I can get remotely wistful about the shore scene, Bodie is tugging me like he's in some kind of Drag Your Owner race. 'Easy!' I plead, breaking into a trot to try and keep up, which only causes him to transition into a run.

As soon as we hit the beach, he's on a mission to get to the water, still pulling me behind him. Is he a swimmer? I wonder as he trots in up to his belly. But then a wave advances in his direction and he makes a sploshy retreat, clearly happy just to paddle.

'Give me a sec to roll up my jeans,' I request, even though they're already wet through from the knee down. 'Oops!'

He pulls me on to a great straggly island of seaweed, sniffing agitatedly at all the slithery tails and plump pods. And then he wees all over it.

I look around me – is that allowed?

'What's the problem?' Bodie seems to say. 'It is sea*weed* after all.'

'Fair enough,' I shrug. And then, since there's no one else around and he's straining so hard at the lead, I can't see the harm in letting him loose a little early.

'Ready?' I say as I prepare to release the clip.

He pants excitedly and then bolts with such joyful abandon I can't help but laugh out loud.

'Wanna go for the ball?' I ask as he returns to me. His eyes lock on to it, sitting at a tilt, ready to take off again.

And he's away! Bounding ears down, back legs pounding at the wet sand like Thumper. It takes him a few tries to actually get the ball into his mouth, but he brings it back prancing as proudly as a Lipizzaner.

We continue this ritual all along the beach. This really is a lovely spot – old wooden pier to our left, woodsy headland to our right. The water is cool but not painfully so and I find myself drawn back to the water's edge, even if the ball does fall with a thud into the sludge.

For a moment I think I see the head of a swimmer wearing a dark cap, but then I realise it's actually a sea lion bobbing his slick head above water. I look back to Bodie, suddenly nervous that he might dart in and start chasing it, but there's something more interesting moving in the bushes at the back of the beach, something he urgently wants to meet.

'Bodie!' I call and call again. He pays me no attention. I start getting anxious as he progresses up the bank, tangling with twigs and branches. I'm not sure what lies on the other side of the copse, how close we are to the traffic. I can't imagine facing Marina if he got hit.

'Bodie!' I try for an authoritative tone, but even I can hear the panic in my voice.

He's out of sight now, so there's nothing for me to do but claw my way up and try to follow his tracks. When I get to the top, I see him snuffling busily around a cutesy wood-slatted building labelled, 'Sebastian's General Store, 1852'. To me, it looks like something out of *Little House on the Prairie*. I smile to myself as I remember the opening sequence of the TV show – Laura and her sisters in their pioneer frocks, running down the hill after their dog – and then I wonder . . . Marina did say Bodie loves 'the thrill of the chase'. Dare I do the counterintuitive thing and run away from him in the hope that he'll chase me?

Praying that there is no one watching from inside the store, I give a wild whoop and then start charging back down the bank, imagining my pigtails flying, pounding at the dirt and jolting my body in a way it hasn't experienced in years. It's working! He's coming after me! I hit the sand and run harder and faster, luring him right back to the water's edge. Oh thank God! For a good twenty minutes we play chase, splashing and hurtling and leaping, until we both fall exhausted onto the sand. I lie flat out beside a large piece of driftwood only to be half buried in damp, dark sand as Bodie starts burrowing himself a cool resting place. Even his pink tongue is loaded with gritty sand now. When he stops digging, I try to brush myself off but only serve to spread a cement-like layer over my jeans. Same goes for the assorted spatterings across my face.

I didn't think it was possible to look any more dishevelled than when I left my room, but the difference is that now I feel good.

It's only when the runner collects us and we pass a plaque on the way out – 'Blue Star Memorial Highway: A tribute to the Armed Forces that have defended the United States of America' – that I realise I haven't once thought of Jonathan.

'What the . . . ?' Marina hoots with mirth when she sees the state of us standing in her doorway, both equally bedraggled and encrusted. 'Let me get my phone!' She snaps and then shows me the pic, saying, 'How's that for a new seaside memory?'

I look back at her with a surprised smile. 'You did that on purpose, you little minx!'

'Well, you really helped me turn my mood around last night,' she smiles. 'I wanted to return the favour.'

There it is again – that toasty feeling in my heart. Now I have two people looking out for me!

Though Bodie gets a bubble bath – I swear he just reclines in the water like he's soothing his muscles after all that running – there's no time for me to shower. Marina needs me to get straight to her make-up because Carrie has called to say they want to do some promotional shots before the actual scene.

'Let's just do it here,' she suggests. 'Far more atmospheric than a trailer!'

Considering the state of me, I'm not going to argue. I simply position her in the lightest part of her room and cover the surrounding area with a protective sheet.

'You know, the first time I made you into Marion, you got sprinkled in doughnut sugar, now it's sand!' I laugh. 'What's next? I wonder.'

'Diamonds!' she exclaims, leaping to her feet. 'Look at this.' She hurries back to me with the most gorgeous sparkling marquise-cut necklace set upon a swathe of velvet. 'While you were at the beach, they brought this up to me. It's one of Marion's actual pieces. Isn't that something?'

I nod, slightly in awe. I don't think I've ever seen real jewels up close like this before.

'Put it on,' Marina urges.

'What?' I snort. 'Have you seen the state of me?'

'Just for the feel, while you're doing my make-up.'

And so she fastens it round my neck and then steps back to admire it.

'Beautiful,' she coos, and then she closes her eyes, tilts her face to me and commands, 'Begin!'

I don't know whether it's the setting inspiring me, the sea air in my lungs or the jewels resting upon my collarbone, but the transformation is more convincing than ever.

'You're so good!' Marina raves as she peers close to the mirror.

Fortunately Lloyd agrees. He's come up to the room to inspect my work before Marina goes on set.

'Just wonderful,' he enthuses. 'Your shading skills are exceptional.'

'Thank you.'

'I'm looking forward to seeing what you do with Milo.'

'What time is he scheduled for?' I reach for my notebook.

'He's waiting in Marina's trailer now.'

'What?' I gasp. 'Already?'

'Yes. You'd better pack up your kit and head on down.'

'B-but I haven't even showered!' All I've had time to do is change out of my wet clothes into dry ones.

'If you'd rather I sent Francesca—'

'No, no!' I fluster. 'I'll do it. Just give me a minute.'

With trembling hands I restock my kit, then grab Marina's beanie hat from her dressing table, locate my sunglasses and spritz myself with perfume. As I hurtle down the hill, I pray not too many people see me looking so unkempt – I don't want to appear unprofessional on my first day, especially not in front of Milo. If only there was some way I could see him but he couldn't see me.

And then I get an idea . . .

15

'Oi!' is Milo's opening gambit.

Mine is a rather brusque 'Get in the chair and close your eyes.'

'Oh, I see how it is – you're a bit of the dominatrix in the make-up room.'

I don't do much to disprove this theory as I swiftly 'blind-fold' him with a cooling gel eye mask – crafty, huh?

'Please tell me that the reason I'm wearing this is that you're planning on doing my make-up naked,' he teases.

'Well, there's certainly aspects of me that are all too bare . . .' I peer at my pasty face and then apply the quickest dab of concealer under my eyes. Oh no – it's only now that I remember the violet lenses sitting beside my bathroom sink . . .

'How long do I have to wear this thing for?' he asks, already fidgety.

'The whole time. At least until I get to your eyes.'

He sighs heavily. 'So where's Marina, anyway? I came early because I wanted to see her Marion Davies face.'

'I did her up in the room,' I explain as I clip his hair away from his forehead and start gently sweeping toner over his golden skin.

'So you do boudoir visits, do you?' He jiggles his brows, twitching the eye mask. 'Woman after my own heart.'

'You have no idea,' I mutter to myself.

And then I tell him how the actress Gloria Swanson, most famous for her dramatic role in *Sunset Boulevard*, used to have her make-up done at home by the legendary Mont Westmore. One day he arrived and she was still sleeping, but the maid refused to wake her. He too was reticent, on account of her famously 'changeable' disposition (mostly dependent on how well she had slept the night before).

'So he crept into her bedroom, knelt beside her and did her full make-up while she slept!'

'Now you're talking!' he cheers. 'Do you think we can come to some arrangement? I'll give you my suite key and you can just wake me up when you're done!'

I take a moment to picture sneaking into the creaky darkness, tiptoeing to his bedside and admiring his face as the early morning light filters through the brocade curtains. Maybe I'd bring my cup of tea with me and spend the first few minutes sipping fragrant lapsang souchong and observing the rhythm of his breathing.

There's something about sleeping men that is just so appealing to me. I love the positions they get themselves into – the arm flung back on the bedhead, the face half crumpled into the pillow, leg lolling off the side of the mattress . . . They are so lovely and gentle in repose – for a moment they don't have to shoulder life's responsibilities or be the strong provider or the smartass; they can just be. Certainly some of my most treasured moments with Jonathan were those just before and just after he awoke – his heart was at its most open and receptive in that half-and-half state. If I so much as turned over, he'd instinctively mould himself around me and pull me closer, making me feel so wanted and secure. The sensation would make my heart dance and even though further slumber would elude me, I didn't mind, because my conscious state meant I could revel in the feeling all the more.

He used to tell me that was his favourite time of the day: 'It doesn't get any better than this,' he'd husk. And then he'd look at me with such a doting smile or whisper, 'You're so beautiful.' And what is more disarming than that? Being accepted at your most unpolished. Sometimes I'd go to the bathroom afterwards and I'd see the facial creases and mascara smirches and I'd think, He doesn't even see them. He just sees me.

But mostly I'd just lie there as long as I could – waking up with him fended off the day, delayed me checking my emails and consulting my to-do list. All that mattered was the feel of his skin on mine. I was warm and safe and loved. And as long as I stayed in that bed with him, all was well.

And so it would be with Milo.

I would gently brush his hair from his face, but before I could even attach one clip, he would reach for me, pulling me under the covers and locking me in his arms. For a while he'd just hold me and let my body adjust and awaken to all the possibilities of our bodies merging. I emit a little groan of desire.

'You like that idea?' he enquires. 'Do we have a deal?'

Somewhat reluctantly I shake my head. 'I don't think Lloyd would approve.'

'Really? You won't even try it?'

'Well, I like to think that you'd want to take a shower once you'd got out of bed and then you'd wash off all my hard work.'

'You're saying it's hard work to make me look good?'

I laugh out loud. 'No! But how about this compromise – I won't take offence if you fall asleep while I'm doing your face. In fact, if you like, we can recline you a little right now.'

I reach across him to adjust the lever.

'You realise if I was the make-up artist and you were my subject, I'd probably get done for sexual harassment about now!'

'If you were a male make-up artist, you'd be gay,' I counter.

He opens his mouth and then shrugs. 'I can't argue with that.'

'You want to go further?'

'All the way.'

I really need to get a grip and be more professional, but I'm having too much fun.

'Mmm.' He nestles deeper into the chair. 'Suddenly I'm flying first class!'

'Just think of this as a pampering facial,' I say as I begin to blend the foundation, thrown for a second by the hint of stubble. It's been a long time since I made up a man. Not that it's so very different, the aim is still to accentuate their best features.

'Got any music?'

'How about some Glenn Miller? That always gets me in the mood.'

'Really?' he rumbles flirtatiously.

'In the mood of the era,' I tut.

'Whatever you say.' He listens for a moment, his toes flexing in time to the swishy-tinny hi-hat. 'This is very cool.'

'Just relax and with every breath feel yourself stepping back in time.'

'You sound like a hypnotist.'

I smile, rather liking the idea of planting a few desires in his mind. Perhaps I can do it subliminally with my touch. Of course, as Elena said, it's more hygienic to use sponges and brushes, but nothing beats the finish you get with fingertips. That's my story and I'm sticking to it.

Several times his chest rises and falls in a sigh of contentment. I could do this all day, trace his cheekbones and jawline as if we were lovers, but the time has come to remove the mask.

'Keep your eyes closed for the first few minutes,' I instruct, and then dab on cooling gel and the lightest foundation over his lids.

'Now look up,' I tell him.

'What the . . . ?' He frowns at my sunglasses. 'How can you see what you're doing with those things on?'

'They have a special magnifying lens that helps me catch every flaw,' I lie. 'Look up.'

Oh so delicately I work on his undereye area, applying concealer and then the lightest line of taupe at his lash-line to accentuate his eyes, all the more important for an actor.

I step back and assess his face and then take a tiny dot of balm and massage it into his lips, not to give a sheen, just a suppleness. I half expect him to give my finger a playful bite, but instead he says, 'You have a very tender touch,' his voice low and satisfied.

'Thank you.'

'Five minutes, Mr Vallis.' A runner peeks inside the trailer door.

'Tell them I'm not coming.' He waves him away.

'What?' the runner stalls. 'Is there a problem?'

'*Au contraire*. I'm simply too content to move.'

I giggle again.

'I'm just going to lie here and have this marvellous woman stroke my face all day.'

'Perhaps if I got you a coffee?' he offers.

'Oh, how you people badger me!' he teases as he sets himself upright. 'Stella, what do you think a 1930s movie star would drink first thing in the morning? Latte? Espresso?'

'Bloody Mary,' I decide. 'To counter the night before.'

'Sounds good,' he confirms. 'Make mine a virgin,' he announces, just as a journalist arrives for the set visit.

As we head back up the hill, Milo is called to a pre-scene confab with Marina and Conrad, giving me time to run back to my room and shower away the morning's beach grit. It feels so good to be clean again, and to be seeing the world through violet-coloured lenses, though the vista has certainly changed since last night . . .

The main entrance to Casa Grande now looks strangely industrial with all the cameras and lighting rigs and tracking rails and black-clad bodies walking around with hi-tech communication devices. I just hope nothing bashes into any of the exquisite architecture. At the very least I make a personal vow to ensure I don't leave a single make-up smudge behind, not even on one of the glasses supplied by catering – or, in movie-speak, 'craft services'. Elena told me to have my star sip through a straw to preserve the make-up. I can't see any resistance to that, but I do think I'm going to have to keep my charges away from these oozy, flaky pastries.

'They look so good!' I acknowledge a girl with buttery crumbs on her fingertips as I reach for a pain au chocolat.

'Almost as good as Pret A Manger,' she confirms.

'You're English!' I cheer, delighted that I'm not the odd one out. 'What department are you?'

'Wardrobe,' she grins. 'I'm Carmen.'

'Stella.' We nod at each other in lieu of a mutually greasy handshake. 'I'm make-up.'

'Ooh, who'd you get?'

'Marina and Milo,' I say, unable to disguise the pride in my voice.

'Wow! The two beauties!'

'It's a tough job . . .' I'm about to wonder if she too has a crush on Milo when I notice the intricate gold engagement ring on her finger. 'Unusual ring,' I comment.

'It's a Spanish antique – I've got a bit of a thing for the Latin cultures.'

'Including Latin men?' I cheekily enquire.

She breaks into a huge smile. '*Si!*'

'So, is he in a land far away?'

'Not for long – as soon as the movie is done, he's flying out so we can explore California together. This is actually my first Hollywood movie—'

I'm eager to tell her that it's mine too, but Carmen's boss, Nora, bustles over and sends her on her way, only to turn back to me with a smirk.

'So was Milo all booze breath this morning?'

'No.' I frown. 'Not at all. Why do you ask?'

'Apparently he arrived on set drinking a Bloody Mary . . .'

'Oh, it's a virgin!' I inform her. 'I was there when he ordered it.'

Nora gives a disbelieving snort. 'When Milo Vallis says "virgin", he just means Virgin Vodka!'

My eyes narrow. Apparently it's not just Marina that she disapproves of.

'So who *do* you like, of the cast?' I ask her.

She looks momentarily thrown – 'You want me to be *nice* about someone?' – but I maintain a wide-eyed look.

'Well, Roger Silver – the guy who's playing Charlie Chaplin – has a certain charm.'

'Really?' I say, making a mental note to avoid him, based on her judgement so far.

'Stella!'

'Yes!' I eagerly respond to Carrie's call.

'Marina needs you over in Video Village.'

'Right!' I say, kicking myself that I have to ask where and, more specifically, '*What* is Video Village?' in front of Nora.

Carrie guides me over. 'It's where the director sits and watches the action from different angles on a bank of flat screens.'

'Why has the one on the right got black tape across it?'

'That's to give him an idea of the framing, you know – how it looks on the big screen.'

'Gosh!' I inhale, experiencing yet another flurry of excitement. This really is happening – what I am about to see acted out right here on the entrance steps will soon be projected through the darkness at my local Odeon. I'm so going to see this on one of the mega-screens in Leicester Square!

'Am I shiny?' Marina summons me.

All she needs is the finest dusting of powder. 'I'm beginning to think this look actually suits you!'

'I've told the unit photographer I want copies of everything he snaps – proof that I really was here.'

'Where's Hearst?' I look around the set for a glimpse of Charles Dance, OBE.

'They're just adding a bit more padding to his midriff. He's a lot slimmer than W.R., but facially I think they are so similar, especially in the eyes and the nose . . .'

'Ms Ray?' Carrie leans in. 'We need you in position.'

We exchange a quick hand-squeeze and then I turn my attention to Milo.

He stands before me utterly flawless, until he grins, revealing a set of teeth made from orange peel.

I burst out laughing. 'I haven't seen that done since I was a child!' I happily inhale the citrus fragrance and then hold up my hand to his mouth.

He hooks the peel out with his tongue and pushes it into my palm.

'Ew!' I give a faux shudder. As if I could find this man repulsive in any way.

'You do realise you're going to have to do body make-up on me for the Neptune Pool scene?' He jiggles his brows.

'That's today?' I scrabble for my schedule, trying not to get too flustered at the thought of his caramel contours.

'If the weather holds.' Milo squints at the sky. 'If it clouds over, we're skipping ahead to the movie-theatre interior. No windows there.'

'Mr Vallis!'

Now it's his turn to be placed.

He gives his hair a casual flip. 'Here we go . . .'

'You don't ever get nervous?' I cause him to turn back.

'It's just talking.' He shrugs. 'I've been doing that since I was a little kid.'

I check that I'm not in the way of anyone and then prepare to watch my first ever movie scene. Suddenly I realise I can let go of the notion of being short-changed for not fulfilling my early ambitions as an artist. How could sitting alone in a damp studio compare to this? I smile with pride as I acknowledge the living art upon Marina's face. This is it! This is what I was meant to do!

'Quiet, please!' We are shushed and stilled. 'And action!'

Afraid to even take a breath and disturb the balance of the air, I watch as Hearst and Marion emerge onto the top step, him tall and imposing, her girlish and playful. The first guests to arrive enquire about their recent trip to Europe – Hearst speaks in awed tones about the ancient sites, while Marion compares the cultural excess to being hit over the head with a hammer.

'It feels so good when it stops.'

'Happy to be home sweet home?' suggests the Claudette Colbert lookalike.

'Thrilled.'

Another batch of guests approach – boisterous and joking until they catch sight of 'the Chief', when they immediately straighten up and adopt a fawning reverence.

'Why don't they treat me like an ordinary person?' Hearst bristles as they head inside. 'I'm no different to anybody else. Matter of fact, I'm worse.'

I look down at the script. In voiceover Marion says, 'Everyone censored their conversation around W.R., trying to be elegant, but it didn't really matter what anyone was saying, because he wasn't listening anyway – his mind would be way off, thinking of something else.'

As a young starlet witters on, Hearst's face displays this mental 'absence' so artfully you can almost see the page layout of the newspaper he is working on.

But apparently Conrad wants to try the scene multiple ways and so Milo's canvas chair is brought over – it may be a while before he gets to walk on.

I've heard so much about the *Groundhog Day* aspect to filming – *take after take, after take* – it makes me wonder what it was like for Bill Murray and Andie MacDowell filming so many repetitious scenes, each with such subtle variations. Of course, for me, it's all new and fascinating. Especially when Milo's moment arrives. It becomes quickly apparent that his character is neither in awe of Hearst nor particularly respect-ful, lifting Marion clean off her feet with his twirling hug and whispering in her ear.

She pushes him away, trying to maintain a light tone, but checks to see if W.R. is getting riled. I wonder what the whis-per is supposed to imply – a sexual overture or 'I've got the extra liquor you requested!' Either way, I'm intrigued to see where their relationship is headed. Especially since I like the idea of Marion and Hearst being utterly devoted to each other and it bothers me to think that my beloved Milo could be the one to foul things up. Apparently in real life Charlie Chaplin was always after Marion. He was certainly one of the more regular guests at the castle. Conveniently Hearst's wife, Millicent, was less keen on the place, preferring the high society of New York. While Hearst was famously unpretentious, even given to cooking late-night Welsh rarebit for his guests, she was very status-orientated, which is apparently why she refused to agree to a divorce. Not that there was anything covert about his relationship with Marion – look at them now, playing lord and lady of the manor . . .

After a few more takes I let my gaze leave the stars and take in the reactions of the onlookers. Over in the corner, I see Francesca watching Milo's every move. Then again, what red-blooded woman wouldn't? The men, on the other hand, are probably predicting an affair with Marina based on the way he is sneaking in bottom-squeezes and lascivious glances in subsequent takes. It's easy to see why Marina got romantic notions about him on the previous movie – natural curiosity to want to find out how far their on-camera chemistry could take them. I mean, look at me – he's even got me wondering about our trailer chemistry. And just how much trouble I might get into doing his body make-up . . .

When we finally break for lunch, everyone else is heads down checking out the buffet options, while I stare skyward, preoccupied with the clouds closing in on our sunshine.

Soon it becomes official – too grey for the pool scene, we're going to set up indoors. Well, maybe it's for the best – before Milo strips half naked in front of me, we get to go to the movies . . .

16

Apparently this was quite the ritual: each night after dinner Hearst would roll a film for his guests – typically one from Marion Davies's repertoire, which rather embarrassed her. Marina tells me that she was sure everyone was bored out of their mind, when really there is plenty to look at besides the screen itself . . .

In direct contrast to modern-day screening rooms with their monochromatic design, outsized leather seats and state-of-the-art systems, here the walls are sheathed in rich cranberry-red fabric last seen in a Venetian palazzo. In lieu of pillars there are exotic gold-coated carvings of women looking like a cross between the caryatids at the Acropolis and figure-heads from a creaky old galleon. As for the seats, they appear like regular cinema rows from the back – all bonded together – but peer over and you see each person has the equivalent of an individual armchair, upholstered in dark peach velvet with brocade cushioning. Only five rows remain since the whole back section has been removed to accommodate tour groups, and now assorted light/camera/sound equipment.

'Doesn't it look funny seeing a square movie screen?' Marina points to the far wall.

'Of course, panorama vision didn't arrive until the 1950s,' Orla chips in.

Marina gives her a 'Who asked you?' look and moves us forward, whispering, 'I wish she'd make up her mind whether she's a dumb blonde or a female Rain Man.'

I turn back and watch her twiddling her hair in front of Milo.

'I think she's whoever you want her to be. Or rather, whoever she *thinks* you want her to be.'

Milo couldn't look less enamoured. God love him!

'Well, I wish she'd be *gone*,' Marina huffs as Conrad starts to position the cast.

The scene is basically visual with no dialogue other than from the black and white movie projecting onto the big screen, entitled *Quality Street*. Naturally this gets me thinking of chocolates and soon I have an intense desire to rustle a purple cellophane wrapper and eat at least three of the coconut ones. Deciding it would be fun to order a tin for Marina as a thank-you gift, I take out my phone and start Googling, only to discover that the chocolates were named after the play that inspired this very film. What? I double-check the facts, but it's all here – the play (written by the same man who wrote *Peter Pan*!) opened in 1901. Marion's film version came out in 1927 and Quality Street chocolates were launched in 1936. And there's more! One year later Katharine Hepburn took the Marion Davies role for a remake. Well, I never! I look around for my fellow Brit Carmen, as I know she would appreciate this, but she is nowhere to be seen. When I look back at the screen, I discover that the story is set in 1810, which would explain the abundance of bonnets and breeches featured on the original tin! I always wondered about that! I don't know why I get such a major kick out of this, but I do.

'That's a big smile,' Milo notes. 'What are you thinking about?'

'Chocolate,' is all I manage before Conrad orders him to the second from last row.

Hearst is already in position with Marion beside him, and there are assorted guests dotted around the auditorium as well as extra extras, as, rather sweetly, Hearst would always invite his staff to join the party for the film.

'Okay, so here's the shot I'm going for: we'll start tight on Hearst and Marion, and then pan out to show the rest of the audience – everyone sat behind them isn't watching the screen at all; they're getting it on with whoever is sat next to them.'

I look down at the script to see who Milo is paired with for this scene, but when Conrad calls for 'Evelyn', there is no reply.

A certain buzzing on the walkie-talkies informs us that 'Lloyd is still fixing her hair. She'll be out in five.'

'Okay, can we get a stand-in for her?'

'I got it!' Milo whistles for me to join him.

Surely not? I look around me in disbelief.

'Stella, come on over.'

I edge down the row towards him.

'Take a seat.'

'Don't you want a professional extra to do this?' I fret, still standing.

'Nope,' he says matter-of-factly. 'I want you.'

'Wait!' I protest as he pulls me into position. 'What exactly do I have to do?'

'It's just for camera positioning – no lines, no drama. I'm going to kiss you and all you have to do is kiss me back.'

My heart is rattling like crazy now. My mouth has suddenly gone dry. This isn't quite the intimate idyll I had in mind for our first kiss.

'Where do I put my hands?' I fluster.

'Anywhere you want them!' he twinkles back.

'Seriously, I don't want to mess this up.'

'You'll be fine,' he soothes, placing an arm around my shoulder. 'Settle into the seat a bit more. That's right. Now lean over towards me, get comfortable and just imagine we're at the movies together.'

'H-have you seen this one before?' I default to small talk.

He nods. 'Conrad had a screening at his place just after he cast me. It's basically a comedy about a woman in love with a soldier who leaves her to fight in the Napoleonic Wars. He's gone ten years and by the time he returns she's an old maid and he no longer finds her attractive. What's that look for?'

'Where's the comedy in that?' I gasp. What an utter passion killer. I can't believe this!

'Well, she creates a younger, flirtier alter ego and passes herself off as her own niece. You'll like that bit – the makeover she does to win her guy!'

Oh, this is all too close for comfort. I desperately try and return my mind to chocolates, attempting to account for all the other flavours – toffee penny, strawberry cream . . .

'Relaaax,' Milo urges, placing his hand on the back of my neck.

His touch doesn't help. I couldn't feel any more jumpy and stressed if I tried. This is going to go so badly he's never going to want to kiss me again. I can't bear it.

'Okay, guys,' Conrad gives his cue.

Milo tilts my jaw to his, pauses to give me a look of lusty seduction and then lowers his lips onto mine. My mind experiences a moment more hysteria and then turns to jelly. I don't know if movie stars have more coaching or more technique than regular mortals, but this kiss is in a league of its own. I lose myself to the sensation until a fellow cast member kicks the back of Milo's seat and tells him, 'Enough already!'

I'm in a daze. It's as if my body has just come back to life and is all a-swirl with long-forgotten desires.

'This time I don't want you to start kissing *as* the camera pans,' Conrad instructs. 'The point is that you're at it already, with no regard for the movie. Let's see a bit of variety out there, not just faces merging with faces. Keep in character but have some fun. Again!'

I take a breath, readying myself for round two.

This time he gets so agitated he clambers on top of me, pressing me so far down into the seat only my feet are sticking up.

'Great, great! And, Milo, let's use that move when Evelyn gets here – ah, here she is now.'

I quickly retouch Milo's face, removing any trace of my lip gloss and repositioning his hair, which, from the look of it, I grabbed rather roughly.

He's staring at me the entire time and murmurs, 'To be continued . . .' just as I am obliged to trade places with Evelyn.

'Thanks, sweetie!' she trills.

'No, thank you,' I find myself sleazing back at her.

Back on the sidelines, I find my fingertips tracing my lips, brushing my chin and basically revisiting the areas he just smooched. That was yummy, no other word for it. I want to do it again. He actually said, 'To be continued . . .' All I want to know now is *when*.

Even the sight of him kissing Evelyn doesn't throw me off my game. I'm confident about what I felt. You can't experience that much chemistry if it's just one-way. Can you?

I look on impatiently as they do take after take, longing for the break, eager to see if he follows up in any way. I don't want there to be too much space between that magic moment and the next. It's like when you leave a date all heated and sated and not a little bit giddy and you hope to see them again straight away but then they can't make it until next week and in the meantime all that sexual tension just dissipates and suddenly you're back to square one. I don't want 'To be continued . . .' to slip from the agenda. Momentum counts for a lot. Momentum and opportunity. Oh great, now Marina is slowing things up by having some whispered debate with Conrad.

'Could I just take a peek at your script?' I ask Nora, having no idea where I've left mine.

I'm just trying to figure out how much more filming there is to be done when the end of day is called. Again I feel a surge of nerves. I try to act busy, checking through my brushes. He's making his way over. I prepare to give him a playful smile but – *darn it!* – Jimmy, the lighting guy, has diverted him.

'Stella!' Carrie is by my side now.

'Mmm-hmm?'

'Marina needs you outside.'

'What?' When did she leave the building?

'You can leave by the side door here.'

'Okay,' I say, but I don't move.

'I think it's quite urgent.'

I can't help but roll my eyes as I huff out to find her.

'Marina?' I call into the evening air. 'Oh, Marina?'

'Over here!'

'Why are you hiding in the bushes?' I despair. 'You'll snag your dress. You've already messed up your hair,' I tut, reaching to fix it, but she grabs both my wrists.

'I've got news!'

'Something a little birdie told you?' I smirk, looking up at the leaves.

'Jeff is on his way.'

'*What?*' I screech.

'I know! I know!' She shushes me. 'He wasn't able to tell me sooner because they're so hush-hush about their movements, but he's going to be here by early evening tomorrow!'

My mouth gapes. And then I get my act together enough to pull her into a hug.

'Ow!'

Apparently I'm squeezing a little too tight, but I can hardly believe this – both of us getting such a surge in the romance department within minutes of each other.

'So now I need your help.'

'You've got it.' I nod emphatically. 'This will be the first time he's seen your new look, right?'

'Yes, but it's not that.' She lowers her voice all the more. 'Obviously I can't let on that he is my husband, so I've spoken with Conrad and told him that he's your guy and that he's only got a few weeks' leave so this is the only time you can see him and that I simply can't have another make-up artist so he has to say yes to Jeff joining us on the set.'

I blink back at her, still trying to process what she is proposing.

'What did he say?'

'Well, it took a bit of doing, but he's agreed.'

'So who exactly do we have to pretend to?'

'Everyone,' she asserts. 'And of course this couldn't be any more perfect because you already know everything Navy and so all we need to do is get the story straight about how you guys met and how long you've been together. He's calling back later, so we'll have a little three-way chat and sort it all out.'

'Um . . .'

'Don't look so concerned. You'll do a brilliant job.'

'Are you really saying we can't tell anyone?'

'You know how important it is for me to keep this private.'

'But, I mean, your fellow actors?' I try a little negotiation.

'Oh no, they're the worst gossips of all.'

'What about Milo, seeing as he's a friend of yours?'

'No one,' she asserts. 'I just can't risk it.'

I reach for a branch to steady myself.

'What's the matter?'

'Oh, it's just . . .' I hesitate. What am I going to say, 'I think Milo has the hots for me and I don't want to ruin my chances'? Besides, she probably wouldn't be best pleased to hear that I'm making any kind of progress with the man who rejected her.

'Tell me.'

'I'm just being selfish.' I try to shrug it off. 'You know – the odds of me meeting a guy lessen somewhat if I already appear to be with one.'

She reaches for my free hand. 'I haven't forgotten my promise. I will find a man for you. We're just going to have to wait until the movie is done, that's all.'

I emit a defeated sigh.

'Is this really too much to ask?'

I can't be sure, but her question seems a little loaded, as in 'After all I've done for you!' And the truth is, I wouldn't even be here now were it not for Marina. I'd still be in London, trapped in my agency contract, waiting for something miraculous to occur in my life.

So the fantasy with Milo was short-lived. Who knows, maybe we already peaked – the man just kissed me after all. Can it really get any better than that? Yes, he's flirty, but he's probably one of those men with a knack for making you feel like you're the only woman in the world. It just felt so nice to feel that attraction . . .

'Stella?'

'Yes.'

'All I'm asking is for you to look happy when Jeff arrives and hold hands with him anytime you are in public. Nothing more. The fact that we have interconnecting rooms makes things even easier. He walks in with you, you pass him over to me, and I give him back in the morning. It's perfect!'

There's that word again – perfect. Perhaps a little too perfect.

You almost might wonder whether Marina had this in mind all along.

'I'm going to try and get him on the phone again now, so I'll see you back at the room.' She reaches to give me a hug, but this time my squeeze is positively limp. I don't mean to be ungrateful. If anything, I feel a little foolish. Getting my hopes up like that.

I walk back out onto the concrete walkway. Appropriately this is probably one of the least picturesque aspects of the whole property – a bit of greenery and a view of the white-washed brick surrounding the tennis courts. And then I wonder, Is it possible to get this game back to 'Love all' as opposed to 'Disadvantage Stella'?

Perhaps I could convince Marina that I don't want to look unprofessional or as if I'm getting special favours, so it's best that we try to fly under the radar with this – he doesn't have to arrive to a twenty-one-gun salute. I mean, does anyone really have to know that he's here at all? He could come under the guise of some kind of delivery or maintenance man, knock on the door to my room, I let him in, he crosses to Marina's side and he never leaves. He's used to a tiny grey bunk on a ship – her suite will be pure luxury by comparison. We can bring him all the food and drink he wants. I have dozens of movies on my laptop. They'll be in bed most of the time they're together anyway, and I'm sure he'll be glad of the rest when she goes to work. Plus he'll always have Bodie as company. I take a rousing breath. There. Sorted. Marina just got carried away and I wasn't quick enough to counter her plan, but now we have options.

We could even pass him off as Marina's favourite sushi chef – she decides she can't go on until she has her daily fix of California roll, so they bring him here and, really, so what if people think she's having an affair with him? The only snag would be if someone else got a craving and wanted a taste of his wares. I wonder if there is something Jeff *can* cook – everyone has their speciality, right? Like kumquat marmalade or lavender tomato jam . . .

I'm pacing now as new ideas hit me left and right. I can even do a makeover on him so that even if someone did take a random snap, he could never be identified. His grey hair will be an easy enough fix. Maybe a pair of black-framed glasses, the modern narrow oblong ones—

'What's with the caged lioness prowling?'

I look up and see Milo, leaning against the doorway to the movie theatre.

'How long have you been there?' I gasp.

'Long enough to see your face run the gamut of emotion.' He shrugs himself off the wall. 'Are you thinking of getting in on this acting lark?'

'Noooo!' I laugh.

'It's almost like I could see ideas flashing across your forehead.'

'Oh God,' I cringe as he mimics my cartoonish expressions.

'But you looked particularly sexy when you were brooding . . .'

'Stop!' I plead, feeling my face flush, all the more self-conscious for knowing that everything I was just plotting was to protect my chances with him.

'Anyway, listen. I've been looking over the schedule for tomorrow and it looks like we have the evening free and there's this place in Cambria that does these great peach-glazed baby back ribs . . .' He smacks his lips. 'I was thinking we could maybe share a bottle of Zinfandel. They stock wine from my friend's vineyard in Paso Robles, so I know we'll get a good one.'

He tells me what a cosy place it is. And that he thinks I'll really like the chocolate soufflé torte they do for dessert.

'So, what do you say? Would you like to join me?'

I can't believe this man has made me such a delicious proposition – not just dinner and a movie, dinner and a movie star! But then I'm obliged to ruin everything with my reply.

'I'm going to have to get back to you on that.'

Milo raises an eyebrow, obviously unaccustomed to hesitation in this area, especially from someone who has been visibly swooning over him up until this point.

'They're really good ribs . . .'

'Oh, I'm sure. It's just there's a chance that I'm having a visitor tomorrow,' I explain. 'I'm hoping that they won't be coming, but if they are, then I won't be able to, but I want to. I really want to.'

'A visitor, huh? You don't look too thrilled at the prospect.'

'Well, you know – I'm here to work.'

'So why invite them?'

'Well, it's really an unusual circumstance.'

'Is it a guy?'

Oh, how did I get into this mess? I need to stop talking – I'm making this so much worse. I open my mouth hoping for divine intervention but instead another voice calls, 'Stella!'

Saved by Marina!

She's leaning over the balustrade, beckoning me urgently.

'I'll just be a minute!' I call to her, and then turn back to Milo. 'Whatever happens I just want you to know that dinner with you would be my number-one choice.'

'Stella!' Marina calls again.

Oh, for goodness' sake!

'You have to come now,' she insists, waving her mobile at me. 'Your husband's on the phone!'

For a second I freeze. I can't even look back at Milo now. Mentally I've just turned to concrete and then collapsed in a cloud of grey powder.

Who knew that my best and worst day would be one and the same?

17

So much for options.

It's all the more galling that this lie isn't even necessary. Or at least wouldn't have been if Marina had consulted me before implicating me in all this.

And now I have to watch Milo walk away. I don't know if he cares enough to be disgusted or just has me down as a tease. Maybe he thinks my marriage is on the rocks. Why else would I appear so available to him? Or maybe he's not thinking of me at all, already on to the next.

Collecting myself sufficiently to speak to Jeff takes a grit I didn't even know I had. Fortunately he only has a few minutes, so we simply establish that we've been married the same time as he and Marina and we first met in Portsmouth while I was visiting my aunt Gail. 'Do you think it matters that several people already know I live in London – you know, as opposed to here?'

'No, that's fine,' Marina assures me. 'It makes sense that you would consider that your base since that's where you're from. We'll just say you divide your time between London and California, depending on his schedule.'

Always his schedule.

'And you don't think it's weird that I haven't mentioned the fact that I have a husband to anyone?'

'Well, have you described yourself as "single" at any point?'

I review the conversations I have had along the way.

'I think it's more a case of having *behaved* that way.'

'Well, I think that can be passed off as the life of a Navy wife,' Marina decides. 'Since, in a way, you are single for six months at a time.'

I hear Jeff sigh, but I don't say anything to make him feel better. Why would I? These men need to know what they are doing to their women, however willingly they take it on.

'We can fine-tune when you get here, but basically we'll just have everyone see you guys together when you first arrive, to establish ownership, as it were, and then obviously everyone will expect you to hit the bedroom, so you'll have a chance to get acquainted then, after I've had my way with him, of course.'

I force a laugh. And then make an excuse to exit and fall face-first into my pillow.

In all Marina's talk of matchmaking I never once expected her to be setting me up with her own husband.

I wake the next day with a sense of dread. I don't know who I'm less eager to see – Jeff or Milo. As it happens, the first face of the day belongs to Bodie.

'Who let you in?' I ask as he stands before me, eyes bright and eager, tail wagging optimistically.

'Could you walk him?' Marina calls from next door. 'I barely slept last night.'

'Your wish is my command,' I mutter under my breath.

I'll say one thing: it really is hard to stay angry or miserable when you have a comedian at the end of a lead. Today's water sport of choice is the sprinklers.

Bodie pounces on the head of the jet, trying to contain the multi-directional spurts with his mouth, which must feel like someone squirting your face with one of those soda hoses they have in bars. When that doesn't work, he tries to suppress the water with his paws, redirecting the flow to me.

'Not again!' I look down at my sopping jeans.

'So Marina's got you walking the dog now, has she?'

I look up and see Lloyd approaching, chuckling at the pair of us.

'Compared to the other favours, this is actually one of the perks,' I tell him.

'Well, it's all about keeping the talent happy. Always has been, always will be.'

'And who takes care of us?' I find myself pondering out loud.

'We take care of ourselves.' He shrugs. 'I'm glad I saw you, actually. I wanted to give you the heads-up: Milo may be a little "tired" today.'

He exaggerates the penultimate word, but I want to be sure – 'You mean "tired" as in the euphemism for "hung-over"?'

Lloyd nods.

Oh no.

'Carrie had to fish him out of the Neptune Pool at two a.m., blitzed. I'd heard he was prone to excess, but up until now he's behaved impeccably.'

It's all my fault! I've driven the poor man to drink!

'Don't look so concerned. I'm sure you've fixed bloodshot, baggy eyes before. I just wanted you to be prepared.'

'Right.' I nod. 'I'll bring some ice.'

'And maybe a little hair of the dog?'

'Really? You think I should offer him more booze?'

'I was trying to make a joke.' He motions to Bodie.

'Oh!' I laugh. 'Yes! He is the cure-all!'

'See you shortly.' He gives a little wave as he trundles on his way.

I feel even worse now. Of course, it's perfectly possible that Milo's bender has nothing to do with me springing a husband on him – it is a little egotistical of me to think he would be so disappointed by that. There's got to be a dozen or more women on this hilltop who would dine with him at the drop of a napkin. It's not like he's short on alternatives.

Bodie gives a little whine as if to remind me that we're actually supposed to be in motion as opposed to fretting on the spot.

'Come on, then,' I gee him up. 'Race you back to the room!'

And so the time comes to face Milo. I pause at the trailer steps and try to breathe in a neutral countenance. This does not have to be a big deal.

'Morning,' I whisper so as not to further aggravate his thumping head.

He looks up at me with a mixture of bleariness and wariness. I so want to tell him the truth, but instead I say, 'I brought you some breakfast,' and place my scone peace offering on the table before him. 'It looks like blackberry, but it's actually the local ollalieberry.'

He nods but doesn't speak. Time for Plan B – I reach into my bag and hand him a small envelope.

'What's this?'

Curiosity gets the better of him and he opens it, looking mildly perturbed when he pulls out some blond tufts.

'Hair of the dog.' I give a hopeful smile.

For a second he looks amused and then almost sadder than he did before.

'It's Lloyd's joke really. I just borrowed it.'

'Cute,' he says, setting the envelope down on the counter-top. 'Sorry to make extra work for you,' he says, motioning to his crumpled visage.

'Oh no, it's fine. Well, not fine that you feel bad, but, um, it'll be easy to fix,' I say, wishing the same could be said of our relationship. I don't think there's going to be any playful banter today or any day soon. At least not with me.

He brightens up as Jimmy, the lighting guy, drops by with a Red Bull but quickly returns to his withdrawn self when he's gone.

As I start to paste over the purplish shadows beneath his eyes, the brush seems to make them water, so I switch to my fingertips. No one has ever stroked on concealer more tenderly. But what I really want to do is softly kiss his brow and soothe his aching head. I want to turn back the clock to the movie-theatre kiss and stop Marina from making duplicitous plans. I'm just grateful that he hasn't asked me any probing questions.

'Hey, you with the secret husband!' It's Carrie, the production manager. Apparently she's just heard the news.

My heart plummets as she begins firing questions at me.

'How long have you been married?'

'Not long.'

'You must be very dedicated, to put up with the Navy lifestyle.'

I see a hint of a reaction from Milo at this line.

'S'pose.'

She frowns at me. 'You don't seem very excited at the prospect of seeing him.'

'Can we talk about this later?'

She looks a bit taken aback. 'Yes, yes, of course. I just wanted to let you know that I've settled everything with security and I'll be walking him to you myself.'

I sigh. Now I feel bad. 'That's very kind of you.'

'No problem. Happy to do my patriotic duty. See you on set in two?'

We nod confirmation.

'So he's in the Navy?' Milo asks when she moves on.

'Yup,' I reply, avoiding eye contact.

'I wouldn't have kissed you the way I did if I'd known.'

Now I can't help but gaze at him. He sounds so respectful. Maybe even a little in awe.

'Well, I'm sure we'd all do things differently with hindsight.'

Today we're filming in the dining room, or the 'Refectory' as it was known, quite aptly, as it's definitely reminiscent of *Harry Potter*, with its narrow wooden table seating twenty-two and nearly as many primary-coloured flags jutting from high poles. (They actually turn out to be banners from the Palio horse race in Siena.)

The camera and lighting guys are loving the angles they can get thanks to the 27-foot-high ceilings, but the set designer has to time and again explain that Hearst himself would put actual bottles of ketchup and mustard on the table and offer only paper napkins, reinforcing his insistence that this was a ranch, not a castle. The plates look fairly standard blue and white china, the glassware basic, but no doubt the cutlery is sterling silver.

One of the most interesting features is the fourteenth-century choir stalls lining the walls – with so much standing around the temptation to lean back into them is killing us. One of the extras has already got yelled at for doing that, though – you've never seen Joan Crawford blush so furiously.

Marina, meanwhile, is on form – the excitement of Jeff's impending arrival boosting her energy to play 'hostess with the mostess' over and over and over again. Conrad's idea is for a montage where the guests play a kind of musical chairs – according to lore, when you first arrived at the castle, you were seated beside Hearst and Marion at the centre of the table, new blood being the most interesting. However, as your visit extended you were nudged down a spot until you found yourself at the furthest seat.

'Another day and I should have been feeding on the floor,' P.G. Wodehouse noted.

It's a fun concept but makes for a lot of resetting, not just of the extras but their plates and wine glasses and, of course, their costumes. I do what I can to help Nora and Carmen, making sure all the women cover their head with a silk scarf as they change dresses, to prevent make-up transferring to the vintage silks.

It's helpful that all the rails can be set up in the adjacent Morning Room, so at least we don't have far to go for the switcheroo. On the downside, catching glimpses of Milo stripping a dozen times in one day and being touched by assorted eager dressers is hard to bear. I look at the clock for the thousandth time today. Every time we cross into the next hour I feel a queasy dip to my stomach. Marina has insisted that Jeff and I make a public display of being reunited so everyone gets the visual that he is with me. I've already told her this is a terrible plan, seeing as I won't be able to conjure expressions of delight and longing for a man I've never met, but she doesn't think it'll be a problem.

'He'll be arriving in his uniform,' she tells me. 'Just squint your eyes and pretend it's Jonathan.'

Yup, she really is that insensitive. I've seen a whole more ruthless side to her since his visit was announced. Any needs I might have are out of the window. I am now here entirely to serve her. I feel angry and resentful and maybe a little jealous – she gets the guy, after all. As for me, once again the Navy is obstructing my love life.

We're just shooting what will be an extremely cute moment where Hearst and Marion are having one of their ice-cream-eating contests when I notice the onlookers' expressions change – a sudden curiosity in the air, a couple of salutes. Someone, possibly even Marina, producing a low wolf-whistle.

And then I turn and see him – the man who is about to become my husband. And he is a man, considerably more substantial than I imagined. Marina had failed to mention his height – he has to be at least 6 feet 2 and solid – definitely more Destroyer than Frigate.

Wanting to get our scene over with in one quick take, I hurry towards him, unsure whether to throw my arms around his waist or upwards around his shoulders. As it happens, he saves me the bother of choosing by literally sweeping me off my feet and carrying me directly out of the door and through to the Morning Room. Only when we are safely round the corner does he set me down.

'Sorry, Stella. It was Marina's idea. She wanted to make it clear that we were romantically involved without us actually having to kiss.'

'That's fine,' I say, though inside I'm seething that she stole Milo's move.

'It's good of you to do this for us.'

I wish I could be gracious about it, but I don't quite have it in me. 'Did you want to change out of your uniform?' I ask him.

'Oh yes.' He winces. 'Marina told me that you used to date a sailor.'

'I just thought you might be more comfortable in regular clothes.'

He nods. 'They've already taken my bag to your room.'

So the invasion has begun.

'It's this way . . .' I go to walk ahead.

'Stella?'

'Yes?'

'I think we should probably at least hold hands.'

Suddenly I feel like crying. I didn't expect this to hit so hard, but here I am hand in hand with what-might-have-been – walking with my officer husband in his dress whites. Why is this happening? Why am I being taunted in this way?

'So what did he do, your guy?' Jeff tries to make conversation, picking the worst possible topic.

'ET,' I say. 'Electronics technician. Radar. Planning to go into intelligence.'

'Smart guy.'

'In some ways.'

He looks sideways at me. That could have been a dig at so many things, but he seems to know what I'm driving at.

'I'm sorry it didn't work out.'

I shrug. What can I say? I don't want to have to explain myself, nor do I really need to – as far as he's concerned, I'm just another statistic. If he's been in the Navy for twenty years, he's seen dozens of his friends split up. Still, I hate feeling like I lost the battle.

There's an awkward silence before he offers, 'Marina won't let you stay single for long – she's already been asking me if I know any guys for you.'

'Not Navy guys?' I'm aghast.

'Well, that's mostly who I know . . .'

I snort and shake my head. 'You've got to be kidding – you don't think once is enough?'

'Well—'

'I want a guy who actually wants to be with me, rather than spending eight months of the year at sea.'

He looks a little snubbed.

'I'm sorry, but there is nothing romantic about being left alone that long and any guy who chooses that really doesn't want to be in a relationship anyway.'

'In your opinion.'

I stop just short of the door. 'If it was the most important thing to him, how could he ever leave his woman? There's a million other jobs you could do, but true love is nigh on impossible to find. So if you walk away from that ...' I surprise myself by getting choked up.

'Look, this is obviously a difficult subject for you.' His voice softens. 'Shall we go inside?'

I open the door and then feel the walls closing in on me. Marina could be hours if they don't get the scenes right. I offer Jeff a drink and then look out of the window, wishing I could just scramble out and run off. But where would I go?

'Do you play tennis?' I hear myself blurting.

'I have done, yes.'

'The courts are just across the way. What do you reckon?'

'I think it's a very good idea. Just give me a minute to change.'

'Here, let's put your stuff through on Marina's side,' I say, opening the interconnecting door. 'I'll tell the maid we don't need any service for a couple of days.'

'Okay.' He steps through to her side.

As I sit down to switch to my trainers I take a breath. That was embarrassing – my spewing. Bitterness is so very unattractive. I just don't know how I'm ever going to forgive Jonathan for choosing the Navy over me. I don't know how to let go of the hurt. I thought if I met someone new, it would be all right because then there was a reason it didn't work out – I was destined to be with someone else. I meet Milo and now this?

'Ready?' He returns to my room.

I nod, though how I'm going to traverse the tennis court with such leaden feet I don't know.

I give Jeff a quick overview of the place as we step from our *casa* and cross the main plaza. Remembering his passion for dogs, I pause beside the ornamental pond and point out the little ramp Hearst installed so his dachshunds could climb in and out easily.

'Well, I imagine a dip would be essential on hot days like this,' he notes.

'You know the dog kennels are the only rooms in the whole place that have air-conditioning!'

'What?' He laughs out loud.

This is better. Neutral topics. And soon lots of tennis balls to thwack away my frustration.

Or not.

I guess Milo was bumped to the end of the table fairly soon after we left because here he is now on the tennis court. With Orla.

'Never mind.' I reach for Jeff's arm. 'Maybe a game of billiards?'

'We can still play – there's two courts down there.'

'Oh no—'

'We could even play doubles. I'm sure we could beat them – she's a disaster.'

And she really is – missing the easiest of shots, hitting the ball so weakly it barely makes it over the net or slicing it off into the cosmos.

'I think we should just leave them.'

'Hey!' he calls down. 'Mind if we join you?'

Oh. My. God.

Milo looks hesitant as he identifies the voice of the caller, but Orla is thrilled. 'Oh, it's so much better this way – now we can play on the same team!'

Could today get any worse?

18

It isn't easy tracking the ball when you're desperately trying to avoid eye contact with the person standing across from you. Time and again Jeff looks at me with utter bewilderment.

'Sorry. I didn't see it.'

'You know the ball is coming from the other side of the net, right?'

'Yes, yes.' I nod.

Fortunately Orla's newfound technique has him even more befuddled.

'What's going on?' Jeff asks me as we switch sides. 'She's gone from clueless to Kournikova!'

'Methinks she was protecting his ego before and now it's all about impressing him.'

'You could be right,' he agrees. 'There's definite tennis-lesson pedigree there.'

'Isn't this fun!' Orla cheers as she slams another ace. 'Though I am surprised you guys are playing tennis, rather than, you know, getting *reacquainted*.'

'Maybe it's a courtship ritual for them,' Milo puns, uncharacteristically twitchy. '*Court*ship?' he repeats for her benefit, but she continues to look blank.

Her game may have improved, but she's still playing dumb.

As for me and Jeff, the longer we play, the more we expose our unfamiliarity: we have no sense of teamwork, no secret language, no knowledge of how our partner would behave.

If the ball falls between us, we defer to the other, all very politely, only to see it bounce away unhit.

Meanwhile Orla is high-fiving and whispering strategy to Milo at every opportunity. Every time he hits a winning ball she runs over and hugs him.

'We're so great together!'

Unfortunately I choose just the wrong moment to roll my eyes heavenward and get thwacked full in the mouth.

'Oh my God, are you all right?' Milo hurtles to my side. 'I'm so sorry.'

'It's okay,' I mumble from behind my hand. 'I'm not going to spit out any teeth.'

'I'm sure Jeff will kiss her better,' Orla trills.

'Do you want to stop?' he asks me, looking concerned.

'No, no, let's play on.'

'Whose phone is bleeping?'

I hurry to the sidelines and discover a text from Marina: 'Where are you, and what have you done with my husband?'

'Actually, we do have to go,' I change my mind. 'Time to get reacquainted.' I give Jeff a significant look.

'Wow. You guys set an alarm for that?' Orla gasps.

'Different strokes for different folks,' Milo chips in. 'Strokes – you know, like backhand, forehand . . .'

'Foreplay!' Orla brightens.

Oh God, get me out of here!

'If the guest room's a rockin' . . .' Orla sings after us, though I'm not entirely sure whose guest room she is referring to.

We're almost to the edge of the court, so nearly home free, when things take a turn for the worse.

Yes, really.

'Bodie, come back here!'

We hear Carrie yelling at the top of her lungs, but there's no stopping the furry tearaway. He is pounding the earth, powering a path to Jeff, greeting his master with such rapture you'd think he was entirely made of bacon.

Adorable, were it not for the fact that they have never 'officially' met.

'Hey, boy!' Jeff fusses over him, equally joyous.

'It seems like he knows you.' Milo narrows his eyes.

I see Jeff hesitate for a second as the penny drops and then recover with, 'Well, it's a funny story . . .'

Everyone looks extremely interested to hear it, not least me.

'I actually met Bodie before I met Stella.'

That much is true, so I nod encouragingly.

'I went into Marina's animal shelter with a buddy of mine a while back and, well, we had quite a bonding experience. Lots of fun and games. I guess dogs don't forget in a hurry.'

'Were you thinking of getting a dog for the ship?' Orla looks intrigued.

'Sadly they don't allow them,' he replies. 'It's a shame, it would be great for morale.'

'Just not the dog's,' Milo and I say, at exactly the same time.

'I didn't know Marina had an animal shelter . . .' Carrie mercifully gets us on a safer tack.

'She keeps it hush-hush. I hope I haven't spoken out of turn . . .'

So do I. We really need to get back to Marina and lock down our story – the last thing we need now is for her to turn up here . . .

'So where did you two meet?' Orla delays our exit.

'Portsmouth,' I say, just as Jeff slips up and says, 'Southampton.'

My phone bleeps again.

'We really have to go!' Jeff taps in the vicinity of my ovaries.

Oh great, now everyone thinks we're trying for a baby.

'No, Bodie, you're staying with me.' Carrie holds him back.

'Why don't we take him back to Marina?' I suggest.

At least that gives Jeff something to do with his hands. I need mine to grip in prayer and plead that nothing else hinders our return to the Casa del Sol.

'Was it really too much trouble for you guys to stay in the room like I told you?'

Jeff and I hang our heads as Marina berates us.

'You so nearly blew it in the first hour!'

'Sorry,' we mutter.

She sighs heavily and then grabs Jeff's collar. 'Now get in here and let's have some make-up sex! Oh!' she titters. 'That sounds like your domain!'

I force a smile.

Jeff turns back to me. 'Have a good evening.'

'You too.'

This is so very weird.

So what now?

For a while I just lie there, feeling forlorn and replaying the awkwardness at the tennis court. How different things should've been – Milo and me nibbling on a baby back rib, licking the peach glaze off each other's fingertips. Instead I'm here alone with zero appetite. I take a long breath. I have to do something constructive or I'll drive myself crazy.

Perhaps I'll try out the 'platinum-tip' nail look I want to do on Marina. Apparently it was all the rage in the 1930s to add a silver crescent-moon tip to red enamel. I'm halfway through my first hand when the connecting door flies open and an already dishevelled Marina ushers Bodie into the room.

'Do you mind looking after him? He keeps trying to get in on the action.'

'Of course,' I say, welcoming the company. 'Maybe I'll take him for a walk down to the old bear pit.'

'Oh no, you can't do that!' she gasps. 'Someone might see you and wonder why you're alone!'

'Oh yes.' I flump down again, reaching for the nail-varnish remover – wet nails and overexcitable dog are not a good option.

'Why don't you just make yourself comfy and order room service? Just remember to order for two.'

'Me and my imaginary husband,' I sigh.

'See you later!' she chirrups, shutting the door behind her.

So basically I have to sit here, all too aware of what is going on just a few feet away.

I look at Bodie. He looks back at me as if to say, 'Hey, you weren't my first choice either.'

I do my best to entertain him (not least with two dinners' worth of chicken) but feel all too aware that he'd rather have another dog to wrestle with.

'You know, if you'd been here back in Hearst's day, there would've been dozens of pups.' I show him the glossy book that came with the room. 'It says here he used to breed Kerry blue terriers, Boston bulldogs and harlequin Great Danes. Do you want to look at some pictures of them?'

My phone rings. For a second I allow myself to think it might be Milo, but of course it's not. It's Carrie.

'Hope I'm not disturbing you.'

'Not at all. I'm just reading to Bodie about Hearst's kennels.'

'Where's your husband?'

Damn! I keep forgetting about him!

'He fell asleep,' I whisper. 'Exhausted.'

'Worn him out already?' she hoots.

'I mean from the travelling – jet lag.'

'From a ship?'

I hadn't thought of that.

'Okay, I wore him out!' I backpeddle.

'Anyway, I just wanted to let you know that there's a slight change of schedule for tomorrow – Conrad wants to see Marina for a breakfast meeting, but she doesn't need to be done up for that, so you get a half-hour lie-in and then you can start with Milo.'

'Okay,' I say, ducking beneath the covers as next door's moaning and grunting reaches fever pitch.

'What's that noise?'

Apparently the light silk coverlet is no match for their eroticism.

'Just the TV,' I breeze.

'Stella, these rooms don't have TVs.'

'I mean a TV show I have playing on my laptop.'

'Sounds like porn!'

Oh God. 'I suppose in a way it is.'

'Don't worry – I'm sure he'll be good to go again tomorrow. Goodnight.'

''Night.'

I put down the phone. This is going from bad to worse. I really need to keep on my toes. There's just so many more ways to be caught out than I anticipated.

'Marina!' Jeff cries out.

Jeez! Between the pair of us, the truth will be out in no time. But maybe that's not such a bad thing. I don't know if I can stand another week of this. Overhearing nameless neighbours in hotel rooms is one thing, but listening to people you actually know . . .

I get out of bed and line the base of the door with my dressing gown. Then I look down at my neatly buttoned pyjamas. Ah, sex. I remember when that was a part of my life.

I kept meaning to sleep with someone else after Jonathan. And yet, in a way, I didn't want to sully what we had. To be honest, I couldn't get up the enthusiasm. I suppose it's a good sign that I'm feeling so attracted to Milo. Then again, half the free world is attracted to Milo – that's kind of his job – so perhaps it isn't quite the breakthrough I think it is.

Still. If sleeping with a movie star is what it takes to get me back in the game, I'd be willing to give it a shot. Provided Orla hasn't beaten me to it. I wonder if they went for drinks after tennis. I can't even bear to think that I've blown my chance with him. I keep telling myself this is just a temporary glitch and not to overreact, but the more likely scenario is that our moment has passed.

'Do you want to hear about the elephant that used to live here, Bodie?'

I'm reaching for the book again in a desperate bid to refocus my attention when I hear Marina giggle and my heart pangs – it's those moments in between all the thrusting and friction that slay me. Those besotted looks and delighted smiles that set your heart spinning. Intimacy sounds such a girlie, cringey word, but for me that closeness is the best. One pillow, two heads and all that flows between. There doesn't even need to be any words. Sometimes silent gazing is all you need. And far more than you ever hoped for.

That really seemed to be Jonathan's speciality. I've had boyfriends who couldn't even let you in during those moments, but it's like the Calvin Klein underwear ad says, 'The more I share with you, the more I feel like me. And nothing feels better than that.' And Jonathan actually seemed to revel in sharing. Maybe because it was the diametric opposite of his Navy life, where it's all about suppressing emotion and serving the nation. With me he could really let go and show himself. He taught me so much about that too. I thought I was self-conscious to my core, but it's amazing how liberating it is to feel truly accepted just as you are.

'*I love every part of you, inside and out.*'

Tears brim my eyes. No. No! I'm not going to go there. I have to snap out of this spiralling sentimentality.

'Bodie!' I call, patting the bed so he will jump up and join me. 'Come give me a hug!'

I embrace him and then allow him to settle into a comfy spot, smiling as he shifts position to align his body with mine, his head now resting on my upper arm. I place my other arm around his tufty torso and nuzzle into the scruff of his neck.

'Thank goodness for you!'

As we begin to drop off to sleep, all I feel are his warmth and his heartbeat.

And so it comes to this – I'm actually spooning with a dog.

19

I awake to find Marina shaking my shoulder.

'I'm shutting you in here with Jeff, so there won't be any mix-ups while I'm gone.'

'Where are you going?' I croak.

'Breakfast meeting with Conrad,' she reminds me. 'Seriously, don't go anywhere. You two aren't ready for the outside world, you need to work on your rapport.'

Leaving a sleep-rumpled Jeff standing awkwardly at the foot of the bed, Marina retreats to her room and locks the interconnecting door.

'From one prison to the next.' I give him a sympathetic grimace.

'You think of the Navy as prison?' Jeff challenges, just as I'm about to pull the covers over my head.

Oh, here we go again.

'Don't you?'

'If I did, I'd be something of a fool to keep extending my service, wouldn't I?'

I shrug. 'Maybe we should try to get a bit more sleep? That rug is softer than it looks.'

'I suppose you think I'm institutionalised?' he persists, refusing my offer of a pillow.

I sigh. He's clearly not a cheerful morning person. 'Look, we obviously have very different takes on this and I think it's better we just leave it at that.'

'I don't think that's going to work.'

'Why not?' I blink back at him.

'Two reasons: one, because it's always there festering, threatening to bubble up.'

I can't argue with that. 'And the second?'

'You don't have a very balanced view because you only know one side.'

I can't help but snort. 'And I suppose you were a Navy wife in a previous life?'

'I just mean that you have such a tainted view of the Navy you can't see any of the good it can provide.'

'And what good would it do me to see that?'

'Maybe you'd understand better why it was so important to your guy.'

My lips purse, but before I can reply there's a knock at the door, and delivery of a tea tray.

'I hope you don't mind – I went ahead and ordered . . .'

I watch as he sets the tray down and then prepares to pour.

'Milk and sugar?'

'Just milk. And one of those Viennese whirl biscuits.'

As he brings it over to my bedside I feel like the patient to his doctor.

'It might help to talk about it with someone who's in his position but you have no emotional attachment to.'

What is this – a man who wants to talk about feelings? Better yet a *military* man who wants to talk about feelings! Then again, they're not *his* feelings, so maybe that's why he's so keen.

'Of course, if you're happy with how things are – living with the bitterness . . .'

Right, that's it! I turn and puff up the pillows to prop myself up.

'I just don't understand how something that seemed to make him so miserable would have such a hold over him.'

'May I?' he says, motioning to the end of the bed.

'Help yourself.'

'Go on.'

'What?'

'Just let it all out.'

'They took him away from me!' I wail. 'We were really happy and we were talking about the future and getting married and having children and then almost from the first day he went on the ship he changed.'

'Well, to be fair, that is an extremely stressful time. You go from having classes for just a few hours a day to this all-consuming schedule – they put so many demands on you there is barely room for anything or anyone else. At the end of a twenty-hour day you have so little to give.'

'And you think that's fair?'

'No, that's the military.'

'But why does it have to be that way? It's like they are pushing for pushing's sake.'

'They push you because few people in a sound, balanced state would want to do what they are asking of you. If it's not your priority, the only thing in your mind, you'd start to question and resist . . .'

'So how come so many of them get married and make it work and he wouldn't even try?'

Jeff thinks for a moment. 'Was your guy any kind of perfectionist?'

'He was every kind of perfectionist.'

'Then he didn't want to be anything less than you deserved.'

'Well, yes, he said that, but—'

'What if it's true? What if he thought you'd be better off with someone who could actually be there for you? What if he couldn't bear the thought of letting you down all the time? I know a lot of guys who, even when they are trying their hardest, always feel like they are failing their wives in some way.'

'But isn't that my decision to make – how much I can take?'

'Were you happy the way things were?'

'No,' I pout.

'Then why would he want to prolong the agony?'

I sigh. 'I get it. I do – at least in theory. It wasn't meant to be. But I don't know how to stop loving him or wanting him. Even when someone new comes along.' My hand wafts vaguely in the direction of Milo. 'It's still there, gnawing at me.'

'He's the one that got away.'

'He's the one that was *taken* away,' I correct him.

He nods. 'So it's easier to blame the Navy than blame him?'

'Oh, I blame them both. And myself.'

'Why yourself?'

'Because I handled it all wrong. When he needed space, I gripped on too tight. I should've let him go and miss me. Instead I was desperate to pin down a date when I was going to see him again. It just turned into this almighty tug of war between me and the Navy.'

'And the way you see it, they won.'

I'm silent for a moment, wondering if I am going to tell him what actually happened. But then I hear myself beginning to speak, before I've even given myself permission.

'When we were first together, all we would talk about was getting through the years he'd signed up for and the wonderful life that awaited us on the other side. He said that if he'd met me first, he never would've signed up, never would've left me. I really believed him. He was crushed when he left me. I know he didn't want to go. Then there was the intense indoctrination, very little time for us to speak. Already I felt like I was losing him. Then one day he told me they were so impressed with him they wanted him to sign up for the officer programme.'

Jeff hangs his head, knowing what is coming next.

'I was so excited for him at first – so proud! Of course he'd wowed them – he was a natural leader. It made perfect sense. So I didn't understand the reservation in his voice. Until . . .' I swallow hard.

'He told you about the additional years he'd have to sign up for,' Jeff sighs.

'Ten years!' I cry. 'Bad enough four, but ten was unfathomable – he wanted this torture to last for ten years? I'd be in my forties before I even had a proper day-to-day boyfriend! And what of having a baby? And starting a home together? I couldn't live in this no-man's land for a decade. The fact that he thought being at sea for six months of the year was preferable to being with me . . .' I shake my head. 'It was so humiliating.'

'Of course, you understand the perks . . .'

'It's like making a deal with the devil!' I spit. 'Of course there are incentives! Of course it played to his ego and sense of achievement. How could I compete?' I shake my head. 'I felt such an idiot. I always thought I was his number one, but everything I could offer paled in comparison to the idea of that decorated suit.'

Jeff sighs heavily.

'It would've been one thing if I'd known that he was planning on making it his career – like Marina knew exactly what she was getting with you – but Jonathan always led me to believe that he was just in it until the economic crisis passed. I guess he got his head turned . . .'

'I'm sorry,' Jeff says quietly, surprising me.

I pick at the bedspread. 'All I could think when I was crying myself to sleep at night was that when it came down to a choice between me and the Navy, he chose them. And it wasn't even like they'd bonded over some mission – they hadn't even left the dock!' I reach for my tea and take a sip and then another. 'I don't tell many people that – it's too embarrassing. Not that people ever ask me why it ended. There's such an inbuilt understanding that it's a near-impossible way to live, even at the best of times.'

'For most people.'

'Oh yes, I know there are people who it suits very well. I actually thought I would be one of them. At the time I was freelance, so I had a flexible schedule. I was used to being on my own, so I thought I'd just view the time with him as a bonus. I always liked the idea of travel, so the notion of being sent to some far-flung naval base was almost appealing . . . But in reality, it made me miserable. And resentful. And bitter. Which pretty much brings us full circle!' I force a smile.

'So you never saw him again?'

'Well, the truth is, we were crap at breaking up. We'd say it was the right thing to do and then we'd get in touch again, get all lovey-dovey and nostalgic, and then one day I realised I was getting sucked back in. I was telling myself it was just temporary, that we were helping each other through a difficult time, but I knew if I didn't get out then, I'd still be there in ten years. And then he'd sign for another ten and then another, and that would be my life. I didn't want that.'

'So what did you do?'

'I changed everything – my email address, my phone number, even my name.'

'Your name?'

'Well, surname – there was another Stella Smith at the agency, so when they signed me, they said I had to come up with something different. I went with my mum's maiden name, Conway, and so a new identity was born.'

'Did you give him any warning that Stella Smith was about to disappear?'

'Yes, I told him.'

I don't tell Jeff of the last words I sent him. It seems a little melodramatic and petulant now, but I'd read a verse of a poem that seemed so apt at the time I couldn't resist sending it to him:

> *I prithee send me back my heart*
> *Since I cannot have thine*
> *For if from yours you will not part*
> *Why then shouldst thou have mine?*

Like I say, I cringe now, but it certainly made the point.

'You never heard from him again?'

I shake my head. 'I didn't expect to. He said he hoped I would meet someone else and be happy, and I know he meant it. Deep down, we always had each other's best interests at heart.'

I catch a fleeting reaction on Jeff's face.

'What?'

'Another biscuit?' he distracts me.

'Don't mind if I do.

'You know, before Jonathan, I would see someone in uniform and it wouldn't even register. They were different – I knew that much – but they were doing their thing and I was doing mine. Now I stare at them as they go by and my heart pangs for them.'

'You feel sorry for them?'

'I think in a way I do. They have chosen a tough path. They know more pain in their daily life than most of us.'

'You presume.'

'Well, by the nature of their job.'

'What if their job helped them escape pain? What if that was a step up from their previous life?'

'Well then, that's even more sad.'

'You have to think of it from their perspective, not yours. A lot of these enlisted guys, they want to belong. They want to be a part of something bigger than themselves. Maybe they've come from a bad home situation. Maybe they were poor or beaten or put down.'

'And so they join an institution that pays them very little, physically tests them and yells at them.'

Jeff puffs a breath. 'I'll admit the actual pay may not amount to much, but they have a guaranteed roof over their heads, meals, healthcare, and yes, it is physically testing, but some guys like that – look at all the people who run marathons "for fun". Haven't you ever felt that you wanted to be challenged more?'

Just a week ago, I think to myself. 'Yes,' I concede. 'But they are so restricted.'

'There is a price to be paid for everything. I just feel you are overlooking some major rewards. Now, not from you maybe, but from a lot of other people, they feel respected. They get salutes. They go on liberty in a foreign land and people want to take their picture with them. Can you imagine how that feels for someone who was surrounded by people who said he would never amount to anything?'

I hate to admit it, but he's starting to get through to me.

'You don't feel it's made you more aggressive?'

He thinks for a moment. 'Well, of course it does amp up the testosterone, but then again, you are coming at it from the most girlie profession.'

'The contrast is a little insane,' I admit.

'Like comparing Barbie and Action Man!'

I can't help but laugh. 'It true!' And then I slump. 'I'd always wondered about that – wouldn't he be better off with a GI Jane? There was this woman on his ship that he always sounded so impressed by. Sometimes I imagine that they're together now. You know, when I want to feel even worse about things.'

Jeff smiles. 'Well, obviously I can't speculate about them, but I will say this: there's a good chance he liked coming home to your softness. I mean, would you like a boyfriend who painted your toenails?'

'Actually Jonathan *would* do that!' I brighten. 'It was one of my favourite things – watching this big, muscly guy take such care with this little pink brush.'

Jeff bursts out laughing, just as Marina returns.

For a minute I think she's going to bristle at the fact that it looks like we're having fun, but she's actually pleased.

'That's more like it!' she cheers. 'Now come and put a smile on my face,' she says, beckoning Jeff back to her room.

He gets up willingly enough but then hangs back in the doorway. 'I feel like we're not quite done . . .'

'Go, go,' I urge him. 'I'm fine. Really. I'm glad we had this conversation.'

'I don't want to leave you overloaded with all these thoughts . . .'

'They're not bad thoughts,' I insist. 'It just makes a lot more sense now why he would go.'

'I'm sure he still misses you.'

'That's less helpful!' I tut, getting to my feet and shooing him on his way.

I sigh as I lean back on the connecting door. I wonder if that is true – if Jonathan ever thinks of me, or regrets his decision. I can see now how much I was asking him to give up. I didn't get into this with Jeff, but Jonathan did indeed have a very hard life growing up. I may have seen him as a prince, but he was still very connected to his pauper roots. He expected life to be tough; he expected struggles. I used to tell him that just because he could withstand more suffering than most it didn't mean he had to. And then I remember something he used to say to me, 'Make me proud.' He used to say that all the time.

But I never did. I just made him feel guilty. I certainly never allowed him to be proud of what *he* was doing. I never showed any respect. I was only ever full of hair-brained schemes to extract him from the Navy so we could be together.

'Make me proud.' I say the words out loud now.

And then I ask myself, What have I done with my time since we parted? What have I done with all the freedom I supposedly prize above all else? I have been so fixated on what was taken from me, it never once occurred to me to give back. I want to make amends now. Not with him personally, but there must be some gesture, some action I can take to make things right.

I reach out and set the shower running.

I just need to figure out what it is.

20

Despite the inevitable waiting around on the set, my redemption gets very little attention for the rest of the day. I'm too busy trying to evaluate the body language between Milo and Orla.

Last time I saw them was on the tennis court. I try to tell myself that she couldn't have spent the night with him because her hair and make-up are as ghoulish as ever and that is not a look you can improvise with male beauty products, however comprehensive his range. Then again, she does have a locker here and she could've planned ahead and brought her kit with her. But really, I'm sure I'm being paranoid – there wasn't even any real rapport between them on the court; it's just the thought of his drinking combined with her persistence and availability ... No. He's smart enough to know she'd be an impossible limpet thereafter. And I can't exactly see him taking her on one of his vineyard weekends.

Can I really see him taking me, though? I'm no connoisseur myself. I look around the basement wine cellar where we're filming. Milo seems endlessly fascinated, studying rack after rack between takes, but to me it's just a cool stone room with heavy vaulted doors and a lot of dusty glass. And when I say 'a lot', this place has a capacity for 7,000 bottles of wine.

The thing that is intriguing Milo is that none of the wine is from California. I overhear the onsite expert explaining to him that this was before wine production began in the area, so the majority of the labels are from France and Germany.

'Alsace, Bordeaux . . .' Milo traces his finger over the labels. 'One day I'll go to these places and drink a glass of their finest vintage sitting on a little wooden chair overlooking the vines.'

And I want to be with you when you do, I think to myself, imagining what a relaxing trip that would be and how I might even come up with some wine-based product to rival Benefit's lip stain.

'Stella,' Lloyd calls to me, 'is Milo good to go?'

'Just give me a moment,' I say, reaching for my bronzer to given him a token whisk.

'Maybe one day you'll have your own vineyard,' I tell him as I adjust the flick of his hair.

He smiles at me for the first time today. 'I think that might be the nicest thing anyone's ever said to me.'

We shoot right up until 11 p.m. After so many hours confined in a windowless space, I could do with some air – maybe even a starlit stroll along Azalea Walk – but of course I'm not allowed. I would probably feel more resentful about having to cover for Jeff and Marina were it not for the fact that I'm asleep within minutes of entering the room. (Duplicity really is doubly tiring.)

All too soon it's morning.

'You want to go out?' I see Bodie looking pleadingly between me and the door. 'You and me both.'

Well, I suppose it can't hurt, as long as I have my story straight – Bodie needed a pee and Marina was asleep and Jeff was in the shower or vice versa. No big deal.

'Hi, Lloyd,' I greet my omnipresent boss as we reach the old pergola trail.

'Morning, Stella. Where's your guy?'

'Sleeping.'

'I guess these deployments can take it out of you. I was lucky in that I never needed much sleep. Never bothered me to stand duty all night. Serves me well now too.'

'Wait!' I must be misunderstanding. 'You were in the military?'

'Air Force. Spent two years in England at a base near Cambridge.'

My mouth gapes.

'I had a good time. Even got a taste for Marmite. Is it true that they're making Marmite chocolate now?'

'Um, apparently. I haven't tried it yet.' I'm struggling to think which sounds more peculiar.

'Of course, I'm breaking all the rules now – hair straggling over my collar and ears!'

I smile. 'You know what cracked me up the most when I read Jonathan's grooming guide?'

'Jonathan?'

'Jeff! Jeff's guide,' I quickly correct myself, and then babble onward. 'It was the wording about the hair colouring – "must look natural and complement the individual".' I roll my eyes. 'As if they had some Colour Me Beautiful rep standing by to assess if the men had the most flattering hue for their skin tone.'

'I wonder if they still have the regulations about the sideburns: "Mutton chops and ship's-captain styles are *not authorised*." I didn't even know there *was* a style of facial hair known as ship's captain, but you'd think that would be the one place where it would be all the rage!'

I snuffle a laugh and then shake my head. 'I can't believe it – from the military to make-up artist!'

'Well, everyone was doing a few years as a kid back then – the stranger thing would've been the other way around.'

'From faces to Forces!' I muse. 'I don't think that happens every day. Oh my God!' It's like I just got pinged in the head with a bendy comb.

'Are you okay?'

'Yes, yes, yes!' I squeak. 'You've just given me an idea! I have to go!'

My excitement channels down the lead to Bodie, who bounds back up the hill like he's leading a pack of huskies.

I know how I can give back to the Navy!

This is so much better than my earlier notions of painting their drab grey battleships with the entire spectrum of OPI nail varnishes. I need to start writing this down . . .

No sooner are we in the room than Bodie starts squeaking his Bow Wow Beanie.

'Not now, Bodie!'

He squeaks even more frantically, doing his little paw-prance, desperately trying to engage me. I'm just wondering why somewhere as peaceful as the San Ysidro Ranch sells such noisy toys when my mouth falls open.

'Bodie, you're a genius!'

As ever more advanced ideas start flooding my head, I get to the point where I have to tell the person who can make it all possible or I'm simply going to burst.

'Marina! Marina!' I bang urgently on the connecting door.

'Little busy at the moment!'

'I need to speak to you now!' I press my cheek to the frame.

'*Really?*'

'YES!'

There's a pause, a scuffling and then she opens the door.

'This better be of national importance.'

'It is,' I insist, and then I take an excited breath. 'I know what we should do with your humanitarian fund!'

'Can you tell me later?'

'Well, there's a time factor involved, so now would be best.'
She looks unconvinced.

'Five minutes, that's all it'll take.'

She sighs, sensing I'm not going to back down. 'Jeff, can you excuse me?'

'Actually he needs to be a part of it too.'

Bodie paces eagerly at my feet.

'All right, and you.'

He couldn't look any happier as all four of us heap onto Marina's bed. He twirls on the spot, rucking up the bedcovers, and then collapses in bliss as three pairs of hands fuss over him.

'So what's your idea?' Marina calls our meeting to order.

'Okay. Remember when we were at the San Ysidro Ranch and you showed me the cottage and told me how the memories from that place kept you going because it was like a taste of having your own home?'

She and Jeff huddle a little closer. 'Yes?'

'Well, what if we used your money to give a dozen or so Navy couples the chance to have that same experience? We could take over the place and fill it not just with married couples but also guys with long-distance girlfriends they rarely get to see and who have none of the security or financial benefits of being married.'

Marina looks to Jeff for a response.

'I can name five guys off the bat who, well, let's just say this would make their year. But the odds of the ranch having that many rooms available at this short notice—'

'The wedding cancellation!' Marina pipes up.

'Exactly!' I enthuse. 'There's a chance they won't have rebooked everything yet.'

'When exactly are you thinking of?' Jeff wants to know.

'Saturday.'

'Christ!' he blurts. 'What's the hurry?'

'It's our day off,' I explain. 'We're all here together now, but after the movie wraps who knows which countries we'll even be in.'

'She's got a point,' Marina concedes. 'I can email Seamus at the ranch right now, but what about the logistics of flying the girls in, getting them from the airport . . . ?'

'You said Ruth's getting antsy in the Lake District – she can do the whole thing online.'

'Yes!' she cheers. 'That woman lives for travel arrangements – she'll be ecstatic.'

As she begins tapping correspondence via her phone, I continue talking.

'So here's what I want to do: give all the girls makeovers before they see their guys! And nothing so extreme that they don't recognise them but just enough so they feel glamorous and special.'

'Are you going to make over the guys too?' Jeff teases.

'Actually I do want them to get in on the action – I was thinking about doing a photo shoot with each couple so they'd have a really lovely image to treasure, not the usual snap taken on a night out but something that really captures a sense of intimacy.' I look down at Bodie. 'One of my favourite photos of me and Jonathan was at this hotel that had zebra- and giraffe-print bathrobes and we did all these silly grinning shots lying around on the bed – they would always make me smile.'

'You want to do boudoir shots?'

'Well, they'd be so tasteful there – those lovely four-poster beds, the drapey white muslin . . . I mean, those are the moments you treasure the most aren't they, when you're all cuddled up?'

Marina is sold on that idea but concerned about me turning around so many makeovers in one day.

'I have the feeling that Lloyd might help – I just found out he used to be in the Air Force!'

'No kidding?'

'I know – it's crazy.'

'So you guys do the make-up, Ruth does the logistics, Jeff picks the guys, and I finance the whole operation?'

I nod. 'And I was thinking, if she was up for it, Milo's mum could do a lovely picnic basket for each of the couples.'

Jeff looks bemused.

'She does this special lavender twist to all her dishes – lavender chicken, lavender scallops . . . It's just so unusual and romantic, and I liked the idea of everything being local produce.'

'Milo could pick out the wine,' Marina suggests. 'He really knows his stuff. I'll get them to fax over a list.'

I'm just experiencing a pang for what might have been when Marina's phone dings the arrival of an email.

'We're on at the ranch!' she cheers. 'We can have up to fifteen of the cottages!'

Marina grabs a pad of paper from the nightstand and starts scribbling assorted numbers. 'You know, as extravagant as this may seem, we're still going to have a substantial number of dollars left over.'

'Well, I was thinking about that too, and maybe you would consider starting some kind of fund. This doesn't have to be a one-off, and if we had more time, we could look into setting up support groups.'

'The Marina Arnett Foundation for Lovelorn Sailors!' She looks delightedly at her husband.

'Only, if you used your married name, you'd have to come clean.'

Her shoulders slump. 'Oh yes. Maybe I'll just be the usual anonymous benefactor.'

'Well, we can talk about the details of that later. The key thing now is finding the right couples to fill those cottages . . .'

'I can head back to the base right now,' Jeff offers.

'Are you sure?' Marina looks concerned. 'That's a long drive there and back.'

'Much as I'd love to stay here watching you canoodling on set with another man . . .' He pulls a face. 'Besides, you know I love to drive, and how rarely I get the chance.'

'Pacific Coast Highway in the sunshine . . .' I chip in.

'All right.' Marina gives her approval by pushing him off the bed. 'You'd better get in that shower.'

'Oh, and Jeff?' I call after him. 'If you can get photos of the girlfriends, that would be great – you know, so I can start planning their looks . . .'

'No problem.' Then he pauses. 'How do you feel about female sailors and their boyfriends?'

'Gosh. I hadn't even thought of that, but yes, absolutely.'

And then I call for Bodie to join me and give Jeff and Marina a few minutes' privacy.

'Wait!' Marina halts me. 'Bodie needs to have a job too.'

I crouch down to contemplate his lovely furry face. 'What's your role going to be?' As I stare into his topaz-brown eyes, he starts licking my chin. So that solves that. 'He's my date!'

Truth be told, as the only woman *not* falling into the arms of the man she loves, I'll be glad of the company.

But maybe that's the point. Maybe doing this selfless deed will somehow break what feels like the Navy curse and I can get on with my life.

So let's get to it.

I sit down at the desk overlooking the courtyard fountain and start fanning sheets of paper around me – first is a list for Marina to pass on to Ruth. As well as the flights, we're going to have to make arrangements for the girlfriends (and boyfriends) to get to the airport in their hometown, or at least have petty cash ready to reimburse them for any taxi receipts – chances are, none of them will have excess dollars to spare. They'll probably want to know what to wear and what to pack, so I'll need to do up a little information email for them. Also, we need to check if there are any special dietary requirements, like, God forbid, someone is allergic to lavender. There's also the matter of scanning their IDs to see who can drink legally at the reception, though of course what goes on in the cottage is their business and I think we should probably arrange for a bottle of champagne or some Milo-selected wine to be awaiting each couple. It would be great to get each of them a digital camera so they can take a bazillion photos to remember this weekend for ever, and I think it would be so cute if they recorded special secret messages for each other that they could play back (and over and over) once they've had to separate. I feel a pang of sympathy as I imagine them having to say goodbye at the end of the weekend, but quickly flip back to the cheerier anticipation of it all. We definitely need to book a photographer, and arrange for a group shot to act as a reminder that they are not alone. Here is this group of women who know exactly what they are going through – switching solitary for solidarity.

As I summon the hotel website on my laptop and gaze dreamily at the image of the private hot tub, I can't help but fantasise about Milo joining me – teeny bit of a stretch considering the fact that a) he thinks I have a husband and b) he's banned from the San Ysidro Ranch. But a girl can dream.

There's a knock at the connecting door. It's Jeff, wanting to exit via my room.

'Come on through!'

'Jeez!' He does a double-take at the array of notes and lists around me. 'You're really into this, aren't you?'

'Well, I need something to keep me occupied while I'm pretending to have sex with you.'

He bursts out laughing. 'Good point. Don't think we don't appreciate the sacrifice you're making.'

If only you knew, I think to myself.

'Okay, honeypie,' I say as I escort him to the door in a suitably wifely manner. 'Call me with an update if you get a chance.'

'Will do. Wait – I don't have your number. Your new number!' he quickly adds as Carrie passes by.

'Hey, lovebirds!'

'Hey, Carrie!' we chorus with a geeky wave.

Number logged, we give each other an awkward hug – just in case any other eyes happen to be spying.

'Say hello to the boys for me!' I chime as I go to close the door.

But his hand reaches to block it. 'Stella?'

'Yes?' I lean close to foil any eavesdroppers.

'I'm proud of you.'

Even though I have only known this man for two days, I feel my eyes brim with tears.

It's as if the Navy itself just gave me its blessing.

21

My good spirits are all too quickly dampened when I discover that today is the day we shoot at the Neptune Pool.

All I can think of is how different things were with Milo when this scene was originally scheduled – how he was friskily baiting me with the prospect of making up his naked torso. Of course, I still get to do that today, but there is zero flirtation involved as I play up the definition of his muscles and add a bronzy sheen to his skin – he's on the phone the entire time, making me feel like one of those manicurists who barely registers as a human being to her Upper East Side client.

Conrad has him get up from one of the wicker sun loungers, stroll to the edge of the pool and execute the perfect dive.

'Is there any way you could do it and splash Marion?' he asks as Milo emerges from the blue. 'Don't worry about towelling off.'

'Sure, let me try it again.'

'Perfect!' Conrad cheers as he adds a dolphin flip. 'Ten minutes, everyone!'

Before, I wouldn't have been surprised if Milo had taken this opportunity to pull me into the pool alongside him. Now I just get a distracted 'Thank you' as I offer him a dry towel.

'Oh, Stella?'

'Yes?' I turn expectantly towards him. It feels so good to hear him say my name again.

'Do you have the eye drops?'

'Of course.' I hurry to locate them. 'Here.'

'Thanks.'

'You're welcome.'

This emotional distance is getting me down. I miss his attention. I miss how it felt when he looked right into my eyes. But there's no one I can talk to about this. I actually feel like sneaking off for a little cry, but then a call comes through from Jeff letting me know that one of the lovelorn sailors is a woman, so instead of having an eight-minute breakdown, I quickly read up on the female grooming guidelines. Not that I'll be having too much to do with the hair – Marina is arranging for a couple of her favourite stylists to come up from LA so Lloyd and I can concentrate on the make-up. Still, I think it's best they know what they're up against. I mean, if they're going to go to all the trouble of braiding some girl's hair, they should know that 'Cornrow ends can only be secured with inconspicuous rubber bands that match the colour of the hair – fabric elastic bands are not authorised.'

Now I see where the term 'petty' officer came from. No, no, let it go. I have to be respectful.

'Ruth for you!' Marina sticks her head round my door and hands me the phone.

I have to say she's really rising to the occasion, already underway with travel arrangements and busily liaising with the San Ysidro Ranch, where she will meet us on Saturday morning.

'She may be a humourless curmudgeon, but she's damn good at her job,' Marina confirms as I patch up the splash marks on her face.

'All good?' she asks when I set down my brushes.

'As a matter of fact, you looked your all-time best before I even put on a dab of make-up this morning.'

'It's the elixir of love!' she giggles.

I force a smile. Truth is, the more radiant she becomes, the slumpier I get.

My mood change doesn't go unnoticed.

'It must be tough,' Carrie commiserates, as we take our positions back at the pool, 'knowing he's going to be leaving again so soon.'

I nod. 'The whole thing is very upsetting.'

'I can see it's taking its toll,' she sympathises, 'but you mustn't let it ruin the time you have together now.'

'No. That would be foolish.'

'I mean, really, all we have in life is right now.'

As she witters on, I look over at Milo. Here I am with him in this magical place *right now*. I have feelings for him right now. When am I ever going to have a chance like this again? I want to embrace that, not act out this alternate reality.

'Listen, I'm planning a fun little al fresco dinner tonight, would you and Jeff like to join us?'

'I'm sure the two of them just want to be alone,' Orla offers her passing twopenn'orth.

And I'm sure Marina would say the same, but I need a break.

'Actually we'd love to join you.' I perk up. 'What time?'

'Nine thirty p.m. We're meeting in the main plaza, just by the fish pond.'

'Great. We'll be there.'

'Why did you agree to that?' Marina is less thrilled. 'You know I haven't seen him all day, and it makes things so awkward with an audience.'

'I just couldn't face another evening sequestered in my room with no one to talk to . . .' I appeal to the kindly jailer in her. 'Besides, doesn't a dinner party in the gardens sound fun?'

Marina pouts her response.

'You don't find it a little bit of a turn-on, the idea of you and Jeff stealing glances across the table, not being able to touch but knowing that in a few hours you'll be reunited? I think it'll act as quite the aphrodisiac.'

This she likes.

'Okay. He's already on his way back – come help me pick out a suitably tantalising outfit.'

Having been feeling so defeated and restricted of late, I am now eager to get out there and have a good time. Of course, there's a decent chance I'm going to have to sit and watch Orla try to lap-dance her way into Milo's affections, but not if I can get to him first.

Perhaps it's the time I have spent literally gazing at his navel today, but I have decided I'm going to tell him the truth.

I know Marina has made me swear not to tell a soul, but if I can keep one secret for her, then I'm thinking that he could keep one for me. I get the feeling that if I don't act now, the opportunity will be lost for ever, and I really do want to have that dinner *à deux* or, most importantly of all, another kiss.

Of course, I realise this isn't going to be the easiest affair to engineer, because I am going to have to hide it from the woman on the other side of my connecting door. We'll have to tiptoe and talk in whispers, and if things get truly amorous, I guess we'll find out just how good Milo is at playing a *silent* movie star . . .

I look back at my reflection. While helping Marina choose her outfit – milky silk, almost an exact match for her new hair colour – she said I could pick something out to wear myself. I had fallen in love with a midnight-blue dress with a bazillion little loop buttons running up the sides, but sadly couldn't fit into it, so instead I went for one of her more forgiving bias-cut dresses in – appropriately enough – lavender.

I love the texture of the fabric, the way it can appear dark and still one minute and then gleam brightly the next. The low drape at the back is rather daring for me but not for the siren I hope to channel tonight. I step closer to the mirror and check on my eye shadow – it's the exact same colour as the dress, but you'd only really notice the subtlety of the shimmer up close. And I want him to be close.

'Stella!' There's a rapping on the door.

I reach for my jewelled clutch and crouch to give Bodie a parting tummy rub. He looks up at me, makes what I like to think is an approving noise and then flumps his head back onto his bed.

'Leaving with one man, hopefully coming back with another,' I mutter under my breath as I turn the handle, ready to greet Jeff.

Marina follows a few minutes behind us, keeping her body language in check by focusing her attention on Carrie.

'So where exactly are we eating, and what's on the menu?' she quizzes her.

'Well, we've set up on the North Terrace' – Carrie points over yonder – 'and we've got the Black Cat Bistro to cater.'

Marina scans the page she hands her and then brightens. 'Limoncello mascarpone ice cream? Well, I already know which dessert I want!'

Carrie looks at her watch. 'Actually, we should start heading over there, we don't want the rest of the food to spoil.'

'No, we don't!' Marina agrees, rousing the troops, including Charlie Chaplin, Carole Lombard and Gary Cooper – albeit out of costume – and Wardrobe head Nora, though sadly no sign of her far more palatable assistant, Carmen.

'Follow me!' Carrie goes to lead the way.

'Wait!' Orla calls out, looking agitatedly around the group. 'Milo isn't here yet.'

Her disposition soothes me – if they had got together already, she would be smug rather than skittish. She also probably wouldn't feel the need to be dressed quite so provocatively.

Even Marina does a double-take. 'It's like she forgot part of her outfit!'

'Yeah, her underwear,' I concur.

I see Orla stop and look me up and down. Her apparent displeasure bolsters my confidence all the more. Now, if the man himself would just show up . . .

'Okay, follow me!' Carrie sets the group in motion.

Both Orla and I hold back, looking expectantly at the side door of the Casa Grande.

Come on, come on! I will him to appear.

But the door remains closed.

Suddenly Orla and I look as ridiculous as each other – all gussied up for a man who didn't show.

Though Jeff nudges me onward, I'm guessing Orla will make an excuse so she can stay here and track him down. I just hope he's napping rather than hitting the bottle again.

We're just catching our first glimpse of the candlelit table when – 'SURPRISE!' – suddenly Milo and Jimmy, the lighting guy, burst out from behind the giant oak tree, releasing a series of streamer poppers into the air and yelling, 'Are you guys ready to have some fun?'

I'm glad of all the squealing and cheering because it means my own heartfelt whoop blends in. *Yes, yes, yes!* He's here! All I need now is a few minutes alone. I turn to give him a beguiling smile, just as he releases a confetti air bomb. Now I have a trillion dots of paper peppering my lip gloss and teeth.

'Pah!' I try to spit them away.

'Sorry about that!' He scoots to my side. For a second his hand hovers around my mouth – I would love nothing more than for him to gently peel away every last dot – but then he looks at Jeff and chooses instead to retreat back to Jimmy's side.

I'm just wishing I could fast-forward to the moment when I tell him, 'Jeff is not my husband. He's Marina's. Now kiss me!' when my phone buzzes the arrival of a text. It's from Marina. 'Put your arm around Jeff. You guys are looking way too stiff.'

I sigh and show Jeff the text so he doesn't think I'm making a move. In turn he places his arm around my shoulders.

'How's that?' I tap back, removing yet another dot from my tongue.

'The pair of you could use some acting lessons.'

Or maybe it's time we got a divorce, I think to myself.

The dinner table is a delight: white linen set with dainty tea lights and vases of soft pink flowers from the garden. It's such a romantic sight, enhanced by Cole Porter's 'Night and Day' wending its way to us on the evening breeze . . .

Following the boy-girl-boy-girl seating plan, it's easy enough for Marina to be on one side of Jeff and me on the other. Equally Milo now has me to his left and Orla to his right. I try to shrug off an image of him sitting with a female hand upon both his knees – one with short, dark nails, the other long and pink – both his ears being blown into, and the poor man being eventually torn in two by our clutches.

Fortunately the food is a significant diversion, although I can't help but wish that Milo was popping the deep-fried green olives into my mouth like he did with the Mentos in the car. Thankfully the cool sweetness of the amontillado sherry is easing my pain. And then a Pinot Noir that Milo declares the perfect match for the steak served with melt-in-your-mouth courgette Gruyère bread pudding. For those having the duck with dried cherry risotto, he recommends the local Cabernet Sauvignon.

'You're such a *bon vivant!*' Carrie teases him as the desserts are served.

'Well, if you can take pleasure in your food and wine, you can enjoy every day of your life.'

'I'll drink to that!'

And then, as happens sometimes at dinner parties, all chatter ceases at precisely the same time, producing a disquieting silence. Perhaps it's the stickiness of the salted caramel tart restricting our speech, but none of the ice-cream eaters jumps in with a conversational lifesaver, so of course the next thing said will be given undue significance. But who will be bold enough?

'I've been meaning to ask . . .' Carrie begins.

Oh, good for her! She's such a trouper.

'. . . Stella . . .'

Oh God! Why did she have to drag me into the spotlight?

'. . . how come you don't wear a wedding ring?'

I look down at my bare fingers (along with the rest of the guests) and flash a look to Marina. How could we have overlooked such a significant detail? Probably because she doesn't wear one, it didn't even occur to us.

'Well,' I say, reaching for a stalling sip of wine, 'you can imagine I was constantly picking out make-up goop from the little claws around the diamond, and one time I actually snagged a model's hair, so I decided it was just a liability while I was working . . .'

'So what's your excuse?' Carrie turns her attention to Jeff.

Oh Jeez. I feel my anxiety rising, but he doesn't miss a beat.

'Are you familiar with the term "de-gloving"?'

Multiple heads shake a no.

'It's actually a common injury in industrial environments – obviously there are a lot of metal wires for a ring to catch on and in turn act as a blade, basically slicing away all the skin and tissue and even tendons, exposing bare, bloody bone.'

There's a clattering sound as assorted spoons drop onto the china plates.

'Way to put people off their dessert, dude!'

'Well, you did ask.' Jeff shrugs.

You'd think such a gag-inducing image would be enough to move the subject on, but no.

'Maybe you guys should think about tattooing a wedding band – that way, you could have the symbol without any of the attendant problems.'

'Good idea,' approves Orla, obviously enjoying the thought of me at the mercy of a buzzing needle. 'Jimmy, you could hook them up, couldn't you?'

'I trained as a tattooist before I got into lighting,' he explains to us. 'Take my kit everywhere.'

'He's done me!'

'And me!'

'And me!'

Our faces drop in horror as an assortment of shoulders, wrists and upper buttocks are proffered. Naturally Orla has to go one step further. She gets to her feet and, I swear to God, prises apart her cleavage to reveal some black writing between her breasts.

'What does it say?' Jeff gulps.

' "Help! I can't breathe!" ' I suggest.

Milo bursts out laughing, spurting wine across the table.

I can't believe I said that out loud.

'Maybe it's the signature of her plastic surgeon,' Marina whispers across to me.

'I heard that,' Orla scowls. 'It's actually the Chinese symbol for sex.'

'Oh, classy,' Marina mumbles.

'You know, just because you wish you actually had some breasts . . .'

'Oh, honey, if I wanted breasts like yours, I could simply go out and buy a pair.'

'Off the rack?' Milo suggests, eliciting a high five from Jeff.

This is all getting too weird.

'I think we should finish up here and move on to the game, don't you?' Carrie sets down her napkin.

'Absolutely,' I agree, first to my feet. And then I falter. 'What game are we playing?'

'One of Mr Hearst's favourites . . .' Carrie gets a mischievous look. 'Hide and seek!'

22

Before we scatter into the night, Carrie explains a small twist to the game – 'Every time the tower bell rings, you must change your hiding place. Otherwise we'll all be tucked in our hidey-holes till morning. Oh, and when the bell sounds twice, we're done – everyone has to come back to the pond.'

'So who's "it"?' Marina wants to know.

'Well, I've got everyone's names in a bag here. Why don't you choose?'

Marina puts in her hand, pulls out a piece of paper and then reads the name of the one person I was hoping to have a quiet moment with: 'Milo!'

Oh well, I suppose I'll just have to pick a really, really obvious place to 'hide'.

'Okay, five minutes to empty your bladders and fill your glasses!'

On my way back from the loo, I see Orla standing by herself, taking overly big gulps of Cointreau and trying to steady her breathing, rather in the way I might if I was trying not to cry. Suddenly I feel for her. I just don't know how best to approach her. But then she shifts position and one of the paper lanterns strung in the trees casts a reddish glow over her.

'You know, you'd actually look really good with auburn hair,' I offer.

She turns on me and snorts, 'Too much competition for you as a blonde?'

'Too much competition for yourself – I mean, you live in LA, right?'

She nods.

'I'm just saying that copper hair would really make your blue eyes pop.'

'And why exactly would I want my eyes to "pop"?'

'Because they're your best feature.'

Her brow furrows, unsure of what to make of me.

'You don't think they're too small?'

'Only in comparison to the gargantuan lashes you have on them!' I smile, trying for a bit of levity. 'The proportions are out, that's all.'

'Why are you telling me this?'

'Nature of my job, I suppose.' I pause for a moment. 'Plus I feel bad about what I just said at dinner. It wasn't meant to be out loud.'

She shrugs. 'I'm used to it.'

'Doesn't it bother you?' I ask her. 'All the jokes at your boobs' expense?'

'If I didn't want people to look, I wouldn't dress this way, would I? And before you start psychoanalysing me, this is my choice. This is who I want to be.'

'Okay,' I back down. 'But if you ever feel like trying something different, give me a shout. You'd be amazed at how much a new look can change your life.'

'Who says I want to change my life?' she snaps.

'Nobody.' I hold up my hands. 'If this is making you happy, I won't say another word.'

'There you are, pumpkin.' Jeff kisses me on the forehead as he presents me with a petite glass of port.

'Thank you, my little kumquat.' I turn and chink glasses with him.

'Kumquat?' He frowns as he leads me back to the group.

'You don't like that?'

'Well, it's a very small fruit. I think it implies—'

'Everyone ready to play?' Carrie cuts in, loud and enthusiastic, just like the response she receives from the throng. 'And this isn't just an excuse for you two lovebirds to canoodle in the moonlight!' She swats at me and Jeff. 'In fact I'm going to make sure you head off in two different directions.'

'Deal!' we concur, him with a covert wink at Marina.

Milo then closes his eyes and starts counting out loud.

And we're off!

Most people charge to the furthest-flung points but I bet you anything Orla will be entwining herself with one of the more provocative statues, maybe even disrobing entirely, all in the name of authenticity.

Me, I tuck myself just a few paces away in the doorway nearest my room, hoping I can nip Milo inside for a private conversation.

As I stand there, shivering a little in anticipation, I remember Milo carrying me over this very threshold. I want that feeling again. I want playful, flirtatious Milo back. I'm just about to peek out and see if I can catch a glimpse of him when I hear male voices, but sadly neither belongs to him.

'Did you see which way she went?' the first asks.

'If I did, I'm not telling you!'

'Whatever, dude. You bang her tonight. I'll have her tomorrow.'

I pull a disapproving face in the shadows.

'To be honest, I don't think either of us stands a chance – you've seen the way she hangs around Milo.'

'Yeah, but he'd have had her by now if he wanted. Besides, I'm not asking her to like it; she just has to take it.'

Oh yuck. I cringe back further. That's so horrible.

They make a few more lewd exchanges and then the one with the nastier voice says it's time to find 'Whore-la'.

I shudder, wondering if I should warn her. But what would I say? I heard two men discussing you in an objectifying way? She'd just tell me she's used to that too.

The bell chimes. Time to relocate. No sooner do I emerge from my doorway than I collide with Nora.

'Oop, sorry!' I prepare to dash on my way, but something in her expression causes me to pause.

'Everything okay?'

There's a simpering pity in her eyes as she reaches for my hand. 'Oh, you poor dear.'

'What is it?'

'I'm afraid I've got some bad news.'

Oh no, she's found out about my lack of experience and blabbed to Lloyd or Conrad and I'm off the project. This was all too heavenly and now the dream is over and I'm on the next plane home.

'Go on,' I gulp.

'I'm going to blurt it out, but you won't like it and I don't want you to hate me even though you have every right.'

'Don't shoot the messenger?' I give a wobbly smile.

'Exactly. And I wouldn't say anything were it not for the fact that he's in the Navy and the thought of you putting your life on hold for a man who—'

'Wait – what are you talking about?' I demand.

She takes a pained breath. 'Jeff and Marina. I just saw them kissing. Well, more than kissing . . .'

Welcome to my world! I think to myself.

'You don't seem that surprised.'

I heave a resigned sigh. 'I had a feeling this might happen.'

'B-but how can you not be wanting to kill him right now? Especially considering you've been waiting so long to see him.'

'Perhaps I'm in shock?' I venture, rather unconvincingly.

'If it were me, I'd—'

'Oh, hello, girlies!' Marina breezes round the corner, all a-twirl. 'We seem to have the same idea, don't we?'

Nora looks expectantly at me.

There's only one thing for it. I reach back my hand and slap Marina – a right zinger across the cheek.

'What the . . . ?' She stumbles backwards into the base of the fountain. 'What was that for?'

'For kissing my husband!'

Marina goes to speak, but Nora cuts in. 'There's no point in denying it. I saw you myself.'

Marina looks to me with a 'What do we do now?' in her eyes.

'I can't believe you would do this!' I cry. 'After all I've done for you!' And with that I storm past her and scramble down to the lower terrace.

I need to find a quiet nook to text her and come up with a strategy for our next move. As for Jeff, I'll leave Marina to handle him. As if she hasn't been handling him enough . . .

God, what a mess! I knew this was a bad idea from the start. I slump over the stone balcony, staring out into the starry night, and then drop my head to rest on my arms. I really don't know if I'm up to playing the woman scorned. This is getting way too complicated.

'Stella?'

I look round and see Milo coming down the steps towards me.

'Are you okay?'

'Yes, yes, just a little bit of a headache,' I try to dismiss my angsty pose.

'I'm not surprised,' he says, placing a cool palm upon my brow. 'I can't believe he would do that to you.'

Wow, news travels fast around here.

'I take it Nora's been Tweeting again?'

'She didn't have to,' he tells me. 'I was with her when she saw them.' His hand falls away from my face. 'I didn't know how you'd take it coming from me. I didn't want it to look like I had an ulterior motive because . . .' he pauses '. . . well, because I do.'

My heart does a little leap – all is not lost!

'Not that you need to hear that right now.'

'Actually . . .' I say, reaching for his hand and returning it to my face, only this time resting my cheek against it.

He looks confused for a second and then hopeful. 'Stella,' he breathes as he shifts his body closer—

'What the hell is going on here?'

We startle apart as Jeff and Orla – of all people! – loom into view.

I see Jeff hesitate and then suddenly puff up his chest. 'Unhand my wife!'

'Oh good Lord!' I roll my eyes. *Really?*

Within seconds the two men are but inches apart – jaw thrusting at jaw. 'You've got a nerve after what you've been doing with Marina!'

'Wait, wait, wait!' I squeeze between them. 'Jeff' – I give him an intense look – 'Nora and Milo saw you kissing Marina.'

'Oh crap.'

'Yes,' I concur.

'Here you all are!' Marina rounds the corner, in just the nick of time.

Everyone turns to look at her as though she is somehow the linchpin in all this. Which, of course, she is.

She studies the scene before her, the assortment of expressions ranging from 'I'm going to deck you!' to 'We are so screwed!' and then she sighs and calls to Carrie, 'Ring the final bell – it's time for me to come clean.'

23

As Marina reveals her true relationship with Jeff to the masses, I hear her stutter for the first time and my heart goes out to her. This really is a big deal for her. I can see in her eyes just how afraid she is of exposing her most treasured relationship to the world. It's almost as if she expects paparazzi to abseil down from the sky and start snapping and jostling the pair of them. But when everyone just laughs and moves to congratulate them (with the exception of Nora, who looks miffed that no real harm has been done), Marina begins to relax and I see her heave a sigh of relief.

As for Milo, I can see it's taking him a moment to process my part in the deception, but then his eyes meet mine and a smile spreads over his face.

'So . . .' He sidles up to me.

'So . . .' I beam back at him.

'Tomorrow?'

'Tomorrow,' I confirm.

It's the shortest and happiest conversation I've ever had.

As it happens, tomorrow comes a little too soon, even for me. It's a painfully early start and, naturally, the longest day of shooting so far.

We begin in the main library, where Hearst would display the costumes for his fancy-dress parties, shipping in fantastical wardrobe selections from his film studio in Los Angeles. All the colour and frivolity make a great contrast to the leather-bound books with titles like *Famous Cathedrals Described by Great Writers* and *Cliff Castles and Cave Dwellings in Europe*.

This scene is basically the prelude to the grand finale we'll be filming on Sunday, when we get back from the San Ysidro Ranch. Although everyone already knows their assigned costume, this is a great opportunity for the actors to grab any hat or cloak and improvise. Everyone is in high spirits, especially me when Milo hands over a note with our rendez-vous destination for tonight. It seems he's discovered an all-but-secret room at the top of the Casa Grande. It's called the Celestial Suite but is more commonly known as 'the honeymoon suite'. *Interesting* ... He's even drawn me a little map to get there. I tuck the piece of paper inside my bra so there's no chance of losing or leaving it anywhere.

We've decided to be discreet about our plans for two reasons – Marina and Orla.

Of course, I'm sure Marina wouldn't have any real objec-tion to us getting together, but he did turn her down that time and, considering I am here because of her, I don't want to do anything to peeve her. As for Orla . . . I just don't see the need to rub her nose in anything, especially since she's actually started to open up to me. Earlier today she casually asked me what kind of makeover I would envision for her. 'Just some-thing that allows you to look more like *you*,' I told her. 'What you are projecting at the moment is very one-note. I think there is more to say—' Then we were interrupted.

Presumably she wasn't too offended by my opening gambit because she joins me now as I'm perusing the library's travel section and tells me that her grandfather came from my part of the world, as in Ireland.

'Well, that explains your name!' I smile. 'Were you close?'

'Oh yes,' she says, pulling a photograph from her bag. 'That's him and his daughter, my mum.' She points to a homely-looking lady.

'And who's this?' I say, pointing to the third person in the picture.

'Me!'

I peer closer, trying to reconcile this sweet, bookish girl with the Pammy clone next to me.

'Not exactly a looker.' She seems almost embarrassed for me to see the real her.

'I think you look lovely. Perhaps not the most flattering hairstyle, but who doesn't have dodgy photos from yesteryear?'

'Let's just say I've had a lot more male attention looking like this.'

'Well, I don't doubt that. So is that why you did it – to get a guy?'

She looks uncomfortable. 'I actually had a guy when this picture was taken.'

I look to her to tell me more.

'We were high-school sweethearts, saving ourselves for marriage.'

'Go on . . .' This is going to be good, I can tell.

'I was only nineteen when he proposed and we went straight out to look for a ring – we had the best day, so romantic, sparkles everywhere I looked!' she sighs. 'We went to Cracker Barrel for dinner and then back to his. His parents were out of town, so we decided to raid the liquor cabinet and invent the signature cocktail for our wedding reception and' – she takes a breath – 'we ended up getting completely drunk and sleeping together.'

She stares fixedly at the floor.

'Was it really that awful?'

'I don't think either of us had much recollection of what happened, other than he knew I was no longer a virgin and so he said he couldn't marry me.'

'What?' I splutter, causing a few too many heads to turn our way. 'You're kidding?'

She shakes her head. 'He said his mum would know and that he'd just feel too guilty about it. You have to understand we're from a very conservative area.'

'Are you Amish?' I'm still incredulous. 'So he dumped you even though it was because of him that you were no longer a virgin.'

'Yes. It really messed with my head.'

'I'll bet.'

'I knew I wasn't the prettiest girl, and of course he went and told everyone what happened.'

Now I'm really seething.

'What did your grandfather have to say about all this?'

She smiles. 'He wanted to pay him a visit. "Knock some sense into him." '

'Finally some sanity!' I cheer.

'He was actually planning on coming to live with us, but he passed away before he could make the move.'

'Oh, I'm sorry.'

'It's just as well he can't see me now. He was always telling me, "Find a good man, Orla. He'll be worth the wait." '

'So why this?' I say, motioning to her overall look.

She shrugs. 'I just thought, No one is going to want me now. And all I ever saw were men salivating over these *FHM* babes and I remember looking at them really closely thinking, They're not even that pretty.'

'But they're half naked and acting available . . .'

'Plus I already had the boobs. I'd just never worn anything to show them off.'

'I bet you blew your ex's mind when he saw the transformation.'

'Well, that was the plan . . .'

'Didn't work?'

She shakes her head. 'I know it's wrong and I'm supposed to just let it go, but I felt like I couldn't move on until I made him regret what he'd done. That's when I decided to get it on with Milo – that's his favourite actor . . . Don't look so shocked. Haven't you ever fantasised about an ex seeing you with his hero?'

'Oh, absolutely,' I confess. 'Multiple times. I just didn't realise that was your motivation.'

'Well, I was fighting a losing battle – I could see from day one he was more into you.'

I mull the bombshell for a second. 'You know, if all you need is a picture of the two of you to put on Facebook—'

'Actually, I'm going to hold off on that project . . .' She looks coy.

'What is it?'

'I've kinda got a date tonight.'

My eyes widen. 'With a good man, I hope,' I say as I flashback to the conversation I overheard during hide and seek last night.

'Oh yeah. He couldn't be more complimentary. Said he's had a crush on me the whole time.'

I want to find out more, but we're being hustled up to the next location – Hearst's private floor, aka the Gothic Suite – and as a result only Marion and Hearst are required.

'Have fun tonight, and let's schedule the makeover for tomorrow's lunch break,' I tell her as I leave.

'You're on!' she cheers.

I even find myself reaching to give her a little hug, all the while thinking, We're going to have to find a way to make that lousy ex-fiancé pay!

*   *   *

Of all the rooms at the castle, I had imagined Hearst's would be the most OTT grand, pretty much a cathedral with a bed in it, but in fact his personal space is surprisingly modest, in a classic ebony and ivory palette with portraits of his mother and father on the wall. Perhaps he saved all the glitz for his lady? But no, Marion's room is simple too (relatively speaking!), albeit a little cosier, thanks to the warm red and gold brocade of the canopied four-poster.

'Maybe it's the corridor-creeping that kept the romance alive over the decades,' Marina suggests as she stands midway between the two rooms, in an expansive lounge area.

The scene she is filming is a touching one: Hearst fretting about his inability to make an honest woman out of Marion and her insisting that it is of no consequence to her to become a Mrs.

'Why should I chase after the streetcar when I'm already on board?'

Even though I am a little fidgety, eager to fast-forward to my date with Milo, I can see the takes are going well. Conrad even comments that this may be some of Marina's best work.

'I haven't seen this tenderness in you before,' he compliments her. 'It is very becoming.'

I smile to myself. Perhaps the world will get to see a little more of the real Marina through this movie.

'Can we try it with a softer light?' he requests.

In a bid to step out of the way of the lighting guys, I back round a corner and discover the real showstopper of this floor: Hearst's private library.

I wish Milo were here to tell me more about the hand-painted arches creating a ribcage effect to the room. A passing techie tells me there are a staggering 4,000 books on these shelves. I see a welcoming sofa at the far end of the central table and think how nice it would be to have one of those relationships where you can sit side by side reading contentedly. Maybe looking up and smiling every now and again, sharing the odd line or two and then disappearing back into your respective worlds. I like the idea of that kind of companionship.

'Stella!' I'm called back in to fix a curl that has fallen forward and is obscuring the emotion in Marina's left eye.

A couple more takes after that we're done.

'All right everyone,' Conrad calls it a day. 'Get some sleep and we'll see you bright and early for the kitchen scenes tomorrow.'

As I head back to the Casa del Sol with Marina, I make a big show of exhaustion, yawning and rubbing my face and announcing, 'I think I'm going to have a shower and then head straight to bed.'

Which actually isn't too far off the truth . . .

24

Initially I set out to meet Milo in a flirty floral sundress, but people I can't even see in the darkness call out, 'Hey, Stella! Where are you off to?' so I scurry back and switch to black cigarette pants, a boat-neck T-shirt and ballet flats – all very *To Catch a Thief*. Now I feel like I can scamper and flatten myself against walls and disappear into the shadows.

By staying close to the trees and plant life, I've accessed the Casa Grande. Now I've just got to make it up to the top floor.

'You look like a cat burglar!' a voice startles me as I creak along a low-lit corridor.

It's Mr Hearst himself. Or should I say Charles Dance, looking debonair in a silk smoking jacket.

'Oh! So I do!' I chime, making out that I've only just noticed my ensemble. 'Well, if you wake up tomorrow and all the valuables are gone, you'll know who to blame!'

'You need a swag bag,' he decides. 'You're not going to fit much in those pockets.'

'Well, I could always stuff a few items up my jumper.'

'Maybe that's Orla's trick,' he ponders dryly.

I can't believe he just said that.

'Anyway, I'm just running up to the library,' I chirp. 'I think I left my nail kit up there.'

'In urgent need of it tonight, are you?'

'How else am I going to jimmy my way into the safe?' I brazen.

He nods and allows me to continue on my way – apparently my nerve has outlasted his interrogation.

I trot round the corner and then lean against the wall and wait for my heart rate to return to normal. That was nerve-wracking. As far as I know, it's just him and Milo in the Casa Grande. I've made it past the gatekeeper; all I need to do now is keep going up and up.

I must say I'm not a fan of these staircases, they curve so tightly that at a certain point you feel like you're trapped in a twisted box. I can't get up them fast enough. It doesn't help that it's getting hotter and hotter the higher I go. Once I've made it to the bell-tower floor, I take out my phone and use the light from it to study the map. Okay, this should be the room right here.

'Milo?' I call softly.

Nothing.

I tap on the door with my fingernails. Still nothing. Of course, it's possible he's fallen asleep. He does seem to have a propensity for that. I take a deep breath and venture in.

'Wow!'

Of all the extraordinary rooms I've seen in this castle, this has to be one of the most intriguing – hexagonal in shape, the walls are panelled with carved wood, letting in moonlight through the cut-outs so it's almost like being inside a giant Moroccan lantern. I peer closer at the detailing and see eagles and angels and dragons. What I don't see is a window latch. The room desperately needs some cool night air to temper the stuffiness. There must at least be a vent in here . . .

I reach across the bed – it would have a gleaming gold counterpane, just to reinforce the expectation of Olympic standards. Oh, please tell me that isn't a mirror embedded in the wooden headboard! God, I hope he's bringing wine. And then I tut myself – of course he's bringing wine. I just wonder what the 'pairing' will say about how he sees us. Maybe he'll opt for a blend – something golden and lively to represent him and dark and full-bodied to represent me. Put the two together and you have a rosé to toast our upcoming rosy glow. Only I already have one, I think as I try to fan myself with the drape of one of the heavy gold curtains. This is going to be like Bikram sex. I'm seriously not going to last five minutes.

Perhaps I could dredge up a breeze by flapping the door. I open it, preparing to do a bit of vigorous wafting back and forth, but only get as far as one waft – on account of slamming the thuggish wood into Milo's face.

'Oh my God, oh my God! I didn't see you there!'

'It's okay, bottle's intact!' He hoists the wine aloft.

'But what about your head?'

'Thick hair.' He shrugs. 'It serves me well.'

'I didn't bash your nose?'

'No, I was ducking to come in.' Then he gives me a sly look. 'But I'm sure I could find a few things for you to kiss better . . .'

And with that his lips are upon me. I'm rather taken aback by his ardour and can't quite get into a groove with him. I can taste that this isn't his first drink of the evening. I'm obviously no connoisseur, because if I had to tell you what flavour I'm detecting, I would say cherry cola.

'That's exactly what is it!' he cheers when he takes a breather and I share my theory. 'I mean, you know I love to stay true to my Californian roots, but I was in this wine merchant's a couple of weeks back and the notes said, "Cherry cola," so, even though it was French, I just had to try it.'

'May I?'

'*Mais oui!*'

It's then he realises we don't have any glasses.

'Do you mind swigging from the bottle?'

'Not at all!' I say, taking a rather unsophisticated glug-glug-gulp. (A dainty sip just won't cut it at the moment.) 'I love it!' I enthuse. 'Actually, I know this isn't really the time, but I've been meaning to ask you a wine-related favour for this event that I'm helping Marina with.'

'Tell me more.'

'Well, we want to put a special bottle in each room for these couples who haven't seen each other for a while – something romantic, I suppose. I don't know if any one wine has more aphrodisiac qualities than the others . . .'

I've done it now. Said the word 'aphrodisiac'. He sets the bottle on the side table and hoicks me up onto his hips, staggering into the wall, digging my back into assorted mythical creatures.

I try to wriggle free, but that only encourages him more, so I'm forced to use my feet to launch myself off the wall, causing him to tumble back onto the bed.

'Oooh, you like it rough, do you?'

'Wait!' I pant, grabbing and wielding the nearby candelabra to keep him at a distance.

'You want to play lion-tamer now, do you?'

Before I can explain that I'm finding the room unbearably hot, he dodges the prongs and it's my turn to fall back on the bed. As he rears over me, a big splash of sweat falls from his brow, narrowly missing my eye.

I don't mean to flinch quite so obviously, but at least it has the desired effect – he finally decides it's too sauna-esque in here and we need a change of scene.

'Come on, I know just the place!'

We make our descent in tandem – Milo peering ahead to check that Hearst is not on the prowl – and then, not a moment too soon, we emerge into the cool night. Finally I can breathe. Still Milo leads me onward, round the side terrace, weaving down a path until we end up beside the floodlit tennis court.

'What do you think?' he asks, pulling me close to him.

'Well, it's certainly a lot more airy . . .'

He rolls his eyes. 'I'm not that much of an exhibitionist! Look down.'

Only now do I see arched windows and some low glowing lights. It would seem the court is in fact the roof of yet another building . . .

'What is it? What's down there?'

'Come and see.'

We scamper down and then I gasp as he opens the door.

'Welcome to the most expensive room in the place – the Roman Pool.'

The room is nothing short of breath-taking: shimmering gold and cobalt-blue tiles of Murano glass cover every surface, creating a magical aqua palace.

'The water looks so black.' I stoop to give it a swish, wondering for a moment if Hearst had it coloured with squid ink or some such fancy.

'It's just because there are no lights beneath the surface. Plus it's ten feet deep.'

He starts stripping off and hanging his clothes on the nearest statue of a naked Roman god.

'Milo, what are you doing?' I ask, barely able to tell them apart.

'You said you wanted to cool down . . .' He eases himself into the water. 'Ahhh, that's better!'

'Are we allowed?'

'Well, it's not as if I'm going to damage the water – you're the one standing on the priceless mosaics!'

'Don't say that!' I panic, rising up onto my tippy-toes for minimal impact.

'Are you going to join me?'

I take a breath as my concern moves to disrobing in front of him. I mean, from the angle he's looking up at me—

Suddenly there's a clunk and all the lights go out. I gasp audibly.

'What happened?'

'Just a power cut. They get them a lot in this area.'

'Well, how long do they last?'

'Could be anything from a couple of minutes to a couple of hours.'

Not wanting to miss my window of opportunity to slip in unseen, I quickly wriggle out of my trousers and top, then feel my way to the edge of the water. Of course, the downside is that I now can't see a darn thing. Including Milo. Please don't let him be the type to swim under the water and pull at my leg or anything; I'll scream the place down.

'Where are you?' I ask nervously.

'Here!' he says, appearing in the centre of the pool, where moonlight is beaming down through the vaulted arches of the ceiling via a set of glass blocks.

I smile as I swim towards him, revelling in what an incredible first date this is.

Though we can see each other, it is difficult to touch with our feet pedalling so wildly and our arms swishing to keep us afloat.

'Let's move over to the side area. It may be darker, but there's a shallow pool where we can relax.'

I swim with one hand resting on the small of his back, making sure I maintain contact.

'Here, come to me.' He pulls me to him and then laughs, 'Are you still wearing your underwear?'

'Well, you know, just in case someone came in.'

'No one's going to—'

Suddenly we hear voices.

'Oh no! It's security!' I panic.

He places a hand over my mouth. 'Ssshh!'

I can't believe this! My first movie project and now I'll never work in this town again.

'Shouldn't the lights have come back on by now?' a female voice enquires.

'Orla!' I place her name in Milo's ear.

'Never mind about that. Just bring that fine tush of yours to me and let me get a taste of what you've been teasing me with all day.'

My stomach plummets. It's that same awful voice from last night, the man who intended to have her whether she liked it or not.

'Easy, tiger,' Orla laughs nervously. 'What's the rush?'

'You have to stop them!' I hiss at Milo.

'What?'

'He is not a good man.'

'So they really are real.' The rogue gives a grotesque groan.

'Can you do an Irish accent?'

'What?' Milo hisses back.

'As loud as you can and as deep as you can I want you to say these words . . .'

'Orla Hayes, this is your grandfather here to tell you this is a bad man. Walk away, my darlin'. There's something better coming.'

'What the . . . ?'

'Granda?' Orla calls out.

And then the lights come back up.

I'm gripping on to Milo for dear life, praying we're not visible, but it would seem we are sufficiently tucked into the alcove behind the diving balcony.

'Is someone there?' Orla calls, clearly freaked out.

'Look, it's obviously just someone messing around,' the man grizzles. 'Let's go back to my room.'

'No.' She is emphatic.

'But you've got to finish what you've started.'

'No, I haven't.'

Milo is getting ready to step in, but I hold him back – something tells me that she's going to handle it herself.

'Listen, Miss Thing—'

'No, you listen. If you so much as lay a finger on me, I'll put a picture of your out-of-shape body on the Internet.'

'But you don't have a picture,' he taunts.

A flash illuminates the room.

'I do now.'

Milo and I give each other a mini high five.

We then watch as she walks defiantly in one direction and he, still in the process of dressing, scuffs at the earth in another.

'Charlie Chaplin!' I gasp, realising that I've only ever heard him in character on the set.

Milo nods. 'I'll be having a few words with him tomorrow.'

I give a little shudder. 'That could've gone so much worse.' I reach for Milo's hand. 'Thank you for doing the voice. You were really convincing.'

'I'm surprised you're so protective of her.'

'Well, I owe her. She lent me a pair of flip-flops at a really vital time.'

Milo looks bemused.

'And she's actually not a bad person. It's just her outsides don't match her insides. Did you know she's a history major?'

Milo tilts his head fondly at me.

'What?'

'You're different,' he muses.

'Different to what?'

Instead of replying, he leans close and kisses me.

Now he's the one who's different – at least, his kiss is. Slower. More affectionate. This feels so much better.

My toes slide along the uneven tile and find the water again, swishing back and forth as my hands traverse his slippery skin, gliding over his muscles and sliding down to his hipbones. He pulls me closer, triggering a flare of pure desire, and suddenly any notion I had of holding back . . . Well, it just doesn't seem relevant any more . . .

25

Of course, with the morning light comes morning-after uncertainty – will he ever want to see me again? Should I have held out? Will the sexual tension dissipate now that he knows what I look and feel like naked?

I was lucky with Jonathan – there was no room for paranoia because he was instantly so cuddly and amorous. I felt his lips upon me before I even saw his smile. And what a smile, beaming right at me. Normally I would have averted my gaze, head half buried in a pillow, afraid to detect any trace of disappointment or awkwardness, but with him I couldn't look away – all I saw was celebration in his eyes and can't-get-enough-of-you in his touch.

Maybe it would've been that way with Milo if we hadn't had to sneak back to our separate rooms, who knows? It doesn't help that we have to curb any affection in front of everyone else. I can't even assess his body language for clues – the guy is a professional actor and right now his job between takes is to look like we didn't have sex last night. It doesn't help that the catering staff are poring over a picture of him in *Star* magazine wearing a T-shirt saying, 'REHAB IS FOR QUITTERS.' How do people get used to the fact that their boyfriend is fair game for everyone to either diss or lust over? Not that he is my boyfriend, but last night I had a very personal moment with this most public of property. I really hope it wasn't a mistake.

On the upside, my brushes have never been cleaner.

Lloyd mistakes my obsessive spritzing for eagerness to get going with tomorrow's project and as soon as the end of day is called he guides me to the trailer to divvy up the makeovers and discuss the individual looks. Nine times out of ten I'm working on my own, so having a seasoned expert to bounce ideas off is brilliant. The woman with the small baby, for example, we decide to go ultra-glam on, since she probably rarely even has the time to get a comb through her hair. For the over-styled Jersey Shore girl, we strategise about toning down the Tango tan and liquorice-black hair, wondering if she'll be willing to experiment with something more feminine and natural.

'I think you should take her,' Lloyd decides. 'If you can soften up Orla . . .'

I have to say the lunch-break makeover was a great success. She didn't quite have the nerve to let go of the blonde, but I did convince her to relinquish the skanky hair extensions so I could give her a sexy modern-day Marilyn cut. Her complexion was a revelation behind the mask – soft rosy skin that allowed her to reclaim her youth. Every product I used on her had a shimmer or a gloss to it, so when I asked her to look in the mirror and describe her new look, she said, 'Radiant! I feel radiant!'

By tea break she told me she'd never had so many compliments, including her first from women and a good few from people who had no idea who she was.

I hope things work out as well with the Navy project. As I gather up the pictures of my group, I find myself sighing, 'These poor women . . .'

'Remember you're doing this out of empathy, not pity,' Lloyd urges. 'There's a difference.'

'I know. I just can't help but feel sorry for them.'

'Some would say they are lucky to have found a love that can endure such a test,' Lloyd reasons.

'Yes, but who needs to be tested over and over like this?'

'Well, maybe some of their stories will surprise you.'

'I hope so.'

Lloyd tuts as he gets to his feet. 'Don't make me send you to bed wearing a Frownie – this is supposed to be a happy occasion. For you as well as them.'

As I bid him goodnight, I have to admit he's right.

I mean, how can I expect to lay all my residual angst to rest if I don't do it with good grace?

For the next five minutes I attempt to find a facial expression that is both noble and serene, but when my reflection tells me that is still a work in progress, I decide to focus on the one thing I can control – having an immaculately ordered kit.

I'm just colour-coding my glitter pots when there's a tap on the door and a familiar head appears.

'Hey, Jeff. What's going on?'

'I have a favour to ask.'

'Come on in.' I beckon him. 'What is it?'

He takes a bolstering breath. 'This is something I never thought I would hear myself say.'

I set down my pixie dust and give him my full attention.

'I want to look like a civilian for the party.'

'Okay,' I nod. 'You know that no one is expecting you to wear a uniform – this isn't a military event. In fact, the whole point is that for a few magical hours you belong to your woman, not an institution.'

'I know. And I have the suit and the shoes . . .' He trails off.

I think he wants me to save him from having to say the next sentence out loud. And I would, if I only knew what it was.

'It's my hair.'

'Ohhh!' I smile. 'You want a little trim? I'd be happy to. Hop in the chair.'

He doesn't move. 'I don't want it shorter. I want it longer.' He gets even pinker in the face when he adds, 'Do you have any wigs?'

I'd be tempted to burst out laughing were it not for his very apparent embarrassment.

'Marina has this favourite old picture of me and, for one night at least, I want to look like that for her.'

I can't help but smile. Any man who would wear a wig outside of a fancy-dress party just to please his woman is a true romantic.

'Take a seat.'

'Really?'

'Do you have the picture?'

He hands me a small, tattered snap. 'This is all I've got.'

It's the Harry Connick Jr look she spoke of at the San Ysidro Ranch.

'So Marina's never actually seen you in person with this hairstyle?'

He shakes his head.

'Great. That gives us a bit more flexibility. We'll just go with what suits you best.'

'And maybe without the grey?' he ventures.

I give him a fond look. 'Whatever you like.'

It actually doesn't take too long to find the right mid-brown hairpiece to suit him. I do a minor bit of texturing, then step back to assess the effect.

'You look like a different person,' I marvel. 'A lot more playful.'

'And ten years younger?' he says hopefully.

'Easily. You want me to tidy up your brows?'

I've barely plucked two hairs and his eyes are *streaming*.

'You Navy guys aren't so tough!' I tease.

'I can handle it.' He grits his teeth.

'Maybe it would be quicker if I just waxed—'

'Noooo!' he howls, jumping out of the chair.

'Oh, don't be such a baby – they're just tiny little strips. It's not like I'm ripping hair off your werewolf back!'

'What's Marina been saying?' His eyes narrow.

'Nothing!' I laugh. 'Come on, back in the chair. I'll leave your brows, but you have to let me dip your hands.'

'In what?'

'Paraffin wax. No pain, just silky skin. Trust me.'

He hesitates as he contemplates the tub of pink liquid.

'It's not like I'm going to turn them into little doll hands . . .'

'Okay, okay – do it!'

We wash them and then dunk, dunk and re-dunk in the warm fluid until his hands are coated in layers of soft wax.

'Now I have to tie them in sandwich bags,' I explain as I make little mitts for him.

We're both chuckling by this point. It's our first moment of authentic interaction. Albeit a tad later than originally scheduled.

'I think you just got a text . . .' He nods over to my bag.

I scramble for my phone with certain anticipation. YES! It's him! 'Come sleep beside me.' My heart does a triumphant jig. He wants to be with me again! I am not wholly repugnant to him! Yippeee!

'Good news?'

'Tremendous!' I grin back.

'Are my hands done yet?'

I burst out laughing at the sight before me. He looks like he's about to break into a jazz routine. 'If your shipmates could see you now!'

'The good news is that they wouldn't even recognise me,' he asserts.

I give a little gasp. 'You've just given me an idea.'

'For what?'

'You'll have to wait and see . . .'

Turns out I have to wait and see too. Despite the invitation to his boudoir, Milo is out cold by the time I arrive, so I have to hang on until morning, easing him awake with the aroma of freshly baked rosemary and bittersweet chocolate muffins.

'Holy mother of God, that's good,' he mumbles as he comes round.

'I know you're still half asleep, but can I borrow you for ten minutes?'

'I tell you what, on account of the muffin, I'll give you eleven.'

I reach for his hand. 'Come with me to the make-up trailer.'

'Mmm.' He perks up as he follows me. 'Are we finally going to get to try out that reclining chair?'

'Not exactly.'

'Oh.' He looks genuinely disappointed. 'Listen, I'm sorry about crashing last night. I can't believe I'm going to miss out on you tonight too.'

'Well, not necessarily . . .'

'What's all this?' He blinks at the countertop set with assorted facial props.

'I was thinking about the party and your ban from the San Ysidro Ranch.'

'Go on . . .'

'Well, you're an actor; I'm a make-up artist; between the two of us we should be able to come up with an entirely different persona, one they would actually welcome as a guest . . .'

'My devilish alter ego?' he suggests with a twinkle.

'Well, he won't be much of an alter ego if he's devilish,' I quip. 'On the plus side you have a very strong signature look in all your films.'

'You mean I always look the same?'

'Er . . .'

'We can't all be Philip Seymour Hoffman,' he pouts.

'And that's fine – it hasn't exactly done Robert Redford any harm having the same haircut his entire career. All I'm saying is, if we change your hair colour and maybe add a little goatee, you'll be virtually unrecognisable. Provided you don't speak.'

'I could always do my cockney accent!' he brightens.

'Oh Lord!' I roll my eyes, pretending to make a run for the door, but he pulls me back to him.

'You really want me there?'

I sigh. 'Well, it's going to be such a lovely event. And the cottages do have their own private hot tub . . .'

'Bribing me with sex now?'

'Pretty much,' I concede.

He looks back at the countertop. 'You weren't seriously thinking of making me wear false teeth?'

'Noooo!' I lie. 'Look, I promise we'll find something you're comfortable with – just think of it as customising the avatar on your Wii.'

'Well, when you put it like that' – he reaches for his coffee – 'I'm in.'

I had thought this would just take a few minutes, as it did with Jeff, but it turns out that Milo's hairdresser has already laid claim to the number one most flattering look for his face and the truth is, without that blond tousle, well . . . it's not that he's not good-looking, it's just that he looks borderline ordinary without it.

'I would've had a very different life if I looked like this,' he says as he contemplates his reflection with a short brown crop.

'You think?'

'I know. I look exactly like my brother. He got my mum's colouring; I took after my dad. And let's just say I've had it considerably easier than him.' He looks up at me. 'Ever wondered how different your life would be if you didn't have such distinctive hair?'

'Oh yes. In fact, I very much doubt I'd be here with you now.'

'Whole different persona?'

'Absolutely,' I confirm.

He looks back at his reflection. 'This is kind of depressing.'

'It is just for one night,' I assure him. 'And it's not like anyone will even know except me, and maybe Marina and Jeff.'

'Is there going to be any press there?'

'That's still being debated, but even if there is, it will liter-ally be for the first hour, so we can keep you hidden until then.'

'What's up with this moustache?' He reaches for a broom-brush affair. 'Please tell me that's not real hair.'

'Want to see it on?' I dare him.

As I paste it and press it in place, he twitches his lips from side to side.

'I can't believe it – that actually suits you!' I gasp as I step back to assess him. 'Very Sundance Kid!'

'You like that, do you?'

'I kind of do!'

'Then kiss me!' He pulls me hard down onto his mouth.

'Oh, that tickles.' I pull away, wiping at my face.

'Don't be such a wuss!'

'Let's see how you like it!' I reach for a droopy Fu Manchu number and secure it to my own face. 'Now do you want to kiss me?' I challenge him.

'Oddly I do.' One hand reaches up to the back of my neck; the other hooks behind my leg, easing me onto his lap. Bristle friction aside, it's a good kiss. Maybe our best yet.

'I like you, Stella,' he says as we come up for air. 'I never thought I'd find a girl with so much facial hair attractive, but I do.'

As I giggle back at him, I find my fingers raking through his hair and that's when I get the idea for a Jeff-style grey. Not so far off his natural blond, it might just work . . .

'Close your eyes,' I instruct as I rummage for my hair paint. Now this I like – a debonair, dark silver. I even give his eyebrows a matching tint. It would take a while to perfect the older-man latex stippling, but first I want him to get a glimpse of just how dashing he would look as a silver fox.

'Open your eyes!' I cheer.

His face instantly falls.

'You have to imagine a few Benjamin Button wrinkles here—'

'No.' He grips on to my wrist. His face is serious, if not a little anxious. 'Don't do that.'

'Okay,' I soothe, waiting for him to release me.

He does so and then grabs a towel and starts rubbing frantically at his hair. 'I don't think this is going to work.'

It feels as if he's talking about us as well as the disguise. Why do I get the sense that he's about to storm out of the trailer? *Because he is.* I watch the door close behind him and then kick myself – who wants to see themselves prematurely aged? Especially someone whose job depends on their looks. What was I thinking? I slump down in the chair. I mean, how would I like it?

By way of punishing myself I reach for an old-lady wig and puff a cloud of white powder onto my face and then squint back at my reflection. Not a good look, but I can't help but wish that I could meet my older self for just a few moments – I'd love to know if I ever got this love thing right. What are the odds, I wonder, of me finding someone I can have ice-cream-eating contests with when I'm sixty?

Heaving a sigh, I slide off the wig and dust off my face. Better get a move on – there's less than an hour now before we leave. I gather up my kit and open the door and there at the bottom of the steps is Milo.

'I didn't mean to act so huffy,' he says, looking up at me with remorse in his eyes.

'I'm sorry I tried to age you!' I hurry down to his level.

'You know, my dad died really young and I've always had this feeling I'm never going to make it to be an old man.' He takes a breath. 'Getting a glimpse of how he might have looked if he were still alive . . .' He shudders. 'It just felt weird.'

Now I'm even more mortified. 'I'm so sorry—' I begin.

'It's okay,' he shushes me. 'You didn't know. The thing is, I'm in no rush to join him.' He takes my hand. 'I like being here with you.'

My heart is mid-swoon when he adds, 'Anyway, I think I'm just going to stay here and chill out today.'

'Okay,' I gulp back my disappointment. How can I possibly argue considering the state I've put him in?

There's a moment of silence.

'I wish I didn't have to leave you like this.'

'I'll be fine.' He shrugs. 'Jimmy said he might go into town for a bit, so . . .'

'I should never have tried to change you,' I say as I attempt to remove a little more of the Tin Man taint to his hair.

'You know it's highlighted?' he blurts.

'Really?' I gasp, touched by his sudden honesty.

'I mean, I was white-blond as a kid, but then it started to turn mousey.'

'And you can't have a mousey movie star.'

He shakes his head and then turns his body to face mine. 'So now you know my secret, you have to tell me one of yours.'

I think of all the sentimental things I'd like to say to him, but instead I smile back at him and shrug. 'My hair is dyed too.'

'Really?' he chuckles.

'Really, really.'

You wouldn't think that such a trivial thing could bond two people, but if someone walked by and saw the way we're looking at each other, well, let's just say it's all the more annoying that I have to leave.

Apparently Milo feels the same way because as he links fingers with me, he whispers, 'Do you really have to go? We could have the whole day together, doing exactly as we pleased.' He draws me closer. 'I'd take you down to Sebastian's General Store and we'd get one of their famous French-dip sandwiches, made with real Hearst ranch beef.'

'And the wine?' I play along for a moment.

'A great Cabernet Franc with a raspberry-chocolate flavour profile . . .'

I smile. He could so be a sommelier in another life.

'And then we'd take the path down to the beach and make a little den from the driftwood—'

'Oh, don't!' I wail, the thought of our very own sandy pit pushing me over the edge. 'I'd like nothing better, really, but I can't let those girls down.'

I know I'm supposed to be brimming with altruism and compassion today, but as I'm forced to walk away from Milo and our dreamy day at the beach, resentment swirls within me – I can't believe this: even when I'm making this highly personalised peace offering, the Navy is still interfering with my love life.

All I can say is that today better be an end to it. I'll make this one last sacrifice and then that's it, the war is over.

26

I really need to hurry up and get in the shower, but Marina is, for some mysterious reason, sitting in my bathroom talking to Kendal on her phone.

'So what I'm thinking is this – you bring Frankie the dachshund to the San Ysidro Ranch tomorrow morning, leave your car there and then we'll all travel back up to the castle together and *get this*: I've even arranged for you to be one of the extras in the costume-party scene! . . . Oh, don't be ridiculous! . . . No, you don't! Besides, you've seen the work Stella did on the dogs – she'll make you look great . . . No, I didn't mean it like that. Stella, you talk to her!'

She hands me the phone.

'Hello, Kendal?'

'You have to help me!'

'Of course,' I say, though already I'm thinking, This is all I need when I've already got so many extra extra faces to make up.

'I know Marina is only doing this to be nice, but I really can't think of anything worse than my worn-out visage messing up a scene that is supposed to be full of glamorous Hollywood-starlet types – the director will probably have me escorted from the set.'

'Don't be—'

'I'm serious, Stella,' she cuts in. 'I'm not in the market for a makeover.'

Having just left a traumatised Milo, I can't deny I'm a little relieved to hear this.

'Aren't there any costumes where the face is mostly covered – you know, like an Arabian princess or a genie or something? You wouldn't even have to do my hair then, just my eyes.'

'Let me see . . .' I step back into my room and flip through the booklet of costumes.

'I want to be there, just not as me, if you know what I mean?'

'I do,' I empathise. 'As a matter of fact, there are several looks that fit that bill.'

'Seriously, I'll come as the back half of a horse if that's what it takes.'

'How does a bear sound?'

'*Fantastic!*'

'Really?'

'Yes, that way I don't have to make eye contact with anyone and I can just spy on whoever I like. Brilliant!'

I rather like that idea myself.

'I can even bring the costume up with us just to be sure it fits.'

'You are a star!' she cheers. 'I've got to run now, but I'll see you tomorrow.'

'Okay, do you need to speak to Marina again?'

'No, just tell her I'll see her bright and early.'

'Okay.' I press end call and hand back the phone. 'Marina, why are you in here?'

She rolls her eyes. 'Jeff has been hogging the bathroom for the last hour. He wouldn't even let me get my make-up, so I had to borrow yours.'

Uh-oh. I've got a bad feeling about the wig.

'Let me just go and check on him – I did promise I'd give him a quick trim,' I lie. 'Maybe he's waiting on that.'

★   ★   ★

No sooner have I rapped on the door than I'm yanked in.

The big crisis? He's got the wig on backwards.

'Easy mistake to make with short hair,' I console him.

But when I go to swivel it round, I discover there is a bigger problem – it won't budge.

'I didn't want it shifting, so I had a look in your kit and went around my hairline with this.'

I blanch as he holds up a tube of the adhesive I use to secure wigs to dummies. 'That is not meant for human usage.'

'You're telling me!' he wails. 'I've tried everything to get it off and all I've succeeded in doing is tearing my skin.'

It's my turn to be queasy now. 'I don't do well with flesh wounds.' I reel away from him.

'And I'm not thrilled about showing up at the party looking like half of Dumb & Dumber.'

'Well, don't get mad at me! I'm not the one who glued you!'

'What's going on in there?' Marina raps on the door. 'We have to leave in half an hour and, Stella, you haven't even showered!'

I take a deep breath. Why do I get the feeling that today is not going to go entirely according to plan?

Of course Lloyd saves the day, using mayonnaise of all things. (Apparently the oils in it loosen the glue.) Meanwhile Marina is swooning at Jeff's sweetness.

'I can't believe you went to all that trouble for me!' Marina applies cooling aloe gel to his blistered skin. 'I mean, the potential for humiliation was just vast!'

'*Potential?*' Jeff scoffs. 'You say that like I actually managed to avoid it!'

'Guys?'

We all look up at Lloyd.

'We really should be going . . .'

'Cripes!' I gulp, looking at my watch. 'Let me just have the world's quickest shower!'

'What about this?' Marina draws an air squiggle in front of my face.

'I can do my make-up in the car.'

'Promise?' She blocks the doorway.

I raise a brow. 'Am I really so abhorrent to behold?'

'I just want you to make a good first impression when we arrive,' she explains. 'There's nothing I hate more than a bare-faced make-up artist – doesn't exactly inspire confidence in their work.'

'Fair enough,' I shrug.

'I'm going to start loading up the car,' Jeff announces, clearly desperate to be seen to be doing something manly again.

'Could you grab this costume from Wardrobe on the way?' I hurry after him with the photo from the catalogue. 'Just don't let Marina see it.'

'Stella, would you get in that shower?' She makes me jump.

'Yes, yes!' I pip.

Amazingly, when we do actually roll out, we are only twenty-three minutes behind schedule. On the way down, we see Milo loitering by the gate. I'm desperate for one last exchange and thrilled when Marina asks Jeff to pull over.

'Just wanted to thank you for making the wine selections,' she calls out to him. 'They sent the list over and it looks great.'

'No problem.'

'Just sorry you won't be it enjoying it with us.'

He goes to speak but Jimmy roars up in his two-seater roadster whooping, 'Right, man, are you ready to go get hammered?'

'You're going drinking now?' I can't help but judge – it's not even happy hour in the UK yet.

'It's all strategic,' Jimmy insists. 'Sooner we start drinking, sooner we get the hangover over with – that way, we'll be fresh as a daisy for the last day's shooting!'

'I like your thinking!' Milo gives him a high five.

I don't, I grimace, getting a vision of them passed out on the beach amid the elephant seals. But of course that's not my problem. Not unless they burn themselves.

'Just remember to wear sunscreen,' I call back as Jeff starts to roll away.

'Yes, Mom!' Jimmy groans.

Great. Not exactly the image I wanted to leave Milo with. I twist round, hoping to catch his eye one last time, but it's too late, he's already turned away.

As it happens, we make such good time with the drive we get to stop by Sephora in Santa Barbara and speed-buy personal make-up kits for each girl so they can maintain their new look.

Overwhelmed by the choice of brands, I suggest we choose from just two – Benefit (my personal favourite on account of the cutesy-cool packaging and their essential Dandelion face powder – the most flattering ballerina-pink flush your cheeks will ever know) and the sleek, professional Smashbox range because of the connection to Max Factor – it is the creation of his great-grandsons, Dean and Davis Factor.

'I never knew that!' Marina looks impressed.

'I only found out at the Max Factor Museum,' I confess. 'I like the fact that they didn't want to trade off his name. Plus they have the best selection of primers.'

By the time we get to the till we've amassed such a bumper purchase the sales assistant throws in dozens of extra samples, which I know everyone will love.

'Oh, I do love a freebie!' Marina paws over the goodies.

'Oh, me too!'

'You girls.' Jeff rolls his eyes. 'Both of you with more make-up than a person could wear in a lifetime.'

'It's never enough,' Marina and I chorus.

Jeff goes to give Lloyd a 'Women!' look but realises he's barking up the wrong tree there, not least because he's asleep.

Bodie, on the other hand, seems to sense that he's just a few minutes from one of his favourite places on earth and is clambering all around the car with no consideration for where he's putting his paws. Up starts the nasal whining, more fidgeting and then no sooner is the car parked; he's out, bounding up to reception, where he receives multi-handed belly rubs from the assembled staff.

Ruth looks on with mild disdain. 'If we could get on with the business in hand . . .'

I can't help but smile. I see she didn't mellow any in the Lake District.

'So, I have everyone's cottage keys. Marina, you and Jeff are back in Eucalyptus. I have Stella and her assigned girls in Rose and Lloyd and his group will be next door in Acacia.'

'Thank you.' He accepts his key.

'At the moment we've got the guys hanging by the pool and the girls having coffee out of sight in the Plow and Angel restaurant. As soon as you are ready for them, I'll send them in for their makeovers.'

'So they haven't seen each other at all yet?'

'No,' she confirms. 'As you can imagine, the energy is pretty high, but the girls are bonding well. I think for a lot of them it's the first time they've had someone to talk to who knows what they are going through.'

'And what a difference that makes.' Marina smiles at me.

'I'm going to check on the party area now, but any problems call me. And please be vigilant regarding the time.'

Lloyd and I give a 'Yes, ma'am' salute and head on our way.

'Wait up!' Marina calls after me.

'You want me to take Bodie?' I turn back to her and her springy-footed companion.

'Only if you want to.'

'Actually, I think he'd be a good distraction for the girls as they wait their turn. Come on, Bodie-boy!'

Still she continues to follow me to Rose.

I look around for Jeff. 'Was there something else?'

'Actually, there is . . .' she says, leading me up the decking steps.

'Oh, Marina!' I burst out laughing when I see the wooden letters she has ordered to be slotted beside the door. 'SALON DE STELLA'.

'You like?'

'I love it! Let me take a picture.'

'In a minute – there's something else . . .' She escorts me through to the bedroom, past the muslin-draped bed and over to the wardrobe.

'Open!'

I frown, intrigued, wondering what to expect beyond slippers and a robe, but when I pull back the slatted doors, I see the beautiful midnight-blue silk dress I had admired of Marina's, the one with all the teeny buttons.

'For you.'

I don't want to seem ungrateful in any way, but I have to speak up. 'You know this didn't fit me.'

'I had one sent over in your size.'

'What?' I gawp back at her in wonder.

'A little reward for all the magic you are about to perform. And for having the idea in the first place.'

'B-but—'

'I'm in the charge of the budget, remember? What I say goes.'

'Th-thank you,' I falter, and then reach and hold it up to me. The fabric feels divinely slippery, both cool and warm to the touch. 'You don't think it's too glam?'

Marina shakes her head. 'I think you should have a photograph of yourself with the girls to commemorate the day. They're all going to be looking their best, why not you too?'

'Why not?' I give a nonchalant shrug. 'And when I get sick of looking at them, I can always PhotoShop in an Oscar.'

No sooner has Marina left than the hairdresser, Jeannie, arrives. We reconfirm the looks for each girl and then decide it makes sense for her to have the bathroom with its double sinks and multiple hairdryer/tong/flat-iron sockets, while I opt for the natural light afforded by the French windows in the lounge. The patio will be the main holding area – what could be nicer after a cramped flight or long car journey than a soak in the hot tub?

The doorbell rings.

'And we're off!'

Bodie is instantly fascinated by the unique sound of half a dozen overexcited females and bounds between them, as if trying to track the origin of the highest-pitched squeak.

Meanwhile Jeannie and I decide to start with the girl with the long blonde hair who just needs giant rollers, so I don't have to wait too long for my first 'client'. In the meantime I introduce myself to the group and try, as best I can, to answer the barrage of questions.

'Is it true that Marina Ray is really here?'

'Yes. In fact, this is her dog!'

'And we're going to get to meet her?'

'She's going to be presenting you to your men.'

'What's with all the Beanie Babies?' one girl asks, holding up today's mascot, Amore the Dog.

'As a matter of fact, I just learned on the way here that the man who created Beanie Babies actually owns this place.'

'Nooooo!' I'm greeted by a chorus of disbelief.

'It's true.'

'Wow! He must be even richer than Marina!'

'Can I open these?' Another girl holds up the complimentary cocoa-dusted almonds.

'Help yourself.'

'What exactly are you going to make us *into*?' The one *au naturel* girl gives my kit a wary glance.

'Just your prettiest selves,' I assure her. 'Nothing over the top.'

'I want to go over the top!' another girl protests. 'There's so many regulations at work – nails can't be more than a quarter-inch from my fingertip, no false lashes—'

'You're the one in the Navy?'

'Mitchell.' She holds out her hand to me.

I furrow my brow.

'Sorry, force of habit. Stephanie.'

'Well, Stephanie, we're going to take you from Code Red to red carpet!'

'That's what I'm talking about!' She high-fives me and then disappears into a huddle of girls desperate to get the female perspective on the Forces.

From what I overhear, she's had a particularly tough time – her first husband divorcing her and actually seeking custody of their young son while she was away on a six-month deployment and couldn't be there to fight in person. The good news is that she's now met a new guy, the one who is here today, who is nothing but supportive. And romantic . . .

'Every day he sends me a different love poem or quotation,' she tells them. 'Look at what he texted me today: "The simple lack of her is more to me than others' presence." '

'You know the line I cling to?' another girl joins in. ' "Absence diminishes small loves and increases great ones." '

'That's so cool. I'm going to text that to Brandon now.'

'What's your name?'

'Gemma!' She grins.

I look on fondly as they shake hands, glad now that Milo isn't here so I can join in with them and not feel self-conscious talking about my experiences with Jonathan. Like now, as the blonde with the big rollers sits in my make-up chair, I can relate as she says that none of her friends seems to get how hard the separation is.

'When Craig first went away, they were all, "Oh, six months will pass in a flash, you'll see." And then their husbands would be gone on a business trip and they'd all be commiserating with each other, "Oh, two weeks is just too long!" '

'I so know what you mean,' I say as I find the right foundation match for her skin. 'Plus you've got to listen to them moaning about how his dirty socks never make it to the laundry basket or how he was home an hour later than he promised when he'd been drinking with his mates, when you're thinking, Oh my God, don't you realise the luxury of being together every day? What I wouldn't give to see his dirty socks on the floor!'

'Did any of your friends try to talk you out of the relationship?' she asks me.

I nod. 'When they'd see how upset I was when he left.' I replay the conversation for her.

' "Is this really what you want from a relationship?" '

' "No, of course it's not." '

' "Well then . . ." '

' "Well then, what?"

' "Maybe you should just chalk it up to experience and let it go. That way, you can look back fondly on the affair you had with the hot Navy guy."

'That's how they saw him, "Hot Navy Guy". But to me he was everything. Every hope and dream I had ever had for my heart. How was I supposed to let go of that?'

'Where is he now?' Blondie looks at me with concern.

'I don't know,' I say, quickly adding, 'Close your eyes,' so I don't have to look at the disappointment in them.

My next subject is a lawyer. Which she tells me is particularly trying as with every new state her husband gets relocated to, she has to resit her bar exam.

'What? That's nuts!'

'On the upside, Michelle Obama is trying to change that – you know she used to work for a law firm? That's where she met Barack.'

'Really?'

She nods. 'It's so cool, it's like she's totally on our side. She gave this big speech all about military wives and pretty much invited the nation to offer us more support and I have to say I am beginning to notice a difference in how people view me now.'

'Wasn't that great?' Another girl perches on the edge of the sofa so she can join in. 'It was the first time I felt "seen", you know, like she really understood what we were going through.'

'For me, the hardest thing was going through pregnancy without my best friend.' A new face appears. 'Going to the hospital and the classes by myself, the morning sickness, painting the nursery and wishing he was there to look at the colour charts with me.'

'It's tough when you don't even have your family or friends around you because you followed him to a new city.'

I sigh – I can't believe that was so nearly my life. I suppose I should be grateful for the near-miss, but, oddly, I just feel my heart panging for Jonathan. I hope he's all right. I hope he's happy.

'Stella?'

'Yes? Sorry!' I realise I've asked my final charge to tilt her head back and then just left her hanging. As I apply her volumising mascara, I ask her what personally keeps her going – 'It's been three years, hasn't it?'

She nods. 'It was basically when I stopped wishing for things I couldn't have and instead took a bit of time to consider how much worse things could be, which I know sounds negative, but I really am glad he didn't choose the Army because their deployments are even longer – up to fifteen months.'

'But what do the Army wives and girlfriends say? I wonder.'

'Well, probably the same as me when I'm feeling really low – that they are so grateful to have met the love of their life. Some people never get to experience that kind of passion and devotion. It might not be ideal, but it's worth it.'

'You have a good attitude,' I commend her.

'Well, I tried it the other way and it only made things worse!' she shrugs. 'I just had to accept that he's the only one for me. There's a certain peace that comes with that. Do you know what I mean?'

'I do.' I sigh. And then I see my phone bleeping Ruth's name. 'Time to go!' I quickly finish up with a spicy red gloss. 'All done. What do you think?'

'I love it!' She beams back at me. 'I feel like a movie star!'

Turning my attention to the rest of the girls, I check, 'Everyone happy with their look?'

Cheers resound.

'Thank you, Stella!'

'Yes, thank you.' Each girl steps forward and shares her appreciation. I feel so good in this moment, so bursting with compassion for them, so glad that they are all going to have a special weekend.

'You know, this whole day has been really cool,' Gemma tells me as we head to the door. 'On the way here, all I was thinking about was seeing Brandon, but now I've met all these other girls in the same situation as me . . .'

'Yes?'

'I don't think I'm going to feel so lonely on the way home.'

27

I give my girls a final once-over as they file out of the cottage, merging with Lloyd's group as we head over to the main buildings.

As they excitedly admire each other's new looks and best frocks, even I garner a few compliments – Jeannie kindly tonged me a few soft waves and added a sapphire hairclip, so now I feel more in keeping with the elegance of my dress.

As we enter our holding room – aka The Old Adobe – each girl is offered the hotel's signature cocktail: a blood-orange margarita. It's a welcome warmer, but the room itself does much to calm them – built in 1825, it has a lovely earthy, almost warren-like quality. Soon we will be passing through to Hydrangea, typically the venue for wedding receptions, and there is also a charming terrace we can spill out onto after the ceremony. It's amazing how well things come together when they are meant to be – there's even one door for the men to enter through and a set of French windows for the women.

'If I could have everyone's attention . . .' Ruth shushes the anticipatory chatter. 'So this is the plan – your man's name will be called, he'll step forward, and you'll be announced and presented to him by Marina. A photographer is going to snap that first-look moment and then together you will step down into the main room, where you can enjoy a glass of champagne and watch the next man being called and the next, until you are all paired up.'

Cue squeaks of excitement.

'I know you'll all be eager to get some alone-time, but we ask that you stick around long enough for the group shot at the end, secure in the knowledge that you have forty-eight uninterrupted hours of cottage time awaiting you.'

'Along with a bottle of almond champagne and a picnic basket so you don't even have to be disturbed by room service on your first night!' Marina chips in, creating a fluster of celebratory squeezes.

'Okay, settle down!' Ruth urges, and then turns to her boss. 'Ready with your welcome notes?'

'Yup. Good to go.'

'Okay, I'm going to start bringing the men in next door.'

I can't resist peeking round the corner as they start to file in, looking expectant and eagerly accepting and downing their margaritas.

The room itself looks so fresh – white walls and china-blue tablecloths offsetting the dark wood of the ceiling beams. I spy one of the men taking a flower from the main display, obviously intending to present it to his girl, and I sigh – that really is so sweet.

'Can you see my guy?' Gemma nudges me, reminding me of his face via a picture on her phone.

I peer back into the room. 'Not yet – wait! Yes, he's here!'

'I love you, Brandon!' she calls out, creating a domino effect down the line, all the girls calling out the name of their beaus.

I look back at the room and smile at the reaction from the guys – the grinning and jostling, a few looking almost teary-eyed at the prospect of a reunion. And that's when my heart stops.

It can't be.

And yet there is no mistaking that face. Or my reaction to it – as if my heart has just tried to long-jump from my body to his side.

'Marina!' I grapple blindly behind me for her.

'What's with the clawing?' She retracts her arm from my flailing nails.

I pull her to my side and, barely able to speak, hiss, 'Jonathan is out there!'

'I know.'

'What?' I gasp. 'Why didn't you say something? Why didn't you warn me?' Suddenly I feel nauseous. 'Who is she? Which one is his girl?' I scan the assembled line. 'Is she one of mine or one of Lloyd's?'

God, I can't believe this! Please don't tell me I just finessed a woman for his pleasure. Even though I should wish him well, I just can't stand the thought of having to see him with the woman who could give him everything I couldn't.

'Stella, did you hear me?'

'What?' My tortured eyes turn back to Marina.

She smiles beatifically. 'You're his girl.'

'What are you talking about?'

'The dress was just a teaser. This is my real gift to you.'

My mouth gapes, but I can't speak.

'I arranged the whole thing!' she continues. 'With Jeff's help, of course.'

I'm still reeling in confusion when Ruth sticks her head round the corner and tells us there's going to be a short delay – one of the guys has gone AWOL.

'If anyone needs to pee, now's the time.'

'Ooh great, I'm desperate!' Marina goes to dart off, but I yank her back.

'Does he know I'm here?'

'Of course – why else would he have flown across the country to be here today?'

I feel the blood draining from my face. This can't be happening. 'Why would you do this, Marina?'

'What do you mean, *why*? Because you're still in love with the guy!'

'What does it matter if I am?' I despair. 'Seeing him again won't solve things. If anything, it makes it a thousand times worse!'

'Oh, how can that be?' Marina tuts me.

'I can't believe you're being so blasé about this! Do you have any idea how painful it was letting go of him? Little by little, every day. Saying goodbye to a million things I loved about him. And now you've brought them all back to me!'

'I know it's tough, Stella. You know that I know. But don't you think it's worth it?'

I sigh, defeated. 'I'm not as strong as these women here today. I tried to be, but I failed. I was miserable every single day he was gone. I can't do that again.'

Marina rubs her brow. 'I thought I was doing you a favour – I wanted you to be happy.'

'But you don't know me!' I blurt. 'You don't know that the me you've spent the past week with is *way* happier than I was before. If you'd seen how I was when he left . . .' My voice catches.

'We've all been there.'

'That doesn't make it okay.'

'But if we stick together—'

'Is that what this is about? You want to have your own two-person Navy Wife Club?'

'I thought we could help each other.'

'But you didn't think to ask me if I *wanted* any of this?'

'Found him!' Ruth darts back. 'Two minutes, Marina.'

She nods at Ruth and then grimaces at me. 'It just seemed so meant to be – all these years on, neither of you seeing anyone . . .'

'I am seeing someone,' I object.

'Since when?'

'Since two nights ago.'

Her eyes dart around, as if mentally scanning the crew. 'Jimmy, the lighting guy?'

'No,' I say.

'Conrad?'

'*Are you crazy?*'

'Well, who then?'

I sigh. 'I'm not sure how you're going to feel about this.'

'Not Milo?'

'Yes, Milo.'

'Oh, Stella, you can't be.'

'I know, it's all wrong – the movie star should have him, not the crew.'

'It's not that.'

'Out of my league?'

'Of course not.' She shakes her head. 'I just don't think he's good enough for you.'

I can't help but emit a snort.

'I mean, he's fun for a while, but don't you want to be with someone you can really have a future with?'

Before we can debate this further, Ruth cues Marina for her welcome speech.

'Hello, sailors!' she whoops as she walks out onto a raised platform, to much whistling and hooting. 'I'm going to keep this short, as I know exactly what you'd rather be doing right now!'

They holler some more.

'I also know, from personal experience, how hard it can be to be apart from your loved one. Now, I know this weekend isn't a solution. This is a Hollywood fix. But it's a start, and one thing's for damn sure – you all deserve a good time.'

She raises her margarita and her audience return the favour. They sip as one and then Marina gives a wry smile, 'You know, a dear friend of mine told me a story about a group of sailors relocating to the Pacific. They were told, "In Guam, there's a woman behind every tree . . ." '

I look up, startled, as she gives them the punchline: ' "But there's only two trees!" '

As the room erupts with laughter, my eyes fly to Jonathan – watching him illuminate with both recognition and delight, I feel all my old affection come flooding back, taking me right back to our first date. But instead of hitting me as pain, I am surprised by an incredible rush of joy and familiarity.

Though my eyes don't leave him, I hear Marina continuing, 'Well, here at the San Ysidro Ranch, the odds are a whole lot better, because we've got a girl for every single one of you!'

More cheers. Then she begins the name-calling: 'Richard Bartlett!'

A sunny-faced fella hurries to her side.

'Allow us to present your beloved Donna Moravec.'

As the couple are reuniting, Marina darts back to me.

'I'm going to ask him to leave.'

'No' – I'm in a daze now – 'don't do that.'

'I'll explain it was all me and oop—'

Ruth hoicks Marina back to the platform.

'Dale Walker,' she calls the next sailor.

I don't know what position Jonathan is on the list, but I have to talk to him before Marina either calls his name or sends him packing.

'Lloyd?'

'Yes?'

'Can I leave you with the girls for a moment?'

'No problem.'

Seconds later I'm easing myself into the back of the reception via the last set of French windows.

Something causes Jonathan, and Jonathan alone, to look back. It takes him a millisecond to process my black hair, but then he begins a smile and the warmth in his eyes is unmistakable and utterly magnetic – I can't get to his side quickly enough.

'Stella.' My name is a sigh on his lips.

I always wondered how it would be to stand face to face with him again. I imagined a tension, a politeness, a distance, but my heart is instantly flung wide and as our bodies collide, it is with a euphoric force. Clinging tight, I try not to let my torso become overcome with shaking. I just need to feel him a moment longer – that sensation of safety and protection surrounding me – so I burrow into the nook of his neck and he holds me there, one hand on the back of my head, the other across my back, until my heartbeat steadies.

'I've missed you so much!' he breathes into my hair before searching out my eyes. 'I can't believe I've finally found you!'

Now it all seems so futile – changing my name, my email address, my phone number – all I was doing was postponing the inevitable. Of course we had to see each other again. If I'm honest, I've had a candle burning in my window the whole time, trying to lure him home to me.

There's a whistle as one of my more dramatic glamorisations – the female Navy officer – hits the stage.

'You've done such a spectacular job with these women.' Jonathan looks back at me with pride. 'I feel kind of left out, but I suppose there's not too many options with me!' He rubs his hand over his shaved scalp.

'You don't need a makeover,' I assure him, hooking my fingers in his belt-loops. 'You're perfect just as you are!'

He pulls a face. 'I do recall you getting me wearing flip-flops, which I was very reluctant about.'

'Well, you have such good-looking feet!' I grin.

Of course, when I look down now, I see a pair of black shiny dress shoes, but as my eyes work back up his body I may as well have X-ray vision, I know so well what lies beneath the fine, charcoal-grey fabric of his suit. I know the curve of his calves, the power of his thighs, the angular hipbones and bumped stomach that varies a little according to his workout regime, the chest where my head has rested so many times . . .

By the time my gaze reaches his softly shaped mouth, my whole body is cleaving to him.

'Care to step outside for a second?' he husks. 'I have something for you.'

He takes my hand (best feeling ever!) and leads me to the car park, where he opens the boot of his hire car. Inside is a compact wooden box, which he invites me to open.

I'm really curious now, especially when I see the squared-off sections and the bubble-wrapped items slotted into each one.

'Go ahead, take one out.'

I pick randomly from the centre, unravelling the plastic to discover a slender pottery jar with a loop handle.

'Well, that's an appropriate first choice,' he cheers. 'I got that for you in Athens. It's called a *lekythos*. They say that perfume originated when the goddess Venus pricked herself on the thorn of a white rosebush – her blood dyed it red and the rose became so beautiful to the eyes of Cupid he kissed the petals and gave it its gorgeous fragrance.'

'That's so romantic!' I enthuse.

'I thought this was pretty cool . . .' He hands me a light, slender package.

I give him a quizzical look.

'Open it,' he encourages.

'It's a fan!' I take in the intricate cut-outs of the stained emerald-green wood.

'From the Seychelles,' he says as he takes it from my hand and wafts it in front of my face. 'What do you smell?'

'Jasmine!' I gasp.

'The wood is infused with scented oil.'

'That's amazing! What a great idea.'

He nods for me to choose another.

I take a breath, a little overwhelmed.

'From Russia, with love,' he smiles as I unwrap a two-tone bottle with an onion-domed stopper.

As he highlights the details with such a delicate touch, I find myself flashing back to the sensation of his fingertips on my skin and I feel a little giddy.

'There's a little treasure from every place I've been,' he says. 'I always hoped that one day I would have the chance to present them to you.'

I feel myself swooning again at his gentrified phrasing – and then revel in the realisation that everywhere he went he was thinking about me, just as I was always thinking of him.

I open my mouth, trying to find the words to thank him, but then we hear the photographer calling everyone together for the group shot.

'We should—'

'Wait, Stella.'

'Yes?'

As I turn back, he clasps me to him and kisses me.

It's the kiss.

His kiss.

The only kiss.

'I couldn't go another minute without doing that.'

Again my eyes blur with tears. I feel a weightless, floating sensation. All I want is to melt into him. My hand reaches for his cheek and my lips find his again. Even though I can't find the words, I want to somehow tell him *yes*.

As we all assemble for the picture, Jonathan's arms wrap round my waist and it feels so natural and so right. I know my face is zinging with glee. I don't want to part from him for a second, but the photographer is now calling for a shot with just the girls. I try to catch Marina's eye, but she is busy in the middle and I'm over at the far end. I feel terrible for freaking out at her now – I have to say, she's done a fantastic job today, really come through for everyone. And then the camera flashes and I have the surreal awareness that I am one of them now. We really are all in this together.

'Now all the guys,' the photographer calls the switch.

I watch Jonathan laughing along with the guy next to him and I feel so besotted and . . . What is this other feeling? Ah yes! A sense of belonging – he's still mine and I'm still his. Even after all this time! Suddenly I can't believe my luck. I've always dreaded the thought of bumping into him again and facing the changes that have taken place between us, but all I feel right now is happy. *So very happy!*

If I could live my life with him looking at me the way he is right now—

My phone interrupts my train of thought.

Presuming it's Lloyd or Marina, I answer without looking at the display, only to hear Milo's sloppy-slurry voice.

'Ah, there she is – my kiss-and-make-up girl!'

I scurry out of the nearest door. 'Milo, I'm right in the middle—'

'I need your help – we're all out of booze here and all the runners are off, can you sneak a few bottles back with you?'

'Well, yes, I suppose,' I falter. 'But you know we're not heading back until the morning.'

'What? Nooo! I'm going to send Brent to pick you up.'

'Who's Brent?' I frown.

'Friend of mine from Ojai. He'll come by with his town car. You'll be back in no time.'

'No, wait, I'm not done here.' I glance back into the room, eager to check on Jonathan.

'But I need you!'

I sigh. Shouldn't this make me feel wanted? Desired? Maybe it would if I could be certain it was me he needed, not the extra bottles of fizz.

'I'm sorry, I have to go. I'll call you back later.'

I switch off my phone and take a moment to compose myself, amazed at how swiftly Milo has been bumped from the top spot – then again, how could our brief affair compare to the years of hardcore emotion with Jonathan?

'Margarita or champagne?' A passing waiter offers me his tray.

It's then I realise I have a genuine choice to make. Not that it really seems like too much of a wrangle – do I cut short my time here to go back to a man who will most likely be passed out and snoring, or do I stay and watch the sun play out its magnificent coral and gold light show before heading back to the cottage for a fireside picnic and some steamy stargazing in the Jacuzzi? Did I mention that the second option comes with the Love of My Life?

It's only when my mind flashes from sunset to sunrise that I experience a moment's hesitation – am I asking for my heart to be broken all over again? It feels so good to be with Jonathan now, but how will I feel when we part tomorrow and he heads back to Virginia? I take a deep breath and in doing so inhale the syrupy sweetness of the night jasmine. Oh, who am I fooling? As if any of that even matters right now! Maybe it's the tequila talking, but whatever price I have to pay for this time with Jonathan, I'm willing. The mere thought of tangling in the clean white sheets with him is giddying. I want to feel that closeness, that bliss, one more time.

When I step back into the reception room, I find the group has dispersed. The couples are heading off to their cottages, and the photographer is now focused on polishing off the platter of coconut fried shrimp.

'Marina!' I run up to the belle of the ball. 'Have you seen Jonathan?'

'I'm so sorry I messed up.' She reaches for my hand.

'Never mind about that now,' I urge. 'None of that matters – just tell me where he is!'

'You don't have to worry any more.' She gives me a solemn look. 'He's gone.'

28

'What do you mean, he's gone?' I feel stone-cold panic.

'I told him I'd made a mistake inviting him here – explained that you were seeing someone.'

My heart tips over. '*WHAT?*'

'I was just trying to clean up the mess I made.'

'By making it *worse?*' I am incredulous. I want to fall to the floor, but I can't waste a second. I have to catch up with him. 'Which way did he go?'

'But you said—'

'Marina,' I halt her, 'do you know where he was going?'

She shakes her head.

I turn away not knowing whether to punch the wall or burst into tears. How could she? How could she do this? Bring a man here, reunite him with his lost love and then say, 'Yah boo! You can't have her!' I imagine how I would feel if the situation were reversed – if I'd been invited to a party by a friend of Jonathan, only to be told that he'd moved on so would I kindly mind doing the same . . . I'd be hysterical, feeling like the world was playing the cruellest trick. Then again, that's just me. Knowing Jonathan, he'd be pleased for me. It would justify his decision – see, it's all meant to be! I was meant to choose the Navy so you could find this great new love!

I wonder if Marina told him who it was? I'm guessing not. He believed her enough to leave, after all.

'Jeff!' I pounce on him as he steps onto the path. 'Have you seen Jonathan?'

He shakes his head but does give me his mobile number, which I ring and ring to no avail.

'Do you know where he was planning to stay tonight?'

'Well, we kind of presumed he was going to be in with you, so we didn't make any other arrangements for him.'

Oh God, now I feel just awful – he's come all this way and doesn't even have a bed for the night. I run straight into reception.

'Excuse me, do you have a list of hotels in the area?'

'Montecito or Santa Barbara?'

'Both!' I say when she tells me there's really just a couple locally, one of which is the Four Seasons and I know he couldn't stretch to that. But now I have a list of seventy. I step back outside and start frantically dialling each one, looking up and around me as I wait for the call to be connected. Could he still be here, wandering the grounds? I roam and dial and get teary and fight the wobble in my voice so I can be understood by the person on reception, but I'm getting nowhere. I'm just considering heading the mile down to the beach wondering if his first instinct would be to stare out to sea when my phone goes. I'm so shocked and scrabble so eagerly to answer that it flies out of my hands, landing in the flowerbed. I fall after it, muddying my beautiful dress, only to realise that it is Milo calling back.

'How'sitgoing?' he slurs three words into one.

'Um . . .' What can I possibly say?

'Just wanted to let you know, Brent is waiting at the end of the driveway for you, whenever you are ready to leave.'

My mouth falls open.

'Stella?'

'Yes, yes, I'm here.'

I don't know if it's the delirium but suddenly putting 150 miles between me and the scene of my misery doesn't seem an entirely bad idea. What was I thinking anyway? Of course it was divine seeing Jonathan, it always was. But how will I feel when he leaves me, not just tomorrow but again and again and again?

'Hurry back!' Milo cheers, and then clicks off.

I try to get to my feet but instead find myself too leaden with sadness to move. I don't want to go anywhere. I don't want to be anywhere. I just want this feeling to go away – this feeling that I'm in love with someone who only ever makes fleeting appearances in my life. This is always how it is with Jonathan, euphoria followed by a crashing sense of abandonment.

And then, out of nowhere, a cat appears.

I sniff and wipe away my tears. 'Are you Bentley?' I ask, having heard of the resident tabby, so named because he was found hiding beneath one of the fancier guest cars. 'Oh, you're so delicate after Bodie!' I smile as he winds his petite fluffiness around my legs. 'Tell me, Bentley, what should I do?'

I convey the rest of my thoughts telepathically just in case anyone can hear me. 'I'm not going to find Jonathan tonight, and even if by some miracle I did, all it would mean is that I'm hooked all over again, committing to a lifestyle I want no part of. How long could the happiness last, really? Then, on the other hand, there's Milo . . . And maybe he is just a good time, but he's new and different, and isn't that what we're all supposed to do? Keep moving forward!'

I wait for Bentley to give me a sign.

'To the cottage or the castle?'

Bentley hops off my lap and starts walking purposefully down the path, towards the driveway.

'Really?' I ask.

Onwards he goes.

'Well, I have to get my things from the cottage.'

In response to which he just lays down, as if to say, 'I'll wait here until you're done.'

One more blow awaits me: the name beside the door now reads, 'STELLA & JONATHAN'.

Marina obviously thought this would be a delightful surprise for us both. Suddenly I get a rush of wild hope and dash inside – but all is still and quiet and empty.

I know if I stay I'll spend the entire night rushing to the door at every rustle and creak and I just don't think I could take the disappointment over and over and over again. At least if I leave now, I won't have to drive back with Jeff and Marina in the morning, that would be too awkward after my tantrum. Marina said she wanted blunt, but she never asked for rude and ungrateful.

Oh, how can everything have gone so wrong? A week ago we were lying on the heated bathroom floor together with so much to look forward to. We didn't even know Jeff was going to be joining us then. I hadn't met Orla or Carrie or Lloyd. I'd never even seen a picture of Hearst Castle. Of course, I wouldn't give up my experiences there for anything, but I would like to turn back the clock to that day I suggested this mega-makeover. But then I imagine taking away the looks on those couples' faces when they reunited and I realise I can't wish that away.

'Stella?'

A short man steps out from a long car, opening the door for me chauffeur-style.

'There's a blanket in the back, feel free to sleep,' he tells me. 'I know you've had a long day.'

It's a kind invitation, but my eyes remain peeled, still looking for any sign of Jonathan along the roadside.

As we merge onto the freeway, I realise any chance is well and truly gone, and I feel physically sick. I can't believe I am speeding away from him like this. Almost worse than the yearning for him is the thought of hurting him. The thought of him being upset and alone ... Against my better judgement, I try his old phone number half a dozen more times and then I give up. I've been here before, clinging on to something that will never work. Just because I feel way more for him than anyone else doesn't mean we are meant to be together. I can't let this ruin the good things in my life or I'll just end up back at square one again. I don't want to go back to that lifeless state, I really don't.

The further along the coast we get, the more implausible it seems that I even saw him tonight. Perhaps I can convince myself than none of it really happened. I never really left the castle. When I get back to my room, everything will be back to normal.

'Here we are!' Brent helps me from the car. 'Do you need help up the steps with your luggage?'

'No, that's fine!' I tell him. 'I know an easier way up. Thank you so much for driving me.'

'No problem. Say hi to Milo for me.'

'Will do!'

I'm just getting level with the Casa Grande when I catch sight of the man in question. And immediately dodge behind a palm tree. Okay, that's not the ideal reaction, but let's not give it too much weight. If anything, it's the natural response – I just need a little more time. Besides, the last thing he needs is more booze. I'll let him go on his way, creep back to my room, have a good sleep and awake in the morning refreshed and ready to embrace the day. And Milo.

I take a breath and step out from the shadows, slap-bang into Milo!

'Baby girl!' He reels joyfully. 'Where did you spring from?'

'Oh, I . . .' I stumble. 'I was looking for you!'

'And here I am!' He throws up his arms.

'Yes, you are,' I wince as he staggers like a broken marionette. 'Whoa, let me help you . . .'

'Did you bring the champers?'

I nod.

'Fantastic! Come on over to my suite! No need to hide any more! We can shout our sinning to the stars!'

'Yes, well, not that there's any real need to do that . . .'

'So how was your do?' he asks as his arm leans leadenly on my shoulder.

'Good, good,' I reply. 'It was a great success.'

'I bet you made a lot of sailors very happy tonight.'

'Most of them, yes.'

Fortunately he doesn't quiz me any further – it takes all our focus to make it up the twisting staircase and then, once inside his loft-style suite, I'm the one quizzing him.

'What's with all the rubber ducks?'

I gawp at what must be fifty or more dotted around the room – propped on sofa cushions, swinging from the chandelier, balanced on the window ledge, not to mention an entire shooting range lined up along the balcony bar – the yellow plastic making an absurd contrast with all the dark antiquities.

'Is this Hearst's "guilty pleasure" collection?'

'Nooo,' Milo laughs as he starts to peel away his clothes. 'I got them in town today – me and Jimmy came out of Mozzi's saloon and there was an entire shop window filled with them. Thought they'd make the coolest gifts for everyone. Look! I have one for you . . .' He lunges over to the fireplace. 'Here!'

I can't help but smile. The duck in question is looking into a silver compact and applying baby-pink lipstick to her beak.

'This one with the clapperboard is for Conrad, and the doggie duckie is for Marina. They didn't have any Bodie-looking ones, so I got her a Dalmatian.'

As I follow him up the staircase leading from the lounge area to the boudoir, I realise every single duck has its own unique styling . . . There's a pirate duck, a painter, a cowboy, one in a bikini (for Orla?), even one done up as a judge with a wig and a mallet (or should that be mallard?).

'This one's for Jeff . . .'

My stomach loops as he hands me a little sailor duck complete with jaunty white hat and Navy insignia on his wing. As Milo goes to kiss me, my knee-jerk reaction is to push him away.

'Hey, you have to give me a chance to catch up with you!' I try to laugh off my response. 'Remember I've been working all day!'

Now I wish I'd popped the cork on the way here.

'Hurry! Hurry!' he says as he begins pogoing on the bed.

I turn away from his naked flip-flopping for just a second when I hear a clunk.

'Milo?' He's disappeared from view.

'I'm okay!' he says as he claws his way back on the bed.

There's no point in asking if he's hurt himself, because he wouldn't be feeling a thing in this state.

'Come here!' he says, yanking me towards him via the hem of my dress. The once-beautiful dress Marina bought for me . . .

I can feel my body tensing at his sloppy vigour. All I feel is resistance. I don't know if it would be any better if he were sober. At least this way he is oblivious to my strange mood. He's still trying to undo all the tiny buttons on my dress when I feel him slowing down.

'It's too hard!' he says, falling onto his back.

Seconds later he's snoring.

I expel a long sigh of relief and sit down on the end of the bed, still holding the little sailor duck.

I had intended to go back to my own room, but sleep, or rather exhaustion, snuck up on me. When I awake, I find I'm still in my dress, remarkably uncrumpled, which is more than I can say for my face.

I blink my sore eyes open. All I really noticed when I came in last night was the rubber ducks. Now I have the ideal vantage point to view the ceiling. I thought the one in my room was pretty fancy, but this is a step beyond, with a dramatic biblical painting at its centre. I wonder if Hearst arranged these intriguing artworks specifically for early morning ponderers. Those among us who open our eyes and immediately start fretting. For a second I lose myself in the fluffy clouds; then my eye is drawn to the balcony, where I notice a vine and grape-cluster motif to the carvings. I'm just wondering if that was a deliberate match for Milo by whoever assigned the suites when I spy the unopened bottle of champagne.

My emotions suddenly flare – a heavy discomfort in my chest and then a pain in my heart as I think of Jonathan, wondering where he is today. Whether he's shrugged the whole thing off or if he too is crumpled.

I reach for my phone and, checking that Milo is still sleeping, I call up the photos from yesterday's event, swiftly sliding through those of the girls until I get to the ones of Jonathan. There it is again, the rush of love I feel at the merest glimpse of that beautiful face.

By rights Milo's movie-star looks should be able to trump that – the guy is paid millions for his decorative ability. And yet as I lean on my side and hold Jonathan's image beside Milo's sleeping face, I can honestly say I find Jonathan more attractive. He just has this quality of grace, which may be a strange word to describe a man, but—

'Whatcha looking at?' Milo startles me as he rears up trying to open his eyes but only fully succeeding with one.

'The shots from the event,' I say, quickly using my thumb to slide back to the girls.

'God' – he grimaces, falling back into the pillow – 'enough with the before, where's the after?'

'This is the after!'

He gives a little shudder. 'Real people scare me.'

'Am I not a real person?'

'No, you're beautiful,' he says, reaching to pull me into a kiss. And then jerks back suddenly. 'Your eyes have changed colour . . .' I hold his gaze until he slumps and says, 'Oh no.'

'What?'

'I know that look – you've seen my true colours and you don't like them.' He rubs his brow. 'Was I awful last night? I don't recall.'

'You were fine.'

'I love wine, Stella. I make no bones about it. Really love it.'

'It's not that,' I begin.

He gives an anguished sigh. 'Marina told you, didn't she? I knew she would!' Before I can reply, he blurts, 'I only slept with Francesca when I thought you were married!'

My eyes widen.

'Wait.' His hand clamps clumsily over his mouth. 'You didn't know about that, did you?'

'No, I didn't.' I take a breath. 'But it's okay.'

'It was just the once. That first night Marina said your husband was on the phone, it threw me for a loop.'

'Does Francesca know about me?'

He shakes his head. 'I am nothing if not discreet.'

'Other than you just told me about her.'

'Yes, but we're friends, aren't we?'

That sounds oddly appealing.

And then something in me finds a little peace. I scoot down the bed so that I am now level with him. 'We were never going to be anything more than the duration of the movie, were we?'

He ruminates for a whole second and then gives a hapless shrug. 'What can I say? I need variety. If I'm around people too long, they tire of me. Or start to worry about me. I don't want that. I just want to have fun.'

And then I see his eye connect with the unopened bottle of champagne.

'We're shooting a party scene today, aren't we?'

'Yes,' I confirm.

'So a little fizz might help me get in the mood . . . Would you do the honours?'

I get to my feet but ignore the bottle and instead pour him a glass of water and shake an Advil from his little white tub. Before he can protest, I ask him where he's put his copy of the Hearst Castle gift book.

'It's downstairs on the table beside the sofa. What about the champagne?'

'Remember when we were first here laughing about David Niven being such a boozer?' I call up from the sitting area.

'Yes.'

'You probably know he used to sneak extra liquor to Marion Davies on his visits, which sounds all very pally, but then I found this other quote from him . . .' I come back up the stairs and perch on the side of the bed. ' "It seemed fun at the time to stoke up her fires of outrageous fun and laughter, and I got a kick, I suppose, out of feeling that I had outwitted one of the most powerful and best informed men on earth, but what a disloyal and crummy betrayal of someone who had shown me nothing but kindness and hospitality, and what a nasty potential nail to put in her coffin." '

I close the book. 'So. I'm not going to judge your drinking, but I'm also not going to encourage it. I'm going to take back the champagne and give it to Marina's friend Kendal, because as of today she just rescued her fiftieth dachshund.'

Milo looks bemused but makes no protest.

'I don't want to be a nail in your coffin.'

'Oh, don't be a downer!' he pleads, pulling the covers up around his head.

I peel the sheet from his face. 'I'm not being critical. If anything, I want to thank you.'

He rolls his eyes. 'You know we have another couple of weeks shooting in LA, are you sure you don't want to save this speech for then?'

I smile but persist. 'Just the thought of you was enough to shake me out of my rut, and being around you has been such a thrill. Before you there hadn't been anyone for a really, really long time. But now I know I can be attracted to someone else.'

'Someone else?'

'Someone other than my ex,' I clarify. 'The thing is, I want the works. That's what I've been holding out for, and in order to find that I have got to keep moving forward.'

He sighs. 'So what now for us?'

'I go back to just touching you here,' I say, reaching for his face, 'instead of here.' I brush his groin.

'Mmm.' His hands reach for my hips. 'How about once more for old times' sake?'

I chuckle but wriggle free, placing a pillow between us.

'Well, at least do me one favour . . .'

'What's that?' I squint at him.

'Can you do my make-up in bed?' He gives me an imploring look. 'Every time I sit upright I feel like someone is taking an axe to my head.'

I grin back at him, remembering our first flirtation in the make-up room. It seems as though we've come full circle.

'Okay,' I consent. 'But just so as you know, from now on I'm going to call you Gloria.'

29

Ultimately I decide to also do my own make-up in Milo's suite so that at least I'm showered and presentable as I make my walk of shame back to the Casa del Sol. I'm just trundling my case past the fish pond when I see Conrad marching towards me cursing the air.

'What is it?' I call over to him, feeling a swell of empathy – it wasn't so long ago that I was in the exact same state.

'That harlot Jean Harlow has some kind of "family emergency" and she's pulled out.'

'Well, I'm sure one of the other extras—'

'Have you seen the dress that she has to wear?' he snaps.

Oh yes. The provocatively diaphanous one. It would take a particularly knock-out body to carry that off. I reach for his arm. 'Orla! Orla would look amazing, even though I think technically her boobs are more Monroe than Harlow, but her hair is definitely the right colour!'

'Already asked her and she won't do it.'

'What? Why?'

'Something about it not fitting with her new image.'

'Oh!' I flush, realising I am mostly to blame for this. 'Perhaps I could have a word?'

'I've already given her every incentive I can think of.'

'There is one more that's worth a try . . .'

'She's in the Morning Room,' he dismisses me, now railing at the prop guy.

Back I go to the Casa Grande.

'Orla!' I spy her fiddling with a tea set.

'Oh God!' She sets down the sugar bowl and hurries over. 'Conrad's in a foul mood with me, says I'm ruining the whole scene because I won't dress up as Jean Harlow!'

'I wouldn't worry about it – it's actually just a fleeting second or two of the movie, no one will miss it,' I shrug. 'But, just out of interest, why are you turning him down?'

She gives an involuntary shudder. 'I don't want to go back to the way I was. Something . . . something unpleasant happened the other night that confirmed for me that I really need a change of image.'

I nod. 'Charlie Chaplin at the Roman Pool.'

She looks startled. 'H-how do you know about that?' And then her face changes. 'You were there! Of course! I haven't told anyone else here about my grandfather.' Then her eyes widen. 'But that voice . . .'

'That was Milo,' I confess.

'Really?'

'He was ready to step in and defend your honour, but you handled it so well yourself.'

She blushes. 'Well, as horrible as it was, I'm glad you were there. It was the wake-up call I needed. I owe you big time.'

'Hmm,' I muse. 'You know you'd be doing me a huge favour if you did do the Jean Harlow scene – I can't think of anyone I could do a better job on facially. I mean, the cleft chin is easy enough to fake, but you actually have a very similar nose and I'd just need to set your hair . . .'

She looks disheartened. 'Please don't ask me to do this.'

'I'm not going to bully you into anything, but I will say this: walking around in broad daylight dressed like an off-duty stripper is very different to a smouldering scene in a classic movie where all you're required to do is walk into a dimly lit room, turn a few heads, have Hearst demand you change your dress and from then on you walk around in a big coat, totally covered up.'

(Apparently this really happened, though this was an outfit she wore to dinner at Hearst's other Californian property, Wyntoon, as opposed to a party at the castle.)

'Plus, wouldn't this be a nice swan song to provocative dressing? One that would have your ex gagging on his popcorn when he sees you waltz into a scene with his favourite actor . . .'

Now I've got her interest.

'I can make you look so luminous, so lovely his jaw will drop to the floor. You can think of him as you stand in the doorway, show him everything he is missing and then, if you really are that concerned, after the filming I can do a warmer honey on your hair and with your new make-up no one need ever know it was you up there on the silver screen.'

'So I get my new look and my revenge?'

'Exactly.'

'There you are!' Lloyd puffs in the doorway. 'I know you've already done Milo, which is great, but you need to get a move on with Marina.'

'Can you do her?'

Lloyd looks a little taken aback.

'It's just that Conrad really needs me to work on Orla.'

'I thought you said no.' He turns to her.

She takes a breath. 'I've changed my mind – there's just one condition.'

'You want Stella to do your make-up,' Lloyd predicts.

'It is the party scene, so if Marion's face was a little different to her usual style, that's totally acceptable,' I reason. 'And I can check it after you've done it.'

'Oh, you're going to check my work now?'

'I didn't mean it like that!' I scurry to Lloyd's side. 'Please, just this once . . .'

'I don't know what is going on with you and Marina, but you need to sort it.'

'I will, I promise. I just need a little bit more time . . .'

The thought of facing her now and rehashing everything to do with the Jonathan fiasco is more than I can bear. We'll have all the time in the world when we get to the set in Los Angeles, but I just don't want to deal with any more drama today. If I'm forced to, I fear I'll lose it completely.

I don't say any of this out loud, but it would seem that my watery eyes are speaking volumes.

'Okay,' he concedes. 'Just this one time.'

'Thank you!' I expel a sigh of relief.

'Come on.' Orla wheels my kit over to the window. 'Let's get this party started!'

Hearst's costume parties were legendary for their extravagance. There was the covered-wagon theme with an abundance of Hiawathas, a baby theme with lots of bonnets and rattles and a Tyrolean evening, which looked very *Sound of Music*, even though it predated the film by thirty years. But, by all accounts, the circus party was one of the most fun – Hearst even borrowed a full-size carousel from the Warner Brothers lot for the occasion!

Today Conrad has opted for an all-encompassing masquerade motif. Smart move – not everyone can carry off lederhosen.

The main scenes are taking place in the Assembly Room, the grandest salon of them all, with its monumental mantel, Renaissance tapestries, Roman busts and yet more medieval choir stalls (though mercifully there's also an abundance of comfy sofas and armchairs).

This is where Hearst's guests would gather for pre-dinner cocktails, play a game of cards or puzzle over a jigsaw. That said, I'm guessing first-timers would be far too busy gawping at the mysterious centrepiece – a sixteenth-century casket made from ebony, rock crystal and lapis lazuli . . .

Just when I think the vista can't get any more opulent, the actors start to arrive – Marie Antoinette in a vast hooped skirt and skyscraper of a wig, a genie glittering jewels from forehead to bellybutton and a disgruntled Charlie Chaplin dressed as a jockey in pink silks.

I'm approaching visual overload when I spot Kendal in her bear costume.

'Everything okay?' I mime over to her.

She gives me the thumbs-up.

'Where's the doggie?' I ask with my hands up in begging mode, possibly doing a better impression of a rabbit.

She guides my gaze across the room to Jeff, standing in the entrance hall with Bodie and Frankie. Bodie is trying to engage Frankie in play, bouncing as enticingly as he can, but Frankie is looking on with such disdain he should be peering through a monocle.

'My dear boy,' he seems to be saying, 'if you want to make yourself useful, go fetch me a snack from that plate of hors d'oeuvres.'

And then Milo appears before me, oh so dashing in his musketeer costume, complete with gold-embossed tabard and feathered hat.

'How do I look?'

The answer is, 'Spectacular.' Whatever Conrad is paying him, he's earning every penny.

'Bet you're wishing you hadn't turned me down now, aren't you?' he teases.

I smile. 'It is a little galling, I must admit.'

'Ah well, we'll always have the Roman Pool.'

'Yes, we will,' I sigh. 'Not bad for my first on-set romance.'

Milo gives a little hoot of mirth. 'Yeah, James Franco, watch out!'

I give him a quizzical look.

'That's Marina's next co-star.'

'Oh. I don't think I'll be around for that.'

Just to confirm my theory, Lloyd walks in with Marina, all frills and ruffles as Little Bo Peep, further enhancing her rosy glow with his favourite pony-hair blush brush.

'She fired you?'

'Not yet.'

Milo is distracted from further probing by the sight of Orla sashaying by in her shimmer-sheer dress.

'Who's that?' he gurgles.

'Jean Harlow.'

'Yes, but who's the actress? She looks vaguely familiar . . .'

'You really don't know?'

He shakes his head.

'Check out the boobs,' I direct him.

'That's Orla?' he gasps. 'Wow. She looks beautiful.'

'Yes, she does. Maybe you should tell her.'

He gives me an intrigued look.

'And no, I'm not suggesting you sleep with her. In fact I'm banning you from doing that.'

'I wouldn't dream of it,' he shudders. 'I don't want her dead grandfather haunting me.'

'Stella!' Conrad is now beckoning me over.

'I'll see you later.'

'Everything all right?' I ask the Boss.

He leans down and plants a kiss on my forehead. I look back at him, stunned.

'Orla looks a dream.'

'Thank you!' I beam.

'Now it's time for you to take back Marina.'

My face falls.

'I don't care what is going on in your personal life, on set I need you to be a professional.'

I take a breath and nod. 'Yes, sir.'

I'm on my way over to Marina when Orla sidetracks me.

'I have to get a picture of the two of us!'

'Well . . .' I check Conrad isn't watching. 'Just a quickie!'

She looks around for someone to hand the camera to, settling on Kendal. 'Would you mind?'

We strike the full movie-star pose.

'Now let's get each of us getting a bear hug!' she giggles.

I'm happy to play along, anything to put off facing Marina.

'Your turn,' she prompts.

As the heavy furry arms envelop me, I feel like I understand just why the term 'bear hug' caught on. What could feel safer than having a bear shield you from all the perils of the world? I rest my head against the synthetic fur, wondering whether there are any similar costumes I could slip into, or at the very least some kind of carnival mask I could put on, so I don't have to make direct eye contact with Marina.

'Hey! I want in on the pics!' Milo strides over, taking the camera from Orla and handing it to Kendal. 'Bear dude, can you get a snap of me with my girls?'

Kendal ignores him and continues to hold me close. When Milo reaches to prise her claw from my back, she shoves him roughly on the chest.

'Kendal!' I gasp. 'Do you know who that is?'

'Your boyfriend?' says a muffled voice, decidedly not Kendal's.

I jump back. It can't be.

'W-what's going on?'

'Let's find out, shall we?' Milo reaches to yank the head off the costume, but again the bear is too quick, deflecting Milo's arms and flooring him with a precision manoeuvre.

There's a sudden flurry of activity with Jeff now restraining the bear – who else but a fellow military man would have the skill?

'J-Jonathan?' my voice quavers before Conrad reaches into the throng and reveals his face.

'Security!'

'No!' Jeff and I speak in unison. 'We know him.'

'He just tried to take out one of my stars!'

'I'm fine!' Milo readjusts his rapier.

But the second he's in range, Jonathan goes for him again.

'Not his face!' I cry out.

Jonathan looks at me with utter incredulity.

'It's all he's got,' I reason.

'No, it's not.' Jonathan shakes his head, suddenly defeated. 'He has you.'

Before Milo and I have a chance to contradict this, Jonathan rubs his stressed brow. 'This was not the plan at all.'

'The plan?' I query.

'When I went back to the San Ysidro Ranch this morning, I was hoping we could talk things through and, when you were gone, I convinced Jeff that all I wanted was the chance to see you with Milo – just to be certain you were happy with him. It was the only way I could think of to let go of the dream of being with you again.' He takes a breath. 'But once you were in my arms, letting go seemed an impossibility.'

He then turns to Milo, who flinches slightly, before realising that all he wants to do now is apologise. 'I'm sorry, man. I lost it for a minute there.'

They shake hands, calling a truce.

Then he turns to me. 'I can't believe I've caused a scene at your place of work.'

I shrug. 'They're used to drama round here – half the people will think it's part of the script.'

He takes a step closer. 'I really want to apologise for all the pain I have caused you, Stella. You're the loveliest girl I know and you didn't deserve any of it. I just want you to know that the Navy was never more important than you, *never*. They were just more in my face, making more demands every single day. I didn't think I had enough in me to satisfy both of you, and I knew the Navy was a commitment there was no getting out of. It's no excuse.' He hangs his head. 'I should never have let you go. But maybe it was meant to be.' He looks at Milo. 'He can give you so much more than I can.'

'Dude, the only thing I've given her is a rubber duck. You're still in the running, trust me.'

Jonathan looks confused.

'We're not an item,' I tell him.

'But I just saw you guys together.'

'There's no ill feelings,' I explain. 'In fact I think we were meant to be friends.'

Milo nods confirmation.

I see relief and then a surge of hope in Jonathan's eyes.

It's time we talked in private.

I lead him over to the secret doorway, hidden in the wall panels beside the fireplace, and huddle in the doorframe with him.

'Jonathan, I have to say something to you.' I reach for his hand. 'I never stopped loving you, not for a minute. And based on my reaction at seeing you yesterday, I probably always will. But it still makes me sick to my stomach – the thought of being apart from you for the majority of the year.'

His face brightens. 'Well then, it's a good thing that you will never have to be.'

My brow furrows. 'What do you mean?'

'Three weeks from now, I'm a free man.'

'*What?*'

'I did put in my application for the officer programme, but these things take a while to be reviewed and approved and by the time the acceptance came through, I was midway through another deployment, spending night after night standing alone on the deck looking up at the stars wondering where you were, imagining how I would feel if I never got to see you again. I knew that if I proceeded with the officer programme, we would never be together, but if I turned it down, I would still have hope. And when there's nothing but black sea all around and you are so far from home, you have to have something to believe in. And I always believed in you.'

I'm still in a state of shock.

'I love you, Stella!'

Before I can reciprocate, my eyes spill over with hot tears and I reach out to embrace him, squeezing him so tight, releasing all the angst I felt last night. He's really here. To stay.

'Are you sure about this?' I ask, suddenly pulling back. 'I understand better now what the Navy means to you – the camaraderie, the respect, the—'

'You're what matters most. There are other ways I can serve my country. Ways I can do that and come home to you every night.'

'That sounds so good!' I swoon.

'Waking up with you every morning . . .' He moves closer and then tilts my face to his and our kisses melt into each other, so warm and cascading with adoration.

'All this time!' I shake my head as we pause to gaze into each other's eyes. 'Why didn't you . . . ?'

'Tell you?' He laughs. 'You think I didn't try? The emails bounced back, your old number was dead, I called every cosmetic establishment in the UK and not one person could give me a lead on Stella Smith.'

'Oh God!' I clunk my forehead on his chin. 'I was just trying to protect myself! I knew if you ever got in touch, I'd get sucked back in and I just couldn't live that way!'

'You don't have to live that way. We can live any way we want, anywhere we want.'

'Can we live here?' I chance my arm.

Jonathan chuckles, tucking my hair behind my ear. 'Well, maybe not here at the castle, but perhaps we could find ourselves a little shack in San Simeon with zebras in the backyard!'

'I still can't believe this!' I blink back at him. 'Is this really happening?'

'It is!' he grins, trying to pull me closer but finding the excess of fur obstructive. 'I guess this costume isn't helping in the realism stakes.'

'Which reminds me!' I gasp, stepping back. 'What ever happened to Kendal?'

'We did a trade – I promised to adopt Frankie in return for wearing her bear costume.'

'We have a dog?' I squeak.

'If that's okay?' He looks suddenly concerned.

'It's wonderful!' I go to kiss him, but Conrad steps between us. 'Stella!'

'Yes!' I quake.

'I'm delighted that you've been reunited with your leading man, but I'm still waiting on my leading lady.'

'Give me two minutes!'

Suddenly I can't get to her quickly enough. 'Marina!' I call. 'Marina!'

'Here.' She beckons to me from the other side of the fireplace.

'I'm so sorry for everything I said yesterday,' I gabble. 'You were being so kind and romantic and only trying to help and I was—'

She places her hand over my mouth to shush me. 'Everything worked out in the end, didn't it?' She winks over in Jonathan's direction.

'Only if we're still friends.' I'm still looking her way.

She smiles. 'I told you I wanted you to be blunt with me, didn't I?'

'Well, yes . . .'

'Well, you were. That's how I always want it to be with us.'

I feel teary all over again. And then I shake my head. 'I can't believe how much has changed in a matter of days – there I was in London, just going through the motions, and then you appeared and invited me into this magical world, reuniting me with my lost love!'

'Trust me, we're in this thing together – I wouldn't be standing here in this magical world if you hadn't made me into Marion, not to mention putting me back together again after my meltdown. I've even officially gained a husband since we met!'

I give a little chuckle. 'All the same . . .'

'All the same, what?' She cocks her head.

I look back at Jonathan. 'I just wish there was more I could do to thank you.'

'Well, there is one thing . . .'

'Yes?'

'You could sort out my eyebrows. Did you see the pig's ear Lloyd has made of them?'

I snicker to myself. They are, of course, perfect, but I am more than happy to give them a touch-up, anything to demonstrate my gratitude.

I'm just pausing to sharpen my brow pencil when William Randolph Hearst approaches.

'Did you see they've added a last line of dialogue?'

Marina shakes her head. 'Show me.'

He extends his script.

' "Dreams are meant to be shared," ' she reads. ' "That is how they live on." ' She looks up at me. 'I rather like it.'

I smile back at her. 'Me too.'

CALIFORNIA DREAMERS PLAYLIST

1930S

Moonlight Serenade – Glenn Miller
A-Tisket, A-Tasket – Ella Fitzgerald & Chick Webb Orchestra
Night & Day – Cole Porter
Begin the Beguine – Artie Shaw Orchestra
All of Me – Louis Armstrong

BILL WITHERS

Lovely Day
I Want to Spend the Night
Ain't No Sunshine
Use Me
Just the Two of Us

STELLA'S FAVOURITE KUMQUAT VANILLA MARMALADE

<u>Ingredients</u>
550g thinly sliced kumquats
1,100ml water (a pint)
900g sugar
1 vanilla bean

<u>Preparation</u>
Halve the kumquats and remove the seeds. Tie the seeds in a muslin bag. Then thinly slice the kumquat halves into slivers, and put them – together with the bag of seeds and the water – into a pan and let it stand, covered, at room temperature for 24 hours. After 24 hours, bring the mixture to a boil over a moderate heat. Reduce the heat and simmer uncovered for about 45 minutes. Stir in the sugar and boil over a moderate heat for a further 15-20 minutes, stirring occasionally and skimming off any foam, until a teaspoon of the mixture dropped on a cold plate gels at room temperature. Ladle the marmalade into a hot jar (heating your jars in the oven on a low heat for 10 minutes will stop the them cracking from the heat of the marmalade!). Then seal, cool and store.

Nb. This marmalade will hypothetically last for years (the sugar acts as a natural preservative) but in reality is so irresistible that it never lasts nearly that long!

MILO'S MOM'S LAVENDER TOMATO JÁM

<u>Ingredients</u>
1.3kg ripe tomatoes, cored, peeled, de-seeded and chopped
1.5kg granulated sugar
140ml fresh lemon juice
12 sprigs fresh lavender (preferably with blossoms)

<u>Preparation</u>
In a large heavy saucepan, combine the tomatoes, lemon juice, sugar and half of the lavender sprigs. Mix thoroughly, until the sugar is dissolved, then bring to boil before reducing the heat. Let it simmer, uncovered, until the tomatoes break down and the mixture becomes jelly-like (about 1 to 1½ hours) stirring occasionally. Remove from heat. Stir and skim off foam, discarding lavender sprigs. Ladle tomato mixture into sterilized jars with a sprig of fresh lavender in each. Seal in hot jars (as with the kumquat marmalade), and cool to room temperature, before storing in the refrigerator. It's the perfect accompaniment to cheese and crackers, but goes just as well on toast!

CALIFORNIAN OLIVE OIL, ROSEMARY AND CHOCOLATE CAKE

Ingredients
85g spelt flour*
170g plain flour
170g caster sugar
1½ teaspoons of baking powder
¾ teaspoon salt
3 eggs
275 ml olive oil
200ml whole milk
1½ tablespoons fresh rosemary leaves
125g bittersweet chocolate (70% cacao), finely chopped into centimetre-sized pieces

Preparation
Preheat your oven to 180°C (Gas mark 4). Rub a 24cm fluted flan dish with a tiny bit of the olive oil. Sift the dry ingredients into a large bowl. Set aside. Using a mixer, whisk the eggs thoroughly on medium speed. Add the rest of the olive oil, the milk and the rosemary and whisk again. Then, using a spatula, fold the wet ingredients into the dry, gently mixing until just combined. Stir in the chocolate chunks, and pour the batter into the pan, spreading it evenly and smoothing the top. Bake for 40 minutes, or until the top is golden brown and a skewer inserted into the centre comes out clean. The cake can be eaten warm or cool from the pan, or cooled, and kept in an airtight container for several days.

*Spelt flour is now widely-available from health food shops as well as many supermarkets. If you can't find it though, never fear. This works just as well with just 85g more plain flour instead (i.e. a total of 255g plain flour).

LIVING LA VIDA LOCA

Belinda Jones

Carmen has been feeling the need to break free for Too Darn Long!

So when her equally frustrated friend Beth suggests the ultimate escape – dancing their way through a series of scorchingly hot countries – she can't resist!

There's just one catch . . . they can only go on this adventure if they participate in a reality TV show, one intent on teaching them the mournful tango in Argentina, the feisty flamenco in Spain and the sassy, celebratory salsa in Cuba!

As they travel from Buenos Aires to Seville and ultimately steamy Havana, each dance has a profound effect on the girls – and indeed the sexy gauchos, matadors and dirty dancers who partner them . . .

But, when the sun goes down, do they have what it takes to go beyond the steps and free their hearts for love?

HODDER